Tooey's Crossroads

Outrageous Tales and Bold-Face Lies

A Collection of Redneck Short Stories.
If you can't take a joke, put the damned
book back where you got it.

PUG GREENWOOD

Heron Oaks, Murrells Inlet, SC

Copyright © 2009 Pug Greenwood

All rights reserved.

Reprinted 2015

ISBN:0692566198

ISBN-13:9780692566190

"This collection of short stories made a great traveling companion during my flight from the authorities to Australia."

- *Malcolm Ironwater, Chief of the Maliqroische*

<>

"Some people don't know when to keep their mouths shut."

- *Alexandra "Big Al" Tooey*

"It's all lies except for that story about that stupid raccoon."

- *Tater Millpond*

PUG GREENWOOD

DEDICATION

To the boys at Beach Creek, who helped me find my way home to Finton County: Rick Lewis, who is my soul brother, Rick Goodwin, who builds campfires that can be seen from space, Bar Ellenberger, who helped me build the cabin, and Winford Tanner, who has gone on ahead of us.

- Pug Greenwood

COMING HOME SOMEWHERE ELSE

When you know the little history of a place, not just the great history of pilgrims and first landings, but everyday history, then a part of you belongs to it. When you know who used to live in the old farm just over the hill and out of sight from the highway, or what store used to be housed among the jumbled splintered boards and crumbling brick foundation at the next crossroads, then you are linked to that place. A place holds a piece of you and wraps it among its own memory when you know something of it, and you get closer to its soul when what you know never made it to the weekly paper or local radio.

There are stories of befuddled relatives and bizarre experiences a community is not quick to broadcast to the world, but still holds and retells in the quiet evening among muted chuckles of those who remember. The stories are told out of time and without sequence as the memory resurfaces, triggered by a name, or sound, or long forgotten aroma. Local stories are told around ancient cast iron stoves, slowly tinking from the heat of burning wood, as cadence to the rhythm of the tale. And the heat and the story combine to wrap both teller and listener within the same warm blanket of 'us'.

It is no longer just another rusting town limit sign along a road occasionally spotted with windowless gray plank buildings, having nothing beyond what you can see from the dashing car. It is a living place full of people with quaint names and humorous deeds to be retold, and you are not merely passing through.

You are coming home
somewhere else.

WELCOME TO FINTON COUNTY

CORNELIUS HOOKER

I stopped by the Park'n'Pump to fill up the Jeep, and bought a glass bottled RC from a tub of ice near the checkout counter. The store had a generous front porch offering welcomed shade from a hot July sun in southern Finton County, so I decided to relax there a while. I dropped into one of the cast off chairs lined in front of a worn lapboard wall, and enjoyed the feel of icy water dripping from the bottle onto the front of my T-shirt, closing my eyes to the glare beyond the porch.

Adam Tooey had seen me in the store and left the back kitchen to join me, letting the screen door screech its own way home behind him. The chipped rattan chair gave a chorus of squeaks as he settled next to me, taking long pulls from a bottle of beer that local law said should not be consumed in public view. I opened my eyes just enough to trade lazy nods. He let out a long sigh, and we watched the starlings gather on the old confederate statue across the gravel road from the store. Out at the intersection, a Sheriff's Deputy car sailed past going south on the Millersville highway, spinning red dust devils along the roadside. Adam pointed at the cruiser with the neck of his beer bottle.

"Heard they gave ol'Corncob five years for Grand Larceny. He told me it was all on account of that CNN story. Had you ever met him?"

"Don't believe I did, Adam. Not that I recall."

"Well you'd have remembered it if you ever met him."

Adam drained the bottle and set it down gently by the neck with long calloused fingertips, and then shifted in his chair to find a more comfortable position. I knew the signs, and stretched my legs out in front of me, sanding ancient planks with red grit under my old hiking boots, waiting for him to begin the story.

"He was the 'Speedo Bandit'. Did you hear about all that?"

"I believe that happened before I settled in down here, Adam."

"Yeah. That'd be right.

"Corncob was Cornelius Cobb Hooker. He was the star full back for the Finton Warriors. They never lost a game while he was in high school – took the state pennant six years running, 'til he finally graduated. He never seemed to do much after high school. He was about like me, had a hard time finding an anchor in his life. I went to see him right after they put him in jail – he didn't have any family except for his Aunt Gracie that he used to live with, but she had given him up for lost.

Corncob told me he got the whole idea watching the news one night. There was a pair of fellas in one of those Pacific island countries that started robbing stores and tourists. They stripped down to just their skivvies and rubbed themselves with cooking oil, so no one could catch hold of them when they ran off.

The next morning after the newscast, Corncob stood before the mirror in his trailer bedroom looking at himself, ready to begin his life of crime. He was stripped all the way down to his naturals, except for an old orange Speedo he had bought at the five and dime store. Halloween was too far off and the five and dime didn't have any serious masks, so he had to settle for a bright yellow two-pipe snorkel mask that went over his eyes and nose - the kind that had ping pong balls in little plastic cages at the top of the snorkel tubes to keep the water out. To help with his getaways, he had smeared himself topnotch to toenail in fresh lard.

Determined to succeed as a criminal, if he couldn't

succeed as a good citizen, Corncob jumped into his faded red Yugo for his first trip into town on the dark side of life. The seats in the Yugo had long since given way in the seams, exposing the foam rubber fill, and Corncob had re-covered the front seats with what was left of an old plastic shower curtain. Just as soon as he slammed the door and brought his feet up off the floor to find the gas and clutch pedals, he started sliding down the plastic in his own grease. There was no stopping. It was like a walrus sliding into the great North Sea. Try as he might, nothing he grabbed for would let him hold on or let him pull himself back up. The more he slipped, the faster he went down, and the more he would slip. It was amazing to think that a six-foot-four man weighing almost three hundred pounds could work himself under the dash of a little Yugo, but Gracie saw it herself.

She came home from working an extra shift at the Double Oak Yarn factory up at Union Rest, and saw her nephew's car just where it was when she left that morning. When she walked passed, she heard him crying in there. She looked in, but didn't see anybody sitting in any of the seats, so started to go on in. He heard her close by and started wailing.

"Aunt Gracie, Help me! Help me! I'm stuck under the dash!"

She looked around to see if he was hiding in one of the boxwoods at the front porch; figured he'd been drinking and thinking of mischief all day, but couldn't see him there either.

"Cornelius! You come out here this instant."

"I can't Aunt Gracie! I'm stuck!"

She heard his voice from within the car and managed to get the driver side door open. He spilled out onto the sandy pebble driveway like a giant pale squid pouring out of a paint can – a giant pale squid wearing nothing but an orange Speedo and coated in runny lard.

She just looked at him with her mouth wide open as he gasped at fresh air and brushed bits of Yugo seat foam off his greasy body. Imprints of the three little Yugo foot pedals were pressed deep into the skin of his left chest. Formed in the fat of his right inner thigh was the perfect reverse likeness of the dash radio that he had just rewired for a CD player. The Barry Manilow CD he used to test the player was in there all day, and he had listened to *Copacabana* repeat itself two hundred and nineteen times.

"Aunt Gracie looked skyward. "Lord God, a'mighty!"

He opened his mouth to speak, but she just turned away shaking her hands back and forth over her ears saying, "I don't want to know, Cornelius. I just don't want to know!"

As Gracie stormed into the house, Corncob slowly worked from his knees to his feet, staggered in fits and stops to the edge of the yard like a walking dead man, and shoved the CD deep into the trash barrel, crushing it in his hand among the discarded green beans and old county newspapers.

The next day, Corncob put some striped beach towels on his car seats, replenished his coating of lard, and set out again to pillage his fortune. On his way into Millersville he considered where he would strike first, but all the stores he could think of that had cash boxes instead of registers and usually had money laying out in the open for easy grabbing, were also places run by people he could not bring himself to rob. He decided he needed to rob a place that was run by people he didn't know and that had so much money they would hardly miss an armload or two. That's when he thought of the Millersville Second National Bank.

Corncob pulled up in front of the bank, and sat there a few minutes working up the nerve to go in there and grab a bunch of money. He rubbed the lard over his body as much as he could reach to reassure himself that no one was going to be able to hold on to him, took in a couple deep breaths, put on his two-pipe snorkel mask to hide his identity, and then stepped out onto the sidewalk. He was nervous as a schoolboy on his first date, and the little white ping pong balls at the top of the snorkel pipe valves went up and down with each breath he took, making a hissing sound followed by a little pop each time.

Millersville is not only the county seat, but it is the economic center for Finton County. Ranged around the town are seven factories, two produce heavy cotton yarn furniture fabric, three make wood furniture frames, and two make fold-out sofas. All the factories hand out their paychecks on Thursday afternoons. On Friday mornings about a third of the workers come in late or lay out altogether and go by the bank to cash their checks, the biggest bank in town being the Millersville Second National, and this was Friday morning.

When Corncob walked into the bank lobby there must have been at least forty five people in lines ahead of him to the three teller windows. Not willing to give up and go home, he picked the shortest line and got in it.

"Sssssssssss-pop. Sssssssssssss-pop."

People turned to stare at him, but he had learned watching old Dragnet shows not to make direct eye contact, so people would not remember seeing him. He waited in line in his snorkel mask, hissing when he took in a breath and popping when he let one out, like a hospital breathing pump, listening to the *Lady From Ipanema* play over the speakers in the background. People stared and he looked around the lobby not making eye contact and acting as nonchalant as he could make himself act, being mostly naked and covered in lard except for his orange Speedo and yellow snorkel mask. The longer he waited the more nervous he was and the warmer he got. That's when the lard started dripping.

Plip.

Corncob was a well-fed man, and what he had in the way of overlap at the waist could only be rightly called a 'spare tire' if what you had in mind went on the back wheel of a tractor. With that much insulation, his body heat began reducing that lard to runny oil in no time. It began to drip off, drop by drop, and form little puddles on the red tile flooring of the bank lobby. Two other people, arriving after he did, slipped in little puddles he had left back there, taking serious falls, but were helped back up by the bank guard who had become fixated watching Corncob.

"Sssssssssss-pop. Sssssssssssss-pop." Plip.

Finally, after listening to a violin and oboe version of *Hey Jude* squeak through the lobby speakers, Corncob got his turn to the teller window, and the guard decided it was time to step in. He raised a questioning finger toward Corncob's mask and opened his mouth to ask the questions he had been working on since Corncob came into the bank, and stepped into a little puddle of melted lard. His feet slipped out forward and up in the air so high, Corncob could see the Cats Paw imprint on the bottom of his resoled neoprene heels, and then he went down hard on the floor like a tossed sack of potatoes that knocked him out cold. Not wasting the moment, Corncob belly up'd to the counter and looked inside the teller window. There to the side must have been a thousand dollars in tens and twenties, stacked high and neatly so the teller could quickly cash all the Friday morning factory checks.

"Sssssssssss-pop. Sssssssssssss-pop."

"C-can I help you sir?" He couldn't take his eyes off all that money until the teller spoke. Her eyes were wide with curiosity, and green the color of an emerald necklace he had once seen in Tater Millpond's store. She had auburn hair and a voice as soft as baby's breath. He looked from her face back to the money then back to her face.

"Sssssssssss-pop. Ssssssssss-pop." Plip. Plip.

"Do you wish to cash a check, sir?"

"Gib be thub moneyb. Ssssssss-pop. Sssss-pop. Ssssss-pop." The melted lard dripped faster onto the tile floor under him.

"Sir, you'll need to give me your signed check first."

"Nobe checkb"

"You don't have a check?"

"NOBE. Gib be theb moneyb! Ssss-pop. Ssss-pop." Plip. Plip. Plip.

She stared at him, unable to take her eyes off the strangest sight she had ever seen in her twenty years.

"Cornelius, is that you?"

"Ssss-pop. Ssss-pop. Nobe."

Then he lunged his arm over the glass partition making a grab for the money stack. The movement made his feet slide over the grease puddle below him and he dropped from her view catching his fall by grabbing the partition and the counter to pull himself back up. His feet began a fast Texas two-step in all directions trying to find a spot where he could stand again, but each movement only forced him to grab firmer to the counter.

"Sss-pop. Sss-pop. Sss-pop!"

He pulled himself up to the countertop, both his arms stretched to the back edge near the teller and framing his masked face, red with exertion and staring at her through the fogging plastic, as his feet and lower body contorted in spasms trying desperately to stand. The slipping thumping of his bare feet and knees bumping against the outer wall of the counter face sounded like a horse trying to escape his stall. His arms and hands began to slip forward over the counter surface. Sadness filled his eyes as he slipped over the edge of the counter and dropped completely to the floor.

The small crowd of people in the lobby was stunned at the sight. Those that could, tried to help the unconscious guard, while the others just stared at Corncob in disbelief. He managed to stand again in front of the second window and grabbed at her stack of bills, but his feet slipped out again and he crashed to the floor. Working farther down the counter looking for unoiled surfaces, he raised up again at the third window and managed to pluck a large handful of twenties just before his feet slipped again and the twenties were freed up into the air to find their own way down to the floor in a race with Corncob. Several bills sailed down under Corncob as gravity took him again and he crashed to the floor on top of them. He slip-crawled-stood-slipped his way back to the front door where an elderly woman held the door open for him to exit, noticing there were six twenties larded on his back.

Once outside he managed to stand again by pulling himself up the stone block wall of the bank.

"Ss-pop. Ss-pop. Ss-pop." Plip.

Then he slipped down again, his feet kicking against a passing man who jumped away to avoid the grease splatter of Corncob's fall. On hands and knees, Cornelius crawled across the sidewalk to where he had left his Yugo, but it was not there.

Since the Millersville Second National Bank shared a back parking lot with the Finton County Sheriff's Department and the County Courthouse, and the bank guard had called them as soon as Corncob got in the teller line, his Yugo had been hauled off to the county lot even before he made his first grab for the money. There was a video feed from the bank to the Sheriff's

Department, and once the Sheriff had determined that Corncob was unarmed, he sent a deputy to fetch Judge Atkins. They both decided to let Corncob keep on for a while longer and recorded the video feed so they could send it into one of those reality TV cop shows.

When Corncob crawled wearily to the curb, his red Yugo had been replaced by a black and white squad car, with a ratty old wool blanket already tossed over the back seat to protect it from the lard. The deputy helped Corncob into the back, peeling the six twenties off his back as evidence. After locking the doors to the back seat, the deputy looked into the rearview mirror and through the wire mesh separating the front and back.

"You might as well take that mask off now."

"Sssssssss-pop. Sssssssssss-pop. NOBE! Sss-pop"

Corncob was charged with grand larceny and malicious greasing, but no one wanted to see him serve time in a federal penitentiary, so it was never mentioned in the court papers that his larceny occurred in the Millersville Second National Bank. He did his time down at the County Farm not far from here, and although his Aunt had disowned him, he was visited every other Tuesday by that little green-eyed teller girl."

I heard the old chair squeak a dozen complaints as Adam got up and went back inside. He said over his shoulder just before the screen door screeched shut again, " 'Course, you know he got out last year. Started his own shop up in Millersville."

I nodded to the bright light out beyond the porch shade. I had been to 'Hooker's Auto Audio' just the previous month to have the speaker for my Jeep radio fixed. That green-eyed girl was still working at the bank, where I had an account now, and the shiny new plaque by the teller window says "Mrs. C. Hooker".

My RC was gone and the bottle was warm and dry, so I took it into the store to get my nickel back, but

Adam said I got it chipped and only gave me 3 cents for it. I dropped the coins into the extra penny bowl by the cash register, knowing full well that Adam would pocket them as soon as I walked out of the store, and I drove the Jeep home.

GENERAL ALPHONSE P. TOOEY

I once blew an engine and the air pressure system on a cantankerous old eighteen wheeler just outside Union Rest. I was standing there in the pouring rain in front of that devil, drinking a pint bottle of Tennessee whiskey and shooting my .357 into the radiator, when Deputy Sheriff Tibideaux pulled up and invited me to spend the night with some other friends of Finton County. After the trucking company paid my bail and set me free, I've just stayed around here.

In my hard-drinking days, I frequently found myself serving the public good as a guest of the Finton County Corrections Department. On one such community spirited exercise, I was afforded the opportunity to clean the statue of General Alphonse P. Tooey, famed Confederate patriot lost during that unfortunate misunderstanding with Abraham Lincoln during the 1860s. My esteemed associate for that civic outing was none other than Tater Millpond of Millpond's Emporium and Pawn Broker, recently closed after criminals broke into Tater's store and stuck several pieces of local heirloom jewelry into his safe, just before a Finton County Deputy happened to look in there with a warrant. Judge Atkins had him brought before the bench eleven times, before he finally passed sentence and gave Tater 18 months, less time already served. The Judge was going through hard times himself, coming to grips with his daughter's announcement that she was gay, and whenever he felt at his lowest he'd have a Deputy go fetch Tater. Atkins said nothing could perk him up more than hearing Tater spin a lie.

Tater was also great with soft metals. He could turn an easily recognized expensive bracelet into the most attractive earring and necklace set you could ever buy; and that skill made Tater the perfect person to help spiff up Gen'l Tooey's statue. It was made of brass marbled lead, and the locals had a habit of cutting small chunks out of it for fishing sinkers when the bass were running hungry in Lake Adolphus. So, they gave Tater a handheld propane soldering torch and me a bag of number eight steel wool when they dropped us off at Tooey's Crossroads without a guard, but with a couple county vouchers to buy sandwiches and sodas across a dusty loose-gravel road at the Park'N'Pump.

Tater had several short thumb thick lead rods that he melted into the larger gashes taken out of Tooey's leg. When he finished one side and moved on, I'd start burnishing his patches with the steel wool. The lead was easy work, but the edges of the brass rippling through the lead would catch the steel wool and yank it back across the palm of my hand, giving me a series of small skin slices like paper cuts; not deep enough to draw blood but deep enough to find a nerve so I knew I was cut. After several cuts, I threw the ball of spun metal to the ground in aggravation.

"Damn, Tater. Why's this got brass runnin' through it anyway?"

"Came from the cannonball that killed him."

Tater squeezed his eyes down at my blank look and decided that nine-thirty in the morning was close enough to lunchtime, and that banishing my obvious ignorance of local history was a higher priority for the moment than soldering General Tooey's legs. We crossed the gravel road to the Park'N'Pump, where Tater convinced the owner that he could charge the county for four RCs and two double deluxe hamburgers with chili cheese fries if he'd just give us each a beer and a pack of nabs. Then we settled onto a single board bench out back by the ice machine where we couldn't be seen from either road, and there began my history education of Tooey's Crossroads.

Adolphus Tooey started a general store in southern Finton County, using the last standing barn left behind when fire swept over his Daddy's failing tobacco farm, and his Daddy, in 1841. His wife and two daughters had finally moved out of the hayloft into a newly built little cottage next to the barn just in time to welcome the son Alphonse. The Tooey's were serious two-name people, so there was no middle name intended when Adolphus penned Alphonse P. Tooey into the family bible. Deep inside he thought it would always be funny to hear his son say "p'tooey" whenever he introduced himself. It was an inflicted omen that forever kept greatness far out of Alphonse's reach.

Adolphus did well with his store, and his family never wanted for anything. He was a shrewd bargainer and found great profit in buying seconds and selling them as firsts. His son always had new clothes of the best fabric, even if the pants were short or the shirt loose, or one sleeve much longer than the other, or the color odd in some way. It was the oddity of color that brought 30 bolts of daffodil yellow heavy wool to Tooey's Store. Try as he may though, he was unable to convince the local ladies and their daughters how stunning they would be at their Cotillions in bright yellow dresses. The color appealed to many, but the coarseness of the fabric was simply too much a challenge for fragile womanly skin in the warm Spring air. After his own daughters threatened to wander the roads of Finton County in their naturals rather than don the yellow wool, and his wife refused to allow the house to be curtained throughout with the fabric, he finally rolled up the cloth for storage in the loft, ever thereafter looking for a way to sell it.

In a similar fashion one day there arrived at Tooey's Store four wooden crates, each half the size of a man's casket, and each harboring four brass figurines in the likeness of De Milo's Rising Venus. The price was extraordinarily low for brass, so he could not help but purchase the entire consignment abandoned by the original owner to the care of the Lynchburg Railroad shipping master. In the single day that one of the brass figurines graced the front window of Tooey's Store, he was threatened with divorce by his wife, disownment by his daughters, charged with lewdness by the Sheriff's wife, caught Alphonse fondling it, and begrudgingly sold it below cost to Mauzy Broadway who ran a 'gentleman's club' up in Millersville. The remaining fifteen lost daughters of Venus were then sent to bunk up with the yellow wool.

When news of the war reached Adolphus he knew there was money to be made in supplies. In a fervor of patriotism heavily laced with capitalism, he had the upper half of one of the daughters of Venus melted down into four small cannon balls. He then boxed them up as samples for sale and sent them via mail train to the new War Department in Montgomery. As soon as he learned the uniform color for the new Confederate army, he brought down the wool and sent it out to be dyed dark gray. He then packed his son Alphonse off to Millersville to join the Finton County Militia, with a note to the Militia Commander explaining that a captaincy for his son would be well received by a store owner who could provide the Commander with many needed items during the coming shortages. It all came to naught, though.

No response came from the War Department. The Militia sent his son home with a note saying that if Adolphus had a good mule instead, the Commander would make IT a Captain, but a commission would be wasted on Alphonse, who was, in the Commander's own written words,

"stupider than owl shit".

Adding further grievous insult to Adolphus' honor, the wool came back from the Dyer with its own note of apology explaining that the local gray dye, which included a small amount of powdered copper, reacted horrifically with the particular Italian dye already in the fabric, resulting in the surprisingly bright key lime green that was the new permanent color of his wool; and therefore there was no charge. The lime green wool was sent back up to the daughters of Venus and Adolphus forbid his family to ever mention it again.

Nonetheless, Tooey's Store prospered during the first two years of the conflict, so much so that the Army cut a second wagon road down from Camp Finton right past Tooey's Store and as far west as Greenwood Cattle Ranch. Supply wagons trudged by seven days a week hauling sides of beef and everything Adolphus could sell. When the big house was built back from the Millersville road, Alphonse opened a tavern in the little cottage beside the store and rented two of the bedrooms out to travelers. Once Adolphus sent his older daughter over to keep the till, the little tavern started making good money, since Alphonse frequently forgot to collect the coins from strangers, and was too embarrassed to charge his friends; of which the number grew as word of his embarrassment spread. It was then the Army asked Adolphus to post mail from the soldiers at Camp Finton, and gave him a commission to operate a post office in the back corner of the store, that the area became known as Tooey's Crossroads.

It was in the third year that the cattle trade gave out, since there were no more to be had from Greenwood, most shelves went bare in Tooey's Store. Beer was only available in the Tavern every other Tuesday, if it was beer. Adolphus had a fortune in Confederate cash squeezed away in his safe, but every day it was worth less and less. At the current rate of inflation, he figured he would be poor in less than a year. He still begrudged the Finton County Militia for denying his son both commission and membership, and with little distraction from the occasional customer, set his daughters to stitching uniforms out of his key lime green wool. With the available remaining men from local farms and Alphonse' hired bartender, Adolphus formed the Southern Finton County Militia Reserves, and appointed Alfonse as Commanding General. The SFCMR boasted a full regiment of one general, two colonels, two majors and three captains. The lieutenants, sergeants, and privates would be added later as they became available, but at the time of the first regimental muster, the eight members of the SFCMR were glorious in their particularly unique regalia. A broad piece of the wool was even used as a battle flag that sported yellow stars for the Confederate States in a rectangle around the letters SFCMR and below them the year 1864.

A Revolutionary War cannon had been abandoned on a hilltop just north of Tooey's Crossroads in 1778 when the left wheel broke, so Alphonse claimed the cannon in the name of the Confederacy, cleared all the briars off it and named the hilltop Battery Tooey. Every morning and evening for nearly a week most of the SFCMR would gather at the hilltop to raise and lower the SFCMR flag, but since there was neither bugler nor bugle, Alphonse' bartender, Captain Hooker, buzzed 'Dixie' on a rusty kazoo during the ceremony.

Early the next week, when flag raising and lowering

seemed to have been set aside for a while, a wagon coming down from Millersville stopped by the Store with a box for Adolphus. Apparently, his four brass cannon balls had never made it to the War Department, and had waited all this time to be returned to sender for lack of sufficient postage. The driver said he wasn't interested in collecting any postage, since he was just dropping them off on his way to his sister's farm to wait until the war was over. Adolphus said nothing to the man but spun on his heels and retreated into his store. Alphonse set the box on the store porch and invited the driver up to the Tavern for a free beer, but suggested he get it drunk before his sister came down from the house.

That evening the flag ceremony was a short one while Alphonse raised and then lowered the flag single-handedly, since he was saluting with the other, and humming Dixie. He then stacked the four small brass cannonballs next to the cannon that now had an empty cider barrel in place of its missing left wheel. The following morning during Alphonse's breakfast Captain Hooker came running breathlessly to the back door of the kitchen.

"The Yankees are coming! The Yankees are coming!"

Alphonse was dabbing the last of his grits and red-eye gravy with a crumbly piece of cornbread and held it in mid-air just in front of his mouth when he turned to look at Hooker. He remembered the bread too late and he turned back just in time to see it fall into his lap. He looked down at his cornbread and then back at Hooker.

"What?" and then back at his cornbread.

"Alphonse, just wipe it off and git out here!"

A patrol of twenty Union Cavalry had managed to get lost and found themselves trotting around southern Finton County when they should have been helping to secure the left flank of a river crossing far to the north.

But to the SFCMR, the invasion of the northern aggressor had finally swept down upon them. To Hooker's suggestion of gathering the troops, Alphonse delivered a decisive

"Yeah, O.K."

Then went upstairs to don his uniform while Hooker spread the word among the SFCMR. The regiment gathered at Battery Tooey by ten-ish and prepared to defend their native soil. Hooker had borrowed one of Adolphus' mules, Suzie, and had her staked out behind the hill in case General Tooey needed to send urgent messages. At noon the order went out and Hooker was sent down to the store for lunches.

At three, Alphonse sent Hooker back up the Millersville road to see what was keeping the Yankees so long. Hooker found them napping under a pair of spready oaks about three miles north of the Crossroads. He approached the patrol in the bright afternoon sun, bobbing on Suzie's bare back, resplendent in his key lime green captain's uniform, straw hat, and rooster feather. The Union soldiers arose in singles, each shading his eyes from the sun with his cap, trying to identify either the allegiance or the species of the oncoming vision. When Hooker approached within thirty yards of the patrol, one trooper finally brought up his carbine into full view and then raised a hand.

"That's close enough, Ma'am".

Hooker drew himself up to his full five-foot-five height and announced that he was a captain in the Southern Finton County Militia Reserve and they, being godless Yankee invaders, were to surrender their arms and prepare to be taken prisoners, or face the full wrath of General Alphonse P. Tooey and the entire regiment of the SFCMR. Captain Richard Lewis, recent of Alpine, New York, crack pistol shot and commanding officer of the patrol, who had suffered severe hearing loss after charging a Confederate gun emplacement at Chancellorsville, turned to First Sergeant Ellenberger.

"What'd he say?"

"Said we were to lay down our arms and surrender to his General."

"Who th'Hell is his General?"

"Sounded like *Alfred P'tooey,* Cap'n.*"

Captain Lewis stepped forward, resting his hand lightly on the holster of his service Colt, and yelled back at Hooker.

"You go tell General P'tooey he can kiss my Yankee ass!" Then he slowly turned around and calmly spoke to his troops. "One of you boys shoot that big mouthed sissy."

Hooker did not hear the command, but saw several carbine barrels come up and rifle stocks slip against their owner's shoulders. Needing no further indication of his peril, Hooker yanked Suzie's head around so far she dropped spittle into his lap, and then he kicked her in the sides as hard as he could. The air exploded in gunfire with bullets zipping past Hooker's head as he ducked and twisted, pushing Suzie to run for all her life. After a hundred yards, no bullet had yet touched him and the Yankee Captain was cussing and slapping his men with his cap for being such poor shots.

At a hundred and fifty yards the Captain drew out his Colt, spread his legs, gripped the pistol in both hands and took a sight on the retreating Hooker. Lewis held no true deep grudge against Southerners, but after years of fighting a plow to keep it straight behind a cantankerous jackass back in Alpine, he absolutely hated mules. At one hundred and seventy-five yards he took in a slow deep breath, let out half of it, and then fired the Colt, shooting the mule dead center in her left haunch.

Suzie bucked and heehawed as close to a blood-curdling scream as a mule can make. It was all Hooker could do to hold on while Suzie set a land speed record unmatched before or since by a butt shot jackass, but she didn't stop. When they got to the tree line and the bullets stopped, Hooker couldn't even get her to slow down. She was shocked and scared and hurt and mad at everything around her. Every trot she took made her haunch feel like it was on fire, but she was terrified that if she stopped, whatever just happened to her in all that noise would happen again, so she just kept up that awful braying and running as fast as she could.

Hooker and Suzie were almost all the way back to Battery Tooey when Suzie finally thought of something that might help her take the edge off her predicament, so she twisted her head back as far as her neck would go and bit the living Hell out of Hooker's right leg. Then it was with bloody mule haunch and bloody leg that Hooker reported to General Tooey that he should expect the Yankees to come along directly. Hooker was treated with such concern and respect due to his wounded leg that he decided not to tell them Suzie had bit him.

Within minutes the sound of twenty pounding horses ran down the Millersville road bringing the Yankees. It was then that Buford Greenwood pointed out that they couldn't see the road from the Battery, and maybe the Yankees wouldn't be able to see them. So, the entire SFCMR, except Hooker, stumbled down the front slope to the roadside to wave their arms and yell "Hey!" at the patrol. Ever on the quick, Jack Dickels was the first to point out that in all their efforts to get uniforms and a flag and the Revolutionary war cannon, none of them had actually acquired a firearm while it appeared that the Yankees had a bunch of them. In a storm of .53 caliber bullets the SFCMR scrambled back up the slope to the safety of the little dirt berm piled before the mouth of the old cannon.

"Load the cannon!" Alphonse yelled and grabbed up

one of his Daddy's postage-due cannonballs.

George Daniels showed his budding mental faculties by asking which one of the group was supposed to have brought gunpowder, but none of them could rightly remember the topic ever coming up before. By then the Yankees had formed a skirmish line at the base of the hill and were preparing to advance. General Alphonse took command of the moment and issued a string of orders that snapped the SFCMR into military discipline.

As soon as the first Yankee took a step up the slope to Battery Tooey, two Colonels, two Majors, and two captains of the SFCMR hunched down together yelling in chorus "KaBoom!". Hooker then tossed up a handful of dirt for smoke effect, and Alphonse threw one of the baseball-sized cannonballs straight at Yankees. The cannonball hit the first soldier slap in the chest and knocked him on his butt, causing the others to stop and stare at him waiting for the gush of blood, but it didn't happen.

Sergeant Ellenberger kicked at the private in front of him and the advance continued, firing as they went. Once again the six men on the hill yelled "Ka-Boom!", Hooker threw up the dust, and Alphonse took a bead on another soldier, breaking the boy's wrist with a savage knuckleball overhand throw.

"Take that damned cannon, Boys," Captain Lewis yelled. He figured the sound of the cannon fire was just muffled by his ruined hearing.

On the next firing, Alphonse broke the knee of Corporal Rushinski and sent him rolling back down the hill in writhing pain, but Sergeant Ellenberger had seen Alphonse throw the brass ball.

"They're just <u>throwing</u> the cannonballs at us, Captain" he yelled through the smoke of their own carbines

But the Captain only heard a few words and kept

bellowing "Take'em boys, Take'em! Death or glory! Go! Go! Go!".

Ellenberger bent down and picked up the little brass cannonball that had hit Rushinski and hefted it in his hand. Ten years working in a Pennsylvania coal mine had put buffalo sized muscles in his arms and back, so as soon as he could see anyone at the top of the hill he pulled his arm up and behind his shoulder like a cocked main spring ready to go. He and Alphonse locked eyes from similar positions and each let fly with all the strength the body could deliver, sending the cannonballs swishing by each other in mid-air. Alphonse's ball burned across the side of Ellenberger's face giving him a cauliflower ear that stayed with him until he died in 1897. Ellenberger's ball landed smack center of Alphonse's forehead and drove him back over the cider barrel and onto the ground, where he watched the lime green flag of the SFCMR and thought a second about his quiet last night before he died.

When they saw their General go down, and knowing all their ammunition was spent, the entire SFCMR charged down the back slope of the battery hill and into the wild swamp peeling off and dropping pieces of lime green wool uniform as they went. So it was in his long johns that former Captain Hooker, late of the SFCMR, tapped lightly on the back door of the big house near midnight to tell Adolphus that his only son had fallen while fighting the Yankees in defense of Battery Tooey.

Alphonse was later buried in the field across the road from Tooey's Store, and a few years later Adolphus consigned the lost daughters of Venus to be melted down for a statue to his son's honor. It was then that he learned only the first two figurines were actually made of brass, while the remaining fourteen were only of lead, and that he had been hoodwinked after all.

When the mold was filled with the molten metal the

brass and lead intertwined like barber pole stripes, shiny yellow brass and dark gray lead. The sculptor, an art student from Millersville, gave Alphonse a manly pose, in full General regalia resting one gloved fist on his waist above the holster he never owned, and held in the palm of his other hand in front of his belt was a three-inch cannonball.

Tater was startled from his last line by the sound of tires on gravel in the parking lot of Al's Tavern next door to the Park'N'Pump. A huge white '84 Coupe de Ville convertible slid to a stop and a muscular shouldered driver hopped over the door to plant silver-tipped cowboy boots firmly into the gravel, and glide a pocket comb in practiced motion through an Elvis Presley style ducktail. The two large breasts under the black and white plaid western shirt were unmistakable, even over the distance from the corner of the ice machine. Tater pointed his long emptied beer can at the car.

"That there is Alexandra Tooey, a.k.a. Big Al, as in Al's Tavern."

I then watched a petite honey brown-skinned cutie in a skirt just quarter inches shy of public lewdness, dainty-step around to the front of the 'Caddy from the other side, plant a blood pressure raising kiss on the lips of Big Al, and waited for Tater to introduce us from afar.

"And that, is none other than Yolanda Atkins. The only daughter, pride, joy, and heartbreak of His Honor, Circuit Court Judge Atkins."

We tossed our beer cans into the trash, noticing with exchanged worried looks how low the sun had dropped in the sky, and walked around front of the Park'N'Pump to find the Deputy's car there with the left door open and the engine still running. We dashed across the gravel road to the statue just as the Deputy emerged from the store stuffing a couple pieces of paper into his shirt pocket. He pointed at us with his sunglasses, put them on and drove the car across the road. We got into the back carrying the soldering torch and steel wool, and he remote locked the back doors. He reached up and flicked a fingernail against the wire cage separating the front and back seats.

"Here I was all upset with myself for letting you boys work through lunch and supper, but Adam Tooey tells me you been working like dogs all day and he fed you each for both meals. Hell, I haven't even had my supper yet."

Tater gave me a silent look that we best not tell the Deputy anything different than what he had already heard in the Park'N'Pump. The Deputy shook his head, pulling out the vouchers and holding them against the steering wheel between his fingers as he drove north toward Millersville.

"Six RCs, Four deluxe hamburgers with chili-cheese fries and two packs of nabs!" He then picked up the radio microphone. "Harry, this is Mike. Go ahead and close up the kitchen and send the help back to their cells. These boys already ate better than us."

We had paid dearly for our beer and crackers far earlier in the day, and the old store owner had doubled up on the meal chits he was charging to the county for food he never served us. I looked back, watching the statue of General Tooey shrink in the distance as we sped away from Tooey's Crossroads, wondering what they were going to have for breakfast the next morning, and my stomach growled.

TOOEY'S CROSSROADS

To meet the requirements for work release, I once took a
job as short order cook, janitor, and night watchman at
the Park'N'Pump in Tooey's Crossroads.   That's in
southern Finton County at the intersection of State Route
535, known locally as the Millersville Road, and a
gravel county road that runs east-west down from
several old farms and then across to the swamp country
out back.   The Swamp Road once ran on through to an
old Confederate army camp, but now just stops at the
edge of a decline into Lake Adolphus, where the locals
use it to launch Jon boats for bass fishing and the
occasional midnight frog shoot.

Since the Park'N'Pump closed at 9:30 each evening,
except for Friday night when it stayed open until 10:00,
and the owner paid minimum salary regardless of how
busy or quiet it got, I thought this would be a piece of
cake.   Adam Tooey, the owner, was a kindly but
larcenous old stoop-shouldered gentleman with sparsely
thin hair combed and sprayed into a wilting pompadour.
On my first day Adam informed me that working for the
Park'N'Pump also meant working for Al's Tavern next
door, and that since all the Finton County deputies knew
that, failing to pull my full load at either place of
business would violate my work release.   Al's Tavern
was open until 2 AM every night, except for Friday
when they just didn't even bother to close it at all, and
that job almost killed me.

The main business for the Park'N'Pump, after
gasoline, was by far the four dollar deluxe cheeseburger
and chili-cheese fries dinner.   Adam would generally let
me sleep until around 10 AM, then roust me out of the

back room to get the grill ready. Heavy duty log haulers would take any passable route they could manage to be near Tooey's Crossroads for lunch. The secret was hand carried each morning by a black woman named Sarah, pronounced with the first 'a' long and heavy, who walked up the Swamp Road carrying two five gallon commercial paint buckets covered with Plastic wrap. One bucket held Coleslaw, the other held chili, and she made them both at home before arriving at 10:30 every morning Monday through Saturday.

I fried hamburger patties, pulled and separated from a white waxy freezer box, laid one slice of generic American cheese across the top after I flipped them, and then slid them off a greasy spatula onto a waiting warm bun as soon as they were ready. Adam cooked French fries in ancient deep baskets that could have taken a full watermelon each, poured melted cheese over them once they were portioned out into small cardboard baskets, and shoved them along the counter to Sarah. Sarah's station was in front of an old double sink, below a high-bottom window with a thick sill that extended several inches outside. Below the inside window sill and above the sink was a narrow unpainted shelf barely holding two old cracked deep plastic bowls that once contained chitterlings. The bowl on the left was marked $1 in red magic marker. In the sinks below the shelf were the five-gallon buckets of Cole slaw and chili, each supporting its own modest sized aged wooden ladle hanging from the lip; the lower end of the chili ladle long stained almost mahogany from the sauce.

Like a general looking along the line of his advancing troops, Sarah looked left then right, to ensure everything was ready, then she nodded to Adam and slid up the window. It was almost a sea of faded John Deere and Ford caps over bushy brows, holding up bills and reaching out for the burger dinners, which brought to mind pictures of feeding the multitude on the hillside. In constantly repeated motions, Sarah gave a ladle of Cole slaw to each burger and a ladle of chili to each order of cheese fries, set them up on the sill and took down the bills. The ones went down into the left and every other bill went down into the right. No one ordered, they only wanted the one thing we were serving, and none of us said anything as we hustled to keep up the pace at the window where they grabbed for anything that went up on the sill.

Only two comments were made during two and a half hours, "That was a twenty" (said almost every day by the same trucker) and "I don't want chili" (from a Yankee passing through), to which Sarah provided the same answer, "Kiss my ass".

When the Cole slaw and chili ran out after the same dinner plate, Sarah reached up and closed the window without looking or asking anything of the remaining people outside, and started cleaning out the paint buckets.

I still had several patties bubbling on the grill, observed by Adam as he took off his apron saying, "You need to pace it better than that, young man."

He took a twenty and a ten out of the right hand bowl and handed them to Sarah, who put them in her pocket.

She said over her shoulder as she finished cleaning the buckets, "I need to take some cayenne along with the cabbage heads and hamburger when I leave."

He didn't look back, but spoke to the ceiling as he carried the money bowls to the front like a proud Papa carrying his twins. "Take what ya'need, Sarah."

By 2:30 PM the kitchen was clean, Adam was counting his money, and I was on my way across the parking lot to Big Al's.

Al's Tavern was run by Adam's baby sister Alexandra, who had come home after retiring from the

Marines as a hand-to-hand combat instructor. Al Tooey was six foot two, had shoulders that would make the Raven's defensive line sigh with envy, and a grip that could hand crush Brazil nuts. It was one of my main strategies of survival to stay on the good side of that woman. I did a fair job and helped behind the bar when the evening crowd belly-up'd, kept the glasses clean and caught up, and stomped down the paper towels in the men's room trash can when I got a chance. Al seemed satisfied with my work and would slap me on the back with a manly "Good job, fellah" when we would close up.

One Friday night Al came in late and kept leaving the bar to make calls on the pay phone by the door. Al wasn't known for having a modest or shy voice, so it wasn't hard to figure out she thought her significant other was cheating on her. Yolanda Atkins was a honey brown skin cutie of such striking appearance she could raise the dead if it ever appealed to her, but she would get confused occasionally and take up with a man for a day or two. During our second happy hour that we had each Friday from midnight to 1 AM to keep business from going up to Millersville, Al tossed me her bar keys and said "Lock up when the business quits", and charged her '84 Caddy out of the parking lot, rooster-tailing arcs of loose gravel over all the other cars.

I still had three guys at the bar and sunlight was just slipping in under the lowest slat in the blinds, when the phone rang with a call for one of the three by a wife who had figured out where they were, and Al's Caddy pulled in. Two of the bar guys were trying unsuccessfully to coach the third through a fantastic tongue-tied excuse, while the third mistakenly held his hand over the earpiece instead of the mouthpiece, as Al walked in. If an extremely large dead man ever cried, he would look exactly the way Al did when she entered the bar. She gave a flat-footed kick to the bar stool that had been nailed to the floor under the phone, sending it crashing into the wall on the other side of the room, grabbed the receiver from the drunk and yanked it from his hands and the payphone without even looking in his direction, and said "We're closed." The three loggers managed to exit the same single-wide door instantaneously and jogged down the Swamp Road, one of them yelling over his shoulder that they would pick up their trucks later on that day.

Al walked by the end of the bar toward the back room, punched her fist through the doorframe as she grabbed an unopened fifth of Tennessee Whiskey, and slammed the door behind her, launching the glass-knobbed door handle out into the middle of the room where it filled the walls with twirling kaleidoscopes from the sunlight. I cleaned up the Tavern, locked the cash box and silently slid the keys under the backroom door, and then pulled the front door closed, locking it from the inside as I left.

I never spoke to Al about that night, and she never invited me to, but she seemed to appreciate that respect for her privacy. In early May, when things were going well between her and Yolanda, Al took me out behind the tavern and flipped a ratty plastic tarp off a primer gray '69 Jeep Wrangler. The rusty trailer hitched to the rear end held an old wooden fishing boat sporting a 25 horsepower Johnson outboard on the transom.

"Guy came up from 'Loosianna a few years ago and ran up a hell-ashis tab, then tried to leave without paying. After he got out of the Millersville Clinic, he said to a deputy he'd come square up with me, but he never showed. Guess he took the bus."

I looked from the Jeep to the boat to Al, then back over the three again in silence.

"You get'em runnin', you can have'em. They're just

in my damned way here."

My next couple of Sundays were enjoyable in a black grease sort of way. Getting the Jeep four-cylinder running smoothly was a tinker's dream. After a good carb and head cleaning followed with a new hot arc plug, the Johnson started on the fourth pull, once Al set it in a water barrel for me. The boat was spruce plank and rope caulked with a two-inch thick oak transom, heavily painted inside and out, and dry as a bone on the water. Sunday evenings in June saw me coming back to the store with a healthy tan and near champion sized bass pulled from Lake Adolphus. The first of July my work release ended and the Finton County Corrections Department cut me loose, but Al and Adam said they'd give me full pay and let me off Sundays and Mondays both if I'd stay on until the end of the Summer. I said I would stay, but I should have left then.

It was the very next day that I found that damned woodpecker flapping weakly on the ground under a briar bush at the edge of the swamp out behind Al's Tavern. I got several thorn scratches and picked a hole in my new T-shirt getting the little feather ball out of the briars. It was one of the smaller eastern species of common woodpeckers and had a broken wing and a split upper bill. It must have flown in front of an empty logging truck running down at high speed from Millersville and it didn't look like it would live long, but it did. There was an old chicken wire rabbit cage next to the dumpster out behind the Park'N'Pump where Adam once tried to raise and sell rabbit meat as duck. His roast duck on a Kaiser roll actually sold pretty well to out-of-towners until they finished the interstate, but all the locals knew it was rabbit. So when the last cooked batch had to be thrown out after going bad waiting on a customer, he let the remaining three rabbits run off into the swamp to save the cost of feeding them, and took the duck off his roadside menu.

I placed the woodpecker in the rabbit cage, pulled up some close by dried grass for a nest of sorts and started looking for something the bird might eat. The dumpster was a cornucopia for the woodpecker. Plenty of young maggots on a jar lid, smeared with drippings from egg shells, and topped off with the residual from discarded packs of headache powder, provided me with all I needed to make a pâté for my patient. I should have quit then.

The woodpecker seemed to perk up a little bit by the next day, so I managed to find enough in the dumpster for another pâté and then came back out after supper and put a dab of Superglue on its beak. It was making a long slow muttering chirp that sounded to me like a whimper, and I thought it was hurting some more, so I went into the Park'N'Pump to ask Adam's help.

Adam had a sort of franchise from an Alabama drug company called Rural Rx, which skirted the law about mailing prescription drugs to people it didn't know, by having licensed distributors verify the buyers' information when they came to pick up their drugs. The distributor didn't have to be a pharmacist as long as one with a state license signed a county license that the local distributor had completed formal drug distribution training, and was an upstanding member of the community as verified by the local police. Since the regional sales rep for Rural Rx still managed to hold on to his pharmacist license, and since Tooey's Crossroads was a civil entity that was entitled to a constable, for which Adam made up a form naming Al, he got his local distributor's license.

Rural Rx paid Adam two dollars for each prescription he released and sold upon recipient verification. Adam made a sign telling customers about the two dollar handling fee and stuck it on the edge of the counter where he did business for Rural Rx, and a local film developing company. So although Rural Rx expected to get back eighteen dollars for a twenty dollar prescription, Adam handed the customer a receipt that showed twenty dollars for the prescription and then that two dollar handling fee described in his sign, took twenty-two dollars, kept four, and sent eighteen to Alabama at the end of the month.

Rural Rx got a lot of their drugs from countries that didn't speak English, and didn't lose sleep at night over U.S. Patent laws, so generic copies of well-known drugs like Rogaine and Viagra made up a large part of Adam's drug business, and most of his recipients were named John Smith, General Delivery, Tooey's Crossroads, Virginia. Adam had so many John Smith's he had to open the packages to see what was in there to make sure they got the right drug, and that led to Adam's Pharmacy days. He would pull out two or three pills from the bottles and save them up until he had more than enough for a full prescription, and then tell that particular John Smith that Rural Rx was running a special if he would just bring in his last empty bottle they would fill it for only 80% of the usual cost, plus Adam's handling fee. So, on those orders, Adam got twenty dollars, John Smith saved two dollars, and Rural Rx didn't get peep.

I was wandering along the short aisle that held over the counter drugs, with my chin in my hand and tapping the end of my nose with my fingertip trying to figure out which drug might do some good for the poor old damned woodpecker. Adam caught me staring at the pain killers and tapping my nose. "What's wrong, young man? You got aches?"

"Naw." I mumbled through my fingers "I got a real sick woodpecker I'm trying to take care of."

He just laid a gentle hand on my shoulder, nodded his head in serious thought, and stepped behind the Rural Rx

/Fujak Film counter. Now, that's when I should have realized he hadn't heard me correctly; when he didn't ask me 'what the hell I was doing with a damned woodpecker', or at least asked 'who the hell I thought was going to pay good money for a stupid wild bird', or something like I would have generally expected from Adam Tooey. He just took it seriously and went behind the counter looking for something to help me without even asking how much I wanted to spend on it. I should have got suspicious right then, but I missed it.

Apparently old Adam's pompadour wasn't the only thing suffering from wilt those days. He had been experimenting among his drug surplus with a concoction of Columbian Viagra, Cuban Rogaine, Duprey's Cod Liver Oil, and bee pollen, that he had come to believe was slowly but surely raising him from the dead as good as a weekend in the woods with Yolanda Atkins, which was a recurring dream among at least half the men of southern Finton County.

Adam didn't tell me what it was; he just slipped a sample of his concoction across the counter inside a re-taped used apple jelly packet. "That one's on me. You're too young to have to deal with that kind of trouble, but see how things are tomorrow." Then he winked at me and went back up to the cash register to ring up a couple six packs to a fellah just coming back from Lake Adolphus, who peeled out and popped open a can before he even got to the door. The upturned can scratched on the screen door spring overhead as the fisherman gulped his way out onto the porch. By the time I got out there he had already sailed his empty can onto the middle of the gravel road and was gulping down another.

I took the mixture out to the rabbit cage and offered a little clump to the woodpecker on the end of a toothpick. He pecked at it gingerly, then scooped it up and gobbled it down like it was the best thing he had ever eaten. I offered it another clump and he met me half way with a wide open beak that looked like the Superglue had set just right. By the fourth clump that woodpecker was standing at the little doorway leaning out waiting for it, and I decided that maybe that was enough, but he whimpered so much when I closed the door that I let him have two more before I finally quit and gauged he had eaten about half of what was in the packet. I locked the cage with a little wooden peg and set the remaining half of the jelly packet on top of it.

I didn't get back to check on the woodpecker until after Sarah left the next day when I swung by the rabbit cage before going over to Al's. The door to the cage was open, with the little wooden latch in tatters, and the woodpecker and the jelly packet were both gone. I thought if he was well enough to get out then I had done my good deed, and hoped he wasn't gone because something got in there and ate him, but I didn't see any loose feathers in the cage. That evening at sundown when Al came back into the Tavern from taking a break out back, she was shaking her head with a funny smile as she stepped behind the bar.

"What?"

She smiled curiously and shook her head again. "Damnedest thing."

"What??"

"I heard a little woodpecker up in a pine just tapping the hell out of the tree, almost like two of them tapping at once. Might have even been two, I don't know, but I only saw the one. Then a flash of red-brown swooped onto the woodpecker and a bantam hawk tried to fly off with him, but he didn't get three feet before that little woodpecker tore into him like a stray cat on a sickly dog. Last I saw of the hawk he was beating his wings for all he was worth and that little woodpecker was right after him."

It was a slow night and we closed at 1 AM after watching an empty bar room for almost thirty minutes. I was walking away from the side door as Al locked it behind us when she stopped in mid-motion. "There. Here that?"

I stopped and listened to the cicadas in the bushes and the frogs out in the swamp, and then above that, like a small electric screwdriver trying to drive a worn screw head, I heard it.

"Tika tika tika tika tika tika tika tika tika tika tika tika."

There was a pause of about ten seconds then it did it again.

"Tika tika tika tika tika tika tika tika tika tika tika tika."

"That's it. That's the sound that little woodpecker was making"

I cocked my head and listened to the sound again, then turned back toward Al in the darkness. "Does sound like two of them, doesn't it?"

I went on to bed looking forward to the extra hour's sleep, but woke up early and went out back to check the rabbit cage one more time before Sarah came. Inside the rabbit cage was the shredded remains of the jelly packet and the half-eaten carcass of a bantam hawk.

"No way," I said to the carcass. "Al's put that there just to mess with my head."

I started back to the kitchen of the Park'N'Pump, when I heard it again.

"Tika tika tika tika tika tika tika tika tika tika tika tika."

It came from the far side of the store, and got around the corner just in time to see Adam throw a stick up at the eves and a little woodpecker flash off into the higher branches of a nearby great oak.

"Damned little shit!" Adam pointed up at the worn plank siding between the eves and the upper window frame where he did his Rural Rx business. "Look at that."

There were four rows of little holes meandering along the upper planks. The first and second rows were perfectly spaced about two inches between upper and lower, as were the third and fourth rows. Altogether there must have been forty little holes. I turned back to Adam. "Well, he's been at it a good while, it seems."

"Th'Hell he has! Those holes are all fresh this morning."

"Ah, Adam, you haven't been around to this side in years."

"Bullshit. I was out here yesterday after you went over to Al's deciding if this side needed painting yet, before you left at the end of the Summer. And yesterday it didn't need painting and it didn't have those damned holes above the window!!"

Now if someone gave me a list of 100 people that included Adam Tooey, Mother Teresa, and Saddam Hussein, Adam Tooey would still be at the end of the list of people likely to take part in a practical joke. I just could not believe Adam had gone in with Al just to play a joke. If Adam was in on it, somewhere this was either going to cost me a lot of money or get me in trouble. But there never came a punch line or a 'gotch'a' from either Al or Adam, and weird stories about woodpeckers floated out of the swamp every day that week.

On Thursday morning a freshman from Finton County Community College collecting swamp samples found three female woodpeckers skewered from behind, and a full-grown vulture dead nearby with two neat little holes drilled into the back of his head. By Friday afternoon boats from all over the three-county area were being towed through the Park'N'Pump parking lot on their way to Lake Adolphus with stories about Mad Woodpecker's Disease and little feathered vampires. On Saturday morning the county ranger brought Mack Wisner, the head of the Finton County Community College Biology Department, and took him up to Lake Adolphus looking for strange birds. Just after 2 PM the Ranger and Mack returned to the store, talking in a hushed buzz over nabs and RCs while they filled up the tank of the Ranger's beat up Bronco, and Mack made a call on the Park'N'Pump pay phone. Adam had an extension wired to the pay phone so he could make free calls, so I listened in on Mack's call.

"It is a new species of raptor! Sure it looks like a woodpecker at first glance, and it's about the same size, but it is a meat eater and has two beaks. Yes, that's what I said – two beaks. It has one in the usual place and then another one about two inches down on its belly, about where you'd normally find its – yeah that's the spot. NO! No way! It's too big and just as long as its head beak. Besides, it drills holes in bark with both of its beaks, so it can't be it's – no, I tell you the thing has two beaks. And it has hair! Yes, hair. It has a very thick top notch, more like an afro, but with thick blonde hair. I've never seen anything like it. I'll write it up when I get back." He hung up the phone when the ranger tapped the horn on the Bronco and he dashed out of the store. I sat there staring at the ceiling ignoring the dial tone coming from the extension when Adam came back to get a fresh case of nabs. He whistled as he opened the case and tapped the last two cases left in the storeroom. He glanced up at me with a huge smile. "Business is damned good young'un. Better get your ass over to the Tavern. You and Al are going to be busy as shit tonight."

"Adam…"

"What?"

"What was in that packet you gave me the other night?"

He told me, and then stood there while I just stared up at the ceiling light watching a moth fly hot touching circles around the edge of the bare bulb. "How'd it do?"

I told him what I had done with the concoction, and then what I had seen over the past few days. His face went blank for a few moments and his eyes just sort of floated around the room while he thought it all out, then he sank down onto a stool with wire wrapped legs set next to the nab cases.

"Ho-ly shit." He looked up at me and shook his head. "Ho-ly shit."

I went over to Al's and told her what I had just told Adam. She agreed that we had a duty to get rid of the woodpecker before things got any farther out of hand. Business was good, she said, but I had created a monster that had to be dealt with. She went into the back room and came out a few minutes later carrying two camouflage painted 12-gauge pump shotguns, two boxes of number eight shot, and a nickel plated .44-magnum in a long holster strapped to her waist and right thigh. We fired up the Jeep and sped down the Swamp Road towing the boat to Lake Adolphus.

We put the boat into the black water, leaving the trailer where it was in the shallows still hitched onto the back bumper of the Jeep sitting on the ramp, and puttered off into the swamp. When we got to where we thought the Ranger had been we cut the motor and waited for the woodpecker. I hadn't thought to grab any Deet from the Park'N'Pump before we left the store and we paid the price for that oversight covered in a roiling cloud of gnats and mosquitoes chewing up our skin while we looked for that woodpecker. We finally decided that even though a wash rag full of gasoline wasn't as good a bug repellant as Deet it still might help, and it did more than I expected, although it worried me a lot as I kept having to remind Al not to light up a cigar while we waited.

After a while we heard a shriek in the tree branches off to the west of us. We saw a full-grown red-tailed hawk drop stone cold dead into the black water, and a flash of black, white and red among the branches above that spot. We both started firing and pumping and firing again like a WWII destroyer laying cover fire at an incoming kamikaze. Tree branches, leaves and pine needles exploded into the air and drifted down through vaporous sunlight mixed with gunpowder smoke as the woodpecker flew from tree to tree, but not giving up its territory and even diving at us as we reloaded. Two boxes of shells were fifty rounds, and we had shot thirty-two before we finally winged it. It spun around like a maple seed corkscrewing down toward the ground and landed on a little muddy rise above the water not more than fifteen feet from us. It propped itself up on its good wing, pecking the ground in front of itself with its belly beak, and chirping that whimper I had heard in the rabbit cage.

Still looking at it I spoke over my shoulder to AL. "Sad, isn't it?"

"Yeah" she said, and the air around us exploded from the barrel of her shotgun. The place where the woodpecker had stood was replaced with a hollow cloud of ripped feathers floating in front of a gaping smoking hole in the mud. The mud and swamp water rushed in to fill the hole, the feathers settled on the water or drifted away like dust particles of twirling smoke in the slice of a slanting sunbeam, and silence returned to the swamp like an old wool blanket. Our ears were still ringing and we did not notice the incoming boat until they were near beside us. We looked up in startled surprise to see Tater Millpond and another man I did not know ease by us.

Tater spoke. "We're going to try to catch one of them vampire woodpeckers. You boys wanna come with us."

We just shook our heads NO and stared at the little plate of mud where the only vampire woodpecker in the swamp had just died.

Tater still looked at me, and winked when he spoke to Al.

"Hey, Al!"

She did not answer, and he spoke again, still looking at my face.

"Al, how're things with you and Yolanda?"

Tater puckered up and blew a kiss at me, spat in the water between our boats, and then laughed.

In less time than it takes to retell it, Al's empty pump gun dropped in a clatter to the bottom of the boat, and at the same moment three tremendous explosions came from the area of her right hip, and with each explosion a fist-sized piece of the outboard motor on the back of Tater's boat evaporated into metal dust and shrapnel. By the time I looked up to see Al's extended hand pointing the .44-magnum at Tater, the firing was over.

Al spoke through the barrel sights down at Tater's face.

"Looks like ya'll had some engine trouble. You boy's want a tow back with us?"

Tater swallowed something large and nodded No.

"No Ma'am. I think we can get back on our own soon enough."

Big Al kept the barrel of the .44 trained on the middle of Tater's ashen colored face.

"You boys be careful. Ya'here?"

"Yes ma'am."

Tater kept his eyes on Al's .44 until they rounded the next tree line and slipped from sight. Al shrugged her huge shoulders and giggled like a school girl as she put the magnum back in its holster.

"That's the smart ass been sniffing around my Yolanda, but she told me she's done with him and that's good enough for me."

I smiled back, with nothing to add, and she went on almost demurely.

"This little run-in just gave me an opportunity to clear the air and purge the animosity from my system."

It was the first time I ever noticed that Al had long eyelashes and freckles across the bridge of her nose. I never really thought of her as a her until that one moment, and it made me feel confused. I let out the tension with a belly laugh of my own.

"Al, I do believe it did just that."

That night the tavern was full of fishermen and tourists and we stayed open until the Sheriff came by and closed us down at 4AM, since it was Sunday then. I slept through the rest of Sunday and didn't wake up until 9AM Monday morning. I didn't have to work, but I spent a lazy morning picking up all the extra trash in the parking lot and in front of the store. I noticed Adam was advertising twenty-dollar 8-by-10 maps of Lake Adolphus, under a new sign announcing that they would show the buyer all the places known to be frequented by the vampire woodpecker that haunted the Lake. I shook my head and hauled the trash bag around to the dumpster, gave a sad look to the ruined rabbit cage, and then took a moment just to look out at the pine trees near where I found that damned woodpecker.

From almost every tree I saw, at about as high as a stoop-shouldered old fool could reach, there was a slit open reused apple jelly pack hanging from a piece of twine. And the birds were all over them.

"Ho-ly shit," I said to myself.

"Adam Tooey, what have you done?"

LAKE ADOLPHUS

Adam Tooey pulled his brush painted '63 Chrysler up in the yard next to the cabin, towing a battered unpainted aluminum boat. The horn was almost gone in the old Chrysler, but it still emitted a wheezing vibrating rasp of a honk when he hit the rusty chrome center of the steering wheel. Adam threw up his hand in a lazy wave and got out of the car. Dawn was a bit early for most folks to come visiting on a Sunday morning, but I was already up sipping fresh brewed coffee on the porch, and watching the sun begin to rise up over the trees at the lower end of the field. I had a clean sheet of paper in the army surplus field typewriter I had found in Millersville sitting on a folding table beside my chair. Adam came up on the porch, went past me to retrieve a cup of coffee for himself and lace it generously with Tennessee whiskey I kept on the top shelf above the cooking stove, then joined me in the rocker next to mine.

"You need to go fishing."

"I need to stay here and do some more work on these stories."

"Yeah? How much you get done yesterday?"

"I'm still revising that last story."

He leaned over and looked at the blank paper.

"That's what you said when you were up at the store the other day. You're not writing anything about me are you?"

"Nope. Wouldn't think of it. They're just silly stories that come to mind sitting down here at the cabin. Probably never do anything with them."

"Well, you still need to go fishing. The bass are jumping hungry down at the Lake."

"I don't know, Adam."

"We can catch a load of bass, then put in at Red Oaks Island and trade'em to Sarah for lunch. You ain't lived 'til you've had some of Sarah Kozlowski's hushpuppies, coleslaw and fried bass."

I smiled and he knew he had me, so he set his cup on the porch boards and headed back to his car. "Get your stuff."

Thirty minutes later we had the boat on Lake Adolphus, puttering northeast across a motionless surface repeating the early morning sky above. I could see Red Oaks Island about a quarter mile back toward the southern shore; ten acres of well-mowed lawn with the neat three-story plantation house sitting in the middle surrounded by great ancient oaks. The ramshackle wooden bridge that connected it to the rest of the world a hundred yards away was just a black line hovering above the water. We slowed as we came to a water buoy that looked to be decorated with an old rooster silhouette weathervane. Adam tied the bowline to it, and I noticed it didn't give or sway when he tied on.

"Must not be very deep here, Adam."

"Hell, boy, it's at least forty foot between the bottom of this boat and bottom of that lake."

"Oh, I thought it must be shallow since that buoy didn't give. Figured it was fixed on a post on something."

Adam looked back at the weathervane, took off his tattered Orioles baseball cap and flipped it against the rooster tail, spinning the arrow around all four compass point marks on the crossbars just above the water.

"That there weathervane is on a barn cap. And the barn cap is at the peak of a three-story barn. Back in the '80s the upper loft was still out of the water and local boys used to dive off it."

Barely two feet down through crystal clear water I

could see the peak of the barn's corrugated tin roof slopping into the depths. We put minnows on Carolina rigs and cast into the deep water just in front of the weathervane and almost immediately got strikes on both lines. Within another thirty minutes we each had our creel limits, the sun was barely over the treetops on the far eastern shore, and the old mercury outboard was pushing us toward Red Oaks Island.

A hundred yards offshore, Adam started slowly circling the boat and looking over the side into the water. When he found what he was looking for, he reached down inside the boat and handed me an oar.

"Here. Stick this down in the water as far as you can and swing it around a little. Don't drop it, now."

I did as he said, expecting to feel bottom, but connected with nothing.

"Little more under the boat."

I hit against something solid with the very tip of the oar.

"Old stump?"

Adam shook his head and gave a gap-toothed smile. "That's a 1961 Massey-Ferguson 202. It was in perfect condition and working the field the day it went under the water."

"How did it get way out here?"

"'Way out here' was in the middle of the cornfield, and I was driving the damned thing when the water came up and swallowed it!"

Adam enjoyed baiting me more than he enjoyed baiting the fish we had just caught, and I refused to ask for the rest of the story just out of friendly spite.

In silence we landed the boat and carried two completely full stringers of bass up to the back door of the plantation. Sarah Kozlowski met us at the door with her hands on her hips. She was fully dressed in a freshly pressed lemon yellow jumper decorated with lavender colored morning glories. Her smooth ebony skin belied her almost seventy years, and her short curly black hair was only lightly touched with silver.

She looked at our catch with a friendly smile. "Adam Tooey, I suppose you expect me to cook those nasty things."

"Just two of'em Sarah. The rest of'em are yours for the trouble."

She opened the screen door and let Adam in to set them on the drain board next to the kitchen sink, while I stayed out on the back porch. She smiled and nodded at me.

"You still like it up there at your cabin, Pug?"

"No better place in the world, Sarah. I still can't thank you …"

"Shush! Those twelve acres weren't doing anybody any good." She smiled again. "It'll be a while, boys. I've still got a few things to do yet."

Adam patted her on the shoulder as he passed back onto the porch. "We got time. I need to tell this fella how the lake got your tractor.

She crossed her arms, shook her head slightly, and tisked under her breath. "If you tell him any of it, you tell him all of it. You hear me Adam Tooey?"

Adam retrieved the ice chest from the boat and we settled onto a cushion of tall meadow grass growing between two leg thick roots in the shadow of the largest oak. Adam reached into the ice chest and pulled out two recapped clear beer bottles containing a dark liquid, and handed me one. Remnants of the original label gum still clinging to the outside.

"Chilled fresh brewed dark roasted coffee…"

I twisted off the cap and took a long pull on the bottle "…mixed with beer"

and then spit it out on the ground.

"Damn, Adam! I hope you have something else."

"Well, I like it."

He reluctantly handed me a factory bottled beer that I recognized and I thanked him for it. He then swept an arc over the lake with his bottle. "All that used to be the best bottom land in Finton County. And back toward the southwest, where the swamp starts now, Red Oaks land kissed up against the original Tooey place 'Alhambra'. Out toward the east was the Atkins place"

"Not Judge Atkins, was it?"

"No, his daddy, Thomas. Don't think I've ever told you anything about Thomas Atkins, have I?"

I shook my head no as I swallowed the next gulp of beer and squinted under my cap in the direction he pointed.

Thomas Atkins inherited a couple hundred acres of what had once been one of the old McClanahan estates, but he never did anything with it until after he moved back down from Philadelphia in the early '70s. He planned to turn the whole property into a housing development. At that time there was a rolling freshwater stream that cut through his property, meandered across Sarah's land, and ended up deep in the swamp to the west in Lake Adolphus. The swamp road ran between Sarah's land and Alhambra next door, crossed the old wooden bridge over Rolling Creek, and then went on for another ten miles or so up to where there used to be an old Confederate fort called Camp Finton.

About the same time, they were building the interstate on the other side of Millersville and needed someplace to dump all the dirt they were scraping away. Thomas went after it, but Adam Tooey got to the State Roads Commissioner before him and convinced the Commissioner that the county could solve a lot of its mosquito problem by using the dirt to fill in the swamp around Lake Adolphus. Adam also got the county to pay him so they could do that.

Adam had heard about Atkins' development plans and knew he could make a fortune selling home sites around his lake. Trouble was, Adam couldn't afford to have all the surrounding swamp land filled in so he could get a license to build. Getting the county to pay him to allow them to fill in part of the swamp for him was pure genius and typical Adam Tooey business, and it made an enemy of Thomas Atkins. Atkins had heard about the fill dirt and was willing to let it go as just a missed opportunity, but when he found out that Tooey did it so he could develop his own land, it made him absolutely bitter.

Signs started going up along the Millersville Road and down the swamp road to Lake Adolphus telling passers-by of the wonderful opportunity to own lake front property at Tooey Acres and urged them to buy lots before they were gone. Adam had Lake Adolphus restocked with every freshwater fish he could get his hands on for credit, until the surface almost boiled with jumping fish. Atkins continued to have his land bulldozed and staked out, but only sold a handful of lots and not getting enough return to pay for the development. All the local realtors told Thomas the same story: between lakefront and backwoods property, the waterfront will almost always win out in sales. So, Thomas chainsawed all the signs to Tooey Acres and dammed up Rolling Creek.

Adam got the volunteer Free Law Office to take his case against Thomas to court, to make him remove the dam. Thomas' younger brother Averill had just become a judge, and it was maddening for him to have to sign the writ telling Thomas to remove the dam, but he had to do it. Just before the dam was opened up, Thomas offered several local sewage tank pumpers the opportunity to dump their loads in the dry creek bed for a small fee, then had the dam tore open sending six tons of human waste back down to Lake Adolphus.

Thomas could not be allowed to cause the 'intentional blockage' of the main water flow into Lake Adolphus. So, he began looking for 'unintentional' ways to do it. He had the dozers dig a new lake bed at the lower end of his property and began offering lake front lots at Atkins Harbor, while the water level in Lake Adolphus began to drop again, drying up faster than Tooey's real estate sales. It was a short-lived success though, since as soon as Lake Atkins filled, the overflow once again fed into the creek bed, and Lake Adolphus slowly returned to its normal depth. The lake also filled with silt from the Atkins development and killed hundreds of fish, so Adam got the Free Law office to take Thomas to court again and make him pay off all the people he owed for fish stock, even though he didn't lose more than a third of what he put in there, the catfish not really minding the sewage.

At that time both Thomas and Adam were still deep in debt for the development, but while anyone dealing with Adam Tooey already knew they'd have to wait a good while to get their money back, Thomas Atkins was in trouble. His debt was hurting Judge Atkins' reputation, and his brother was pushing him to get out of the whole business. Giving in to his brother's demands, he barely broke even, paying off the earth movers and surveyors by selling most of his holding at farmland prices, and was left with only the twenty half acre lots surrounding his lake.

After being paid up, one of the earth movers, Fred Murphy, who was no friend of Adam Tooey, pointed out to Thomas that Lake Adolphus needed every ounce of water coming down from Rolling Creek just to keep up with all of it that drained out into the swamp. He added that even with the fill-in coming from the interstate project, not enough of the swamp would be covered to stop the lake from draining if Rolling Creek did not feed it. The two men stood under the noon sun in silence next to a big dozer for a few moments.

Thomas looked around as he thought it out. "What would it take to slow down the spring that feeds Rolling Creek just enough to affect Lake Adolphus?"

Fred pointed to a large pile of boulders scraped from the building sites. "Most of those rocks."

"How much would it cost me?"

"Hell, Adam Tooey once sold me 10 color sprayed aspirin for a hundred dollars, saying they were Viagra. I'll do it for free."

That evening the boulders were dropped into the shallows at the eastern edge of Lake Atkins and stopped up most of the spring flow. That night Rolling Creek slowed by a half. By the next morning, Lake Adolphus was down an inch. Within 2 days Lake Adolphus was down almost a foot.

Adam suspected Thomas had a hand in the water level decline, but when he called the Finton County Water Commissioner about it, the commissioner said it was probably just a seasonal drop in water flow that no one had ever noticed before, since all the creek ever fed was the swamp. Then the commissioner called his brother in law, Fred Murphy, and told him about it. Fred went to sleep that night with a satisfied smile on his face that made his wife wonder what he had been up to.

Lake Adolphus dropped another foot, and people who had purchased options on lakefront lots started backing out since this was the third problem they'd seen at the lake. Meanwhile, the water level at new Lake Atkins had not dropped an inch, Thomas had stocked it with bass, sold outright his last lot by the end of the month, and moved back to Philadelphia. He put his gains into oil, just before the embargo of '74, and is still a rich man up there to this day.

Adam Tooey was getting desperate as the level of the lake continued to drop, and went to his half-sister Sarah for Help.

"Adam Tooey there is no way in Hell I'm going to put a mortgage on Red Oaks so you can dig a deeper lake in the swamp. You need to get out of that business right now."

"Sarah, there's a fortune to be made. All I gotta do is figure out why the water is dropping."

"Adam, it's dropping because Rolling Creek is slowed down. Any fool knows that!"

"No, it's a seasonal drop..."

"Adam, we Sarahs have been watering cattle and crops from that creek for a hundred years. It doesn't drop unless something is making it drop, and there is no drought out there! Your problem is somewhere in that silly Lake Atkins."

"Well, there's nothing blocking the flow out into the creek bed any more..."

"Then you need to look at the other end, maybe where the original spring feeds it. That's an artesian spring. It used to bubble and splash up out of the ground when I was a kid."

Adam found the telephone number of a man living in Kentucky who had bought a lot by Lake Atkins for a Summer retreat, and asked if he could put a boat in the lake from his property the coming weekend. Saturday evening Adam Tooey and his sister Big Al were rowing around the upper end of the manmade lake looking for the spring feed. Not far from the eastern shore of the lake, Big Al twisted around in the boat looking at several landmark trees that were far enough back from the lake to have been spared by the bulldozer.

"It's right about here, Adam." She leaned over the boat and cupped a hand full of water, bring it up to her nose to smell. She nodded her head with a smile then cupped another sample for a taste. "Yep. This is it. The spring is right under us."

Adam began poking down in the water with an oar.

Big Al watched a moment. "What the hell do you think that will do?"

"I'm trying to see if there's some kind of concrete cap or something over the spring."

Big Al slapped his arm with her flashlight. "Here take these." She handed him her flashlight and the holstered .45 she had clipped in her belt. Before Adam asked what she was going to do, she slipped over the side of the boat and went down in the water. After a long wait she came back to the surface for air, shook her head no at him and then went back down. After her fourth dive she came up with a menacing grin.

"Sarah was right. He's done something to the spring. The bastard has it covered with a stack of big-ass boulders."

Adam tried for days to untie the legal ownership of the lake, but Judge Averill Atkins was happy to cause any delay he could outside of public view. Thomas Atkins' return to Philadelphia, and a confused title arrangement to the lake blocked every path Adam tried to unblock the spring.

Big Al finally suggested they blow up the rocks, and being retired from the Marines she knew some people who could help. An ex-marine demolition specialist blowing up hillsides for the new interstate told her what and how much she would need to do the job. Adam told her to triple it so they would be sure the rocks were gone. At the end of June they had everything they needed, including a second boat to carry the rest of the explosives. Al spent almost all night diving to the rocks and packing them with underwater explosives left over from WW2.

Just before sunrise on Wednesday morning, they lit

the long fuse and rowed furiously to the western shore of Lake Atkins, but the explosives had not yet gone off. They pulled the boats out of the water and trailered them around to Swamp Road, and still the explosives had not gone off. As the sky lightened in the east with the coming of the morning sun, they stood on Rolling Creek Bridge watching the far shore of Lake Atkins. In the gaining daylight the far surface of the lake turned to foam and the lake water rose like a mountain standing up, then the mountain of water exploded like a volcano. Water, flames, steam, fish and bits of rock skyrocketed up as a blast wave raced across the lake to the bridge bringing the concussion of the explosion. The sky rained water, pebbles and bass entrails in a deluge that took almost 90 seconds to fall. Adam and Al remained squatted on the bridge until they were sure the calamity had passed.

When they stood up, Lake Atkins was gone. Fish and tree stumps littered the muddy bottom of the new lake, but the water was gone. A black line zig-zagged along the center of the lake, and as they looked over at it, it grew wider. A ten-foot-wide chasm opened in the bottom of what was once Lake Atkins. The water in Rolling Creek reversed and began pouring back into the empty lake bed from Lake Adolphus, and flowed directly down into the gap.

Adam saw the water flow and knew it was draining from his lake. "Oh Shit. Oh Shit!"

His sister flipped water and debris from her muscular shoulders. "Well, you were the one who said triple the explosives."

"Yeah, but….Shit,…I mean, well…Shit!"

The ground around the bridge began to tremble slightly, then more noticeably. The bridge began to vibrate and the planking wobble. Adam and Al grabbed the aged wooden railing, looking around and then at each other, but then the movement stopped. From the lake came a great hissing sound that turned into a loud gurgle, and the gap in the lake bed filled with water. The water quickly rose back almost to the original level of the lake. Then it stopped. They waited at the bridge, looking over at Lake Atkins, but nothing else happened. The water flow in the creek bed had stopped. The creek bed was empty.

Adam slapped the wooden railing. "Well, Shit!"

Big Al watched a moment longer, gave a short dismissive laugh, then returned to her car and drove away. Adam stood on the bridge for an hour longer cursing his luck and slapping the bridge railing, then went home.

By late morning everything was back to normal, except the level of Lake Adolphus, which continued to drop. At ten in the morning Adam was plowing the cornfield below Red Oaks Hill on a 1961 Massey-Ferguson 202. The water deep in the gap at Lake Atkins began to bubble up, churning the eastern end of the lake surface into froth and sending three-foot waves up the new staked lots. The turmoil in the water gained in strength and turned the entire lake into a cauldron of roiling water. Huge sprays of water shot into the sky over the mouth of the original spring and the water level started rising like a small sink with both faucets open. The full lengths of the new but unoccupied lots around the lake quickly became part of the lake bottom. Water rushed into Rolling Creek bed, instantly overflowing the banks and slipping over the planks of the bridge. Water rushed like ocean waves in all direction, reaching and beginning to fill the lower cornfield within seconds. Adam saw the water and made a dash for Red Oaks Hill, which quickly became Red Oaks Island. By noon only a few acres of each of the three estates remained above water.

The owner of Red Oaks, Sarah, and Adam took the Jon boat leaning against the side of the main house and rowed to higher ground along the Swamp Road. They walked five miles to the Park'N'Pump and called the County Water Commissioner to report another seasonal change in the Rolling Creek water flow. While they toweled off in Adam Tooey's back room at the store, Big Al came in from her Tavern next door and told them what she and Adam had done down at the lake.

When the ambulance arrived at the Park'N'Pump to take an unconscious and badly beaten Adam Tooey to the Millersville Clinic, Big Al had her half-sister locked up in the back of her tavern. She kept her bulky shoulders wedged against the jerking door to keep it from tearing away from the hinges.

"You got to calm down, Sarah. You hear me? Sarah? Sarah?"

The water never did go back down, and the county renamed the whole area Lake Adolphus, since Lake Atkins was never official. At the lake's edge on the last dry half acre of Alhambra sits a little fish bait stand run by one of Adam's cousins. The Swamp Road that used to go on down to Rolling Creek Bridge now dips down into the water just beyond Red Oaks, and the locals use it as a boat ramp.

Adam lifted up his thinning hair on the side of his head to expose his scarred left ear, and grinned. "She just about killed me that day. Would have, too, if it hadn't been for Alexandra. "

Sarah didn't have flood insurance, but still found it in her heart to forgive Adam and Big Al. Now she earns a few dollars a day serving lunch with Adam down at the Park'N'Pump. She walks down the Swamp Road around ten A.M. Monday through Saturday carrying fresh made Cole slaw and Chili in buckets covered with plastic wrap.

Sarah did manage to take an afternoon off right after the flood, but didn't have to go to the Free Law Office, she already had her own lawyer. She now holds the deeds to both the Park'N'Pump and Big Al's Tavern and charges as fair a rent as you could find in southern Finton County.

SARAH KOZLOWSKI

Southerners love to pronounce vowels. That's what adds music to the language as it is spoken in places thought of as Southern. It is the reason we have more syllables in our words than other users of the language, so we may linger among those syllables blessed with vowels; to hover over them, taste them, and to stretch the sound to prolong our joy of them. There are words or names that ring to a certain pitch or meter to a certain cadence, and find preference in particular regions of the South because they add harmony to the local spoken symphony. In that part of our country where speech and geography are both described as southern, and where through marriage or wanderlust the southern accent is most pronounced there sits Finton County, where it is of notable pleasure to pronounce the name Sarah Kozlowski. Sarah, with the first 'a' long and heavy and lingering like a come-home hug, and Kozlowski with the first 'o' as in 'boss' and the second as in 'how'. Somewhere in the time known as early America, between the Polish silversmith that helped settle Jamestown and the Polish prince that lead a cavalry charge against the British in Savannah, Kozlowski joined the ranks of the Smiths and Jones and Jacksons and McClanahans found in town ledgers throughout the old south.

Before she was a Kozlowski, Sarah graduated college with honors among those amazing first pioneers of color to walk across a stage in acceptance of their scrolls, where heretofore they were only allowed entrance to clean. Afterward, she received a scholarship to study a year in Europe, the same year they had more rain and chilly days than even the Parisians could shrug off with good-natured smiles or large cups of café au lait. In damp clothes, fighting influenza and the grip on her wind-blown umbrella, going back to the little second story flat near the Follies, she bumped hard against an ambling American paying more attention to the signs than to the people.

Stanley Kozlowski, late of the U.S. Army in Viet Nam, late of an Army Hospital in West Germany where they seemed to have misplaced most of his right hand, and later still from the affections of a Lynchburg girl once betrothed to him but now wed to a fellow classmate, was totally snockered. When he bumped into Sarah he went down like the proverbial house of cards, and couldn't seem to remember the sequence of steps necessary to either regain his footing or even attain the status of being upright.

Trying to be nonchalant, even while lying on his back in a heavy falling rain, he managed to slip the remainder of his right hand into his pants pocket, and bring his extended left forefinger to his hairline in mock salute, using his best wrinkled-brow John Wayne imitation.

"Sorry, Ma'am. Didn't see you there."

Sarah backed away to return to her path, as an onlooker met Stanley's eyes with his own. Not wanting to be rude, Stanley smiled up at the man.

"How ya' doin? Can you give me a hand here?"

The man moved on quickly without response, but Stanley called after him.

"How 'bout half a hand, I still got the first part!"

He chuckled to himself as he rolled onto his side and began facing the challenge to stand. His left foot slipped on the wet cobblestone and he kicked a passer-by who scolded him in French explicatives. Not yet far enough away, she heard his slurred apology and looked back at him, found his disheveled appearance so much like that of a lost puppy, and yelled at the small evening crowd eddying around him.

"Someone please help that poor man!"

No one stopped, so she went back to help him to his feet and took the wounded veteran to the only warm dry place she could afford, where she brewed him hot coffee and dried both her hair and his with the only towel she had.

Spring came bright and hot, finally baking the chills from their bodies, so that everything she owned was dry and fresh again as she packed to go home to Finton County, and Stanley went with her.

"Momma, this is my husband Stanley Kozlowski," she said as her mother opened the front door and let them both in, not knowing her daughter had married while in Europe, and not prepared to welcome her home with a white man in tow.

Pointing to him with stiff straight arm shoulder-high forefinger, like catching the neighbor's dog crapping on the front lawn, she looked into her daughter's face. "He's Polish?"

"About as much as you're African, Momma." Sarah spoke to the staircase as she began the curved ascent up carved Florentine marble to the second floor.

Sarah's mother stepped directly in front of Stanley who was turning to follow his wife up the staircase. She put a single fingertip gently against the center of his chest.

"Stanley, if you ever cause my baby pain, I will gut you like a catfish. Do we understand one another?"

Stanley swallowed hard, but looked her deep in the eyes. "Ma'am, I'd die for your daughter. She's the only thing in this world that makes it worthwhile staying alive."

They stood there a while, almost nose to nose, with the only sound the tick of the hallway grandfather clock, until she felt she had the measure of that man, and believed what he said.

"Well, get your stuff upstairs. You live here now."

Stanley's first chore settling into his mother-in-law's house, was understanding that her name was also Sarah. In fact, every mother and daughter and granddaughter in her maternal line since 1843 had been named Sarah.

The original owner of the house had it built from highly successful tobacco and cotton profits, just to keep up with his brothers who were doing equally well. The McClanahans were an industrious as well as quarrelsome family, never known to overlook a slight that could lead to a duel. Dueling took a terrible toll on the local gentry and especially the McClanahans, since most of that family was cursed with poor sight and tended to lose most of their duels. Lineage after lineage came to abrupt halts on the back pages of family bibles, while the local woods of southern Finton County rang out with pistol shot all too often.

It was during the month following the funeral of Alexander McClanahan IV, that his father slipped into depression over the realization that he was the last surviving male McClanahan. His second wife had died from yellow fever in 1836, and though he continued to spend time with certain available ladies of the county he was, as his doctor had described it, able to plow the fields but unable to bring forth a crop. Before he put himself down with his handsomest dueling pistol, he bequeathed the plantations of his brothers to their bereaved wives, since as the only surviving male all inheritance went to him by law; and he left his own lands, house, and property to his one true friend, Sarah – his house slave.

In 1843 it had not yet become proper to give slaves last names. Sarah had none, so she took the name of her benefactor and became Sara McClanahan on legal papers. Among the property list of Alexander McClanahan III, along with Sarah, there were 28 other slaves that Sarah freed the day after Third's funeral. The other property, the land, and the house retained its original name of "Red Oaks". Sarah was determined that her daughters and her granddaughters would have ownership of Red Oaks regardless of slave owners or husbands, whom she considered just another form of slave owners, and decided that the last name would not signify inheritance. She came upon the idea of naming the first-born girl in each generation Sarah, since that was really the only name she had ever known herself by, and thus ownership would pass along maternal generations into the future where each Sarah would be landed and self-supporting. Also, as it was obvious to her that each Sarah would have to get married to produce the next generation, it would require no foolish numbering of the Third, Fourth or Fifth, because the husband's last name would be legally forced upon the current Sarah, and that's how they would be told apart.

Sarah Greenwood, the great-granddaughter of Sarah McClanahan, married Augustus Tooey in 1909 becoming Sarah Tooey, in a part of the South that had seen such marriages throughout the years and accepted it quietly, and now her daughter was no longer known as "little Sarah", the appellation each daughter carried until her last name changed. Her daughter was now Sarah Kozlowski, and Sarah Kozlowski was now the owner of Red Oaks. All that was fine with Sarah Tooey, who planned to prop her feet up and not do a damned thing except what she damned well pleased for the rest of her life. She only propped her feet up for six years until she left in her sleep to find all the other Sarah's, knowing she would never again run into Augustus, whom she had outlived for eighteen years and who had assuredly gone straight to Hell.

Stanley opened Kozlowski's Hardware across the Millersville Road from the old Tooey's General Store, that later changed its name to the Park'N'Pump when it started selling gasoline from electric pumps. The Hardware store was something southern Finton County desperately needed, and folks hardly ever noticed his right hand only had a thumb and one finger, except Tater Millpond who called him 'Crab'. Stanley took the nickname with his usual good nature, which was just as well since it caught on and no matter what the sign on the top of the building ever spelled out, whenever anyone went to the hardware store at Tooey's Crossroads, they just said they were going to Crabby's. Eventually Stanley decided that it was better for business not to confuse potential customers when he sent out sales flyers, so he started using the name Crabby's himself, and after that it seemed only proper to change the sign over the store.

Sarah would walk down the swamp road from Red Oaks to the hardware every day to bring him his lunch, fresh from the stove at home. Stanley thought it might be a good way to advertise the new electric stoves he was selling, for Sarah to heat lunch up on the deluxe model, and maybe even make a little extra to let customers sample. That same year Lake Adolphus put out more catfish than the Kozlowski's could ever eat or freeze, so lunchtime became a profitable affair of showing off the deluxe stoves, and selling fried catfish, Sarah's hush puppies, and Sarah's amazing Coleslaw. That's also when the business became known as Crabby's Hardware and Fish Camp, serving weekday lunches and suppers Thursday through Sunday nights. Young Adam Tooey had already started serving lunches from the Park 'N' Pump and at first complained that they were hurting his business, but after a while would stop by Crabby's himself from time to time.

It was a good life for the Kozlowski's, and Red Oaks always had visitors in those days. Being introduced at a hardware store brought people together that otherwise would not have generally been in the same room. Senators, judges, painters, and plumbers found themselves seated for Sunday dinner across from one another at the huge Red Oaks table. The table top was said to have been cut as a single twenty-foot plank from a giant red oak tree in 1822. Stanley got supply contracts for public works projects, and more than once the team to complete the project was pulled from among the Sunday diners at Red Oaks. Anyone who was anyone looked forward to their chance to drive down the Swamp Road on Sunday afternoon for dinner with the Kozlowski's.

In late Summer the Sunday topic was refurbishing the county fairgrounds in preparation for the circus that was due to set up in late August, just a few weeks before the county fair. Young County Attorney, Thomas Atkins, and the County Manager had invited the circus travel manager to town, and naturally she was also invited to Red Oaks when they were. Abigail Schumacher had traveled with the circus for over twenty years, and had been its travel manager for the past ten. She had alabaster skin, striking deep blue eyes, midnight black hair that reflected light like polished onyx, and a womanly figure that only the most dedicated of married men could ignore. She also worked the circus as a performer of sorts. She was in fact, the bearded lady. Her beard matched the beautiful hair on her head, was thick as bear fur, and cascaded from her lower face over her upper chest, and its soft ends swayed gracefully from the plateau formed by undeniable breasts. During dinner no less than two coffee cups and three glasses of wine were spilled by the male diners. Sarah was not pleased that one of the spilled wine glasses lay in front of

Stanley.

It had long been one of the curses laid upon the Sarah's that they all ended life living alone with their menfolk gone to seed ahead of them, or just gone. When Stanley showed up for supper red-faced and unable to look Sarah directly in her eyes, she knew what was happening. She knew what beards did to a woman's cheek, and so knew it when she saw the same redness on Stanley's. She knew it when his shirt came out of the laundry bag with a long silky black hair clinging to the front. She knew it when coming home from the hardware store became later and later. And then she found the note on the kitchen counter.

"Sarah, I have gone off with the circus. Stanley."

The Circus never did come to southern Finton County that year, and most folks thought it was just as well.

Sarah had seen it all coming, and had grown up knowing it would happen. She shook her head at the sadness of it all, and called her lawyer, Thomas Atkins. Since Red Oaks was here, never shared legally with her husband by requirements of her Mother's will, Stanley's departure had no effect on her financial status. And, since Crabby's Hardware was mortgaged by her with Red Oaks as collateral, the store became hers. She had the name changed to Red Oaks Hardware, but came to miss going down the road to meet folks at the fish camp and cooking for everyone. So, she had the name changed once more to Red Oaks Hardware and Fish Camp, and started serving fried catfish again that Fall, but it just wasn't the same for her anymore. That Winter she closed for good and sold all the hardware goods at cost to Adam Tooey across the street, then padlocked the building for good.

The following year the circus did come to Millersville, but it only stayed two days. Apparently one of the sideshows offered the Bearded Lady and the Crab Claw Man in some sort of Duo. Stories also circulated that a local woman brought a pump shotgun on the second night and shot up that part of the circus, paying particular attention and aim to the vicinity of the Crab Claw Man, who barely escaped with his life. Due to some very hard work of newly elected Circuit Court Judge Atkins, the incident did not find its way into the courts or the local newspaper. Co-incidentally Sheriff Poteat added a finely carved English shotgun to his riot gear that one deputy mentioned to Adam Tooey had the name "Red Oaks" carved into the stock.

Adam had spent a good deal of time with his half-sister after she had closed the Hardware, and convinced her it would be good to get out of the house more often, even one so grand as Red Oaks. So, Sarah Kozlowski began cooking again and it made Tooey's Crossroads famous among truckers. Heavy duty log haulers would take any passable route they could manage to be near Tooey's Crossroads for lunch. The secret was hand carried each morning by a black woman named Sarah, pronounced with the first 'a' long and heavy, who walked up the Swamp Road carrying two five gallon commercial paint buckets covered with plastic wrap. One bucket held Coleslaw, the other held chili, and she made them both at home before arriving at 10:30 every morning Monday through Saturday.

THE MOUND

Back when I was almost finished doing my work release at the Park'N'Pump and Big Al's, the lady that cooked there , Sarah, took a liking to me. She said that a neighbor of hers offered to trade twelve acres on a wooded knoll with a pond on her west side, if she would consider letting him have just an acre of her lakefront. Her family place had once been hundreds of acres, but now mostly ringed the edge of Lake Adolphus with much of it under the lake. She told me about that because she said I'd need a place when I got released, and that those twelve acres was as good a place as anyone could find, if I wanted to stay in Finton County. Sarah said she could never sell the land, but she would draw up a paper saying I could live there as long as I wanted. It was the best offer I'd ever had and I made a plan to put a cabin on it where I could get off by myself whenever the need struck. In those days the need struck often and that place taught me that being alone can mean different things.

With the help of a friend I'd met at the Tavern, I re-cut an ancient wagon roadway through hateful briar thickets and thick stands of scrub pines. Where hardwood trees had grown in the old roadbed, we just looped around them. All things not vertical or mache'd in aged leaves were dressed in thick olive drab moss or heavy confederate gray lichen, cast off colors from fleeting times that had dashed past while the woods stood watching.

Weeks later, under an overcast sky threatening rain, I returned to the property to camp alone and explore the center stand of trees separating two little fields on the property. Beyond a large sycamore tree in the middle of the back field, there was a mound of earth and gray rocks on otherwise smoothly sloping ground. It was almost seven feet long by four feet wide and rose about a foot and a half. The mound brought back childhood recollections of my father describing Indian Burial Mounds he had discovered as a young boy down in North Carolina. I walked around it several times looking for some clue to its origin, but without further insight. Within fifty yards of the first mound I found two others like the first. I decided to myself that they probably were Indian burial mounds and I determined to leave them all to rest undisturbed.

The gray gown the sky had worn all day was lifted at the hem just enough to let me see the sun down, and as the moon came up the clouds slipped over the forest tops to some other county. The temperature dropped into the thirties, but it was a glorious full moon night. My campfire was a poor competitor for making shadows in that platinum light. There was a small sycamore tree about fifteen feet tall in the middle of the pasture in front of my campsite nudged against the woods. It still held on to its last three sticker balls in the higher branches, and in the moonlight I could still see those from my campsite.

After roasted venison Al had given me from her frozen reserve of the previous Fall's hunting season, I settled into my folding easy chair with the footrest up high; Tennessee whiskey and concentrated lime juice close at hand. I leaned back and watched a star-filled southern sky that cable television couldn't have done justice.

Occasionally I'd hear a rustle in the woods behind me, and look back over my shoulder in the direction of the mound, but not see anything that hadn't been there during the day. During my second drink I decided that maybe I should go try to make peace with the sleeper in the mound, or introduce myself, or even ask permission to stay. Some positive action with the ancient Indian seemed reasonable at the moment. So, I took my folding easy chair, whiskey, lime juice, and two shot glasses back in the woods to the mound. It was easy to find in the moonlight. I fixed two drinks, set one on the mound and settled into my chair with the other and propped my feet up.

My father used to entertain us with stories of his schoolboy adventures digging up arrowheads from Indian burial mounds. He also told us ghostly stories of levitations and apparitions set upon distant cousins and great uncles who had disturbed such mounds while working their farms. The contradictions between the two types of stories always passed us high overhead in the late quiet night, as we drifted into the tale embraced by his baritone voice and the warmth of slow popping embers. I wanted neither arrowheads not visitors, but only an abiding understanding with the sleeper that we would not be rude to one another. In this place I wanted peaceful nights broken only by my own snoring and the sound of frogs chirping down at the pond.

Alone in the moonlight, my thoughts were interrupted by a scratchy little voice. "What th'Hell are you doing?"

The hair on the back of my neck stood on end. My throat was instantly dry and choked by an enormous cotton ball. My bladder sent a message of extreme urgency that was blindly ignored by my frozen knees, arms, and chest.

"Down here, Dude."

Shivers ran along my spine and out through my lungs with a haggard gasp. I managed to force my neck to bend the quarter-inch required to look down at the mound. Nothing was there but the shot glass. Maybe I should not have been so forward as to place the glass on top of the mound, I thought. Maybe somewhere along the side would have been more respectful. My thoughts were fractured and swirled inside my head.

"Look at me, at least. Over here."

I struggled with my frozen body and managed to turn my head slightly to find a full grown raccoon sitting up on its haunches near the foot of the mound. I blinked wide-stretched eyelids and succeeded in swallowing the cotton ball. I forced a meager breath through my throat only making a sound reminiscent of a strangling cat.

"Shit! I'm in the mood to talk and all I can find is a mute two-legger?" He offered out his paws palms up, in a universal plea of exasperation.

I stared at the raccoon in amazement.

"Hey Dude, cat got your tongue? No, wait. Forget I said that. Bad metaphor. Seen that. Not a pretty sight."

"You're talking?" It was as if another's voice was being forced through my lips.

"Yeah, well, it was either with you or that dead Indian there." He pointed his right paw at the mound. "So far you're only ahead by two words. Speaka da English??"

I raised the Whiskey bottle in the moonlight in front of me to gauge my intake since I broke the seal.

"If there's something on that liquor bottle label I need to know, Dude, you'll need to read it to me. Can't read myself. Doesn't come up much."

"But,…but…"

"Score's only three now, Dude. Repeats don't count."

"You're talking."

"Been doing it a long time, but your score's still only three. No repeats. Look, if this is as far as we're going to get, one of us will have to leave. I'll come back later." He turned and began walking away on all fours.

"No! Wait!"

He raised a front paw off the ground so he could look back over his shoulder at me. "We're up to five now, Professor. You want to try a complete sentence, or was that it?"

"A-are you speaking for the Indian? Is this really an Indian burial mound?"

"No. Yes. Have you met a raccoon that could speak before?"

"I've actually never 'met' a raccoon."

He turned his body around to face me and tilted his head. "So, the first time you hear a talking raccoon, all you can think to do is ask him about the frickin' Indian??"

"Look, I've never been around a raccoon – well, except for the Davy Crockett hat I had, but that wasn't..."

"Oh, Bad! Bad reference, Dude!" He walked back toward me and sat up on his haunches again, gesturing at me with one paw. "How'd you like someone to gut your Aunt Maude and wear her around the house like a hat?! Crude! Very Crude!"

"Sorry, I meant to, well, hell, this is really new ground for me. You've got to admit, it's really strange!"

"Strange? Dude, I'm not the one out here in the woods tossing shots with a pile of dirt!"

"So, then, it's not an Indian burial mound?"

"It is. I already told you that. My family knew his. But, he's not going to share hooch with you."

"Oh. Because I am a 'white eyes'?"

"No. Because he is day-ud!! Been dead since before these trees around here were seedlings – except for that double trunk oak on the other side of the creek."

"You're family knew his?"

"Kinda. We've been coming here for thirty generations..."

71

"What's his name – his Indian name?"

He shrugged his shoulders. "Don't know his Indian name. No one does anymore, but I know what it means in English." He only stared at me from his mask, not speaking further.

"Well? What does it mean?"

He crossed his arms and let out an exasperated sigh. "It means 'Raccoon Hunter'."

"How ironic! You bring homage to his spirit."

"Homage, my ass." He flipped a thumb toward the mound. "This guy went through my ancestors like the frickin' holocaust! If it wasn't for him, we'd be all over this place as thick as gnats! Now you're lucky to find one of us in five acres."

"Then what draws you to him?"

"Nothing 'draws me'. Read my lips, he's dead."

"Then, why?"

"I started to tell you. But you keep interrupting. We've been coming here for thirty generations,..."

"Yeah?..."

"...to take a dump on this mound."

"Oh."

"Look. It's a family obligation. We each take a full moon. I always come in March. The rest of the time I'm living large down at Lake Adolphus, eating fish, mussels and crayfish, and whatever I can lift from the campers."

"Can all your family talk?"

"Nope. Seems to be just one in each generation. Don't know why." He climbed up on the mound and took up the shot glass in his paws. "No sense wasting this." He spoke into the glass taking several tongue fulls. "Really Tasty." He smacked his lips. "What else is in this?"

"Concentrated lime juice."

He drained the glass and then lay down on his side,

resting on his elbow and propping his head in the palm of his paw. He casually flicked a sticker burr from the side of his furred belly and then gently patted the mound. "So, uh, what are you going to do with this mound? Dig it up for stuff? Put a fence around it?"

"I don't think so. I think I'll just leave it alone and let him sleep."

He pointed a dainty finger at me. "Good for you." There was silence for a moment, and then he spoke again. "You know, I was born in a thicket just up the hill from here. The creeks around here were full of minnows and crayfish. Used to love it here."

"Then why'd you leave?"

"Two-leggers. No offense, but two-leggers find a nice stretch of water and the first thing they do is piss in it. Then they let their houses piss in it, then their machines piss in it."

"Not always,…"

He ignored my comment. "Last snail I had from these creeks just about killed me. I've always had a sensitive stomach anyway. Old woman Bessie used to keep antacids for me."

"The woman knew you could talk?"

"She was a loner, a widow. Talked to her plants. Used to shoot her man's gun into the ground once in a while just to keep two-legged prowlers away. She wasn't a risk."

"Like talking to a half-drunk man in the middle of the woods?"

He winked and smiled at me. "She was already in for the night when I ate that snail, and I couldn't find antacid one on the back porch where she kept them for me. So I slipped into the kitchen – done it before – found a couple foil packs in the cupboard and was out in a flash. I was eating my second tablet when it hit me that they weren't antacids."

"What were they?"

"Well, later on I found out they were called 'seltzer' something, but the only thing I knew then was that they were about to explode in my gut! I made it back down to the creek, but by then I was blown up like a decaying possum. White foam was bubbling out of my mouth, my nose and my ears. My guts were rumbling like a coming thunderstorm, and I thought I was going to die right then!"

"What did you do?"

"I went running for Uncle Bob as fast as I could…"

"Who's Uncle Bob?"

"My Uncle Bob. Raccoon.   Taught me to talk. Anyway, I went charging over to his den and found him sucking on a half-empty bottle of wine tossed from a passing car. By then the white bubbles were foaming out of my rear end and I was in pain! I called his name then whirled around and raised my tail to show him what was happening. 'What is it, Uncle Bob', I cried. He looks at me with his one good eye all bloodshot and yells 'Oh my God, Donald, you got ass rabies!!' Then we both spewed, one from each end."

"Did it help?" I took a short sip from my glass trying not to picture the scene.

"Did for me. Most satisfying fart of my entire life! Uncle Bob didn't remember much the next morning. Said he'd had the strangest dream, and I didn't discuss it, but I'll tell you this: I will never eat another snail or anything else from a stream around here." He tapped the rim of his shot glass. "You got any more of that?"

I leaned forward and half filled the glass with Whiskey. He only sniffed at the glass and then fixed me with a wide-eyed look. "Got any more of that tarty stuff?"

I poured some concentrated lime juice in his Whiskey. He stayed on his side, head still propped in the palm of his paw and snaked his tongue back and forth into the glass with quiet little slurps until it was almost dry. He then rolled over onto his back and put his hands behind his head looking up at the moon, now sitting high overhead.

"Well, ..." he sighed. "Got to go. Got work to do."

I drained my own glass, asked him "What work is that?", and then poured myself another. I held the bottle toward him in offering, but he waved it away with his paw.

"I've got three plump fur balls whining 'cause they ain't pregnant yet and it's almost Spring"

"It's already Spring. Five days into it."

He rolled onto his side to get up and let out a yawn. "Dude, it ain't Spring until it feels and acts like Spring." He stood up on all fours, stretched with his shoulders low and his haunch up in the air, and then shook his head vigorously. "That stuff gets to you when you stand up." Then he shook his head again. "Well, it's going to be a long night. Got to go." He mock-saluted with a front paw and then shuffled off the mound. A few feet away he stopped and turned to point a paw at me. "Go easy on that Hooch, Dude. It'll make you see stuff no one will ever believe." He winked and then walked off into shadows of the thicket.

"What about your, uh, dump?" I called after him.

His voice was muffled by the brambles and farther away than I expected. "Do it later. Work first." I heard the chuckle in his voice.

I sat there a while longer while the moon sank low in the sky, but he did not return. Slightly staggered and still in awe of what had occurred, I found my way back to the campsite in the fading moonlight. I woke late the next morning with a splitting headache and grabbed for my pack in the corner with half opened eyes. Putting on my glasses I saw that a hole had been chewed in the corner of my tent, and my pack had been ransacked. All of my antacids were gone.

I try to get down to the mound on full moons whenever I can, but I hadn't seen Donald since then. I let the thickets grow heavy around the center woods and have never told anyone else about the mounds. I leave the sleeper alone, except on those full moons when I leave a little plastic glass of Tennessee Whiskey and lime juice set on top of it, but the glass is always still full the next day when I check on it.

This past March I was at the cabin for the first full moon of Spring. I placed the plastic shot glass on the mound and settled into my old folding easy chair; it's getting shabby now and ought to be replaced. I shared a couple drinks sitting there amongst the moon shadows of the budding trees and listened to the night birds until the moon followed its own arc far down toward the opposite tree line. There was still some lingering Winter coolness left in the air those hours after midnight when I retreated to my bunk under an old wool army blanket.

In the early morning sunshine dewdrops on the grass reflected hundreds of tiny suns, and I meandered along that little trail through the gap in the brambles to the mound, sipping fresh-brewed coffee through its rising steam above a much abused blue enamel cup. I came to the mound and waited patiently while the fog cleared from my glasses, so I could retrieve the plastic cup left the evening before. As my view of the mound and the glass slowly sharpened I saw that the Whiskey was gone, and the little shot glass had been neatly filled with raccoon scat.

That next Friday night I was doing a few hours for Al at the tavern, when Tater Millpond sat down at the bar near where I was washing shot glasses.

"Haven't seen you in a while Pug, not since Al blew away my Evinrude. How you doing jail-buddy?"

Al was busy at the other end of the bar and I could see she had seen Tater sitting there and knew she wouldn't come serve him, so I set up a glass and poured Tater a shot of whiskey.

"I'm fine Tater. Just working a few hours now and then to help out Al."

Tater nodded his glass to me and tossed back the whiskey.

"You still like it up there on those back acres?"

"Yeah. Finished my cabin and its got all I need."

"You know I used to hunt squirrels and camp up there when I was a kid. You ever see any raccoons up there?"

I looked at Tater for a few seconds, studying his eyes, trying to figure out if he knew what I did, but didn't want to say what I'd seen.

He looked at me quietly and then turned over another shot glass drying on the towel, then he filled up both glasses smiling.

"I'm buying."

We both tossed back the shots looking at each other in silence, and then Tater laid ten dollars on the bar. "Tell Al she can have the change." Then he twirled around on the old barstool and stood up to leave, looking back at me over his shoulder out of the corner of his eye and showing the edge of a boy-like smile

"Tell Donald I said 'hey'."

Then he walked through the smoke haze and into the dark beyond the opened door.

VIDALIA MILLPOND

Even at the best of times, Tater Millpond's sister-in-law Vidalia was a rancid woman. There are natural smells that draw a person back, to savor an aroma and sometimes even attach a feeling to it, like the smell of a fresh baby or a puppy, or the breath of your first love after a deep kiss. There are smells that both make you hungry and take you back in time, like coming across a long lost aroma of a favorite ingredient in your mother's cooking and you are at once five years old again wishing you could go in for supper. And then there are smells that give you fear or drive you to boat railings or the far edges of a campsite with your stomach only inches from your throat. A whiff of Vidalia was of that latter category. She was cursed from her earliest days with a body aroma that drove visitors at her bassinet to unviewed corners of the room where they checked the bottoms of their shoes for tracked in travesty. No soap, shampoo, detergent or Eau d'anything could hide the acidic fumes that wafted off her body with the slightest exertion.

Vidalia was cute as a button, and had suffered untold times in her early teens when young men would cross the street just to speak with her, only to rush back shoving their fists into their mouths to retain lunch. She came to deny her affliction and blamed everyone around her for advancing the lie. Hers was an awful existence for herself and her family until the day she met Slick Millpond.

Tater's younger brother was actually named Milford, but he grew up in such constant clutches of nose colds and sinus infections that handkerchiefs could never serve him as well as the sleeves to his flannel shirts. Even after washing, his shirt sleeves exhibited such a noticeable sheen that the nickname 'Slick' just came naturally.

Slick was hell in toddler shoes, and from the moment he could swing something heavy, every other member of the Millpond household was in bruises. It was the afternoon that Slick whomped a fire brick straight down into Tater's crotch, while Tater was driving in a cotter pin under his '52 Ford, that set him on the road to Vidalia. Tater came up screaming and before he really thought it out, Tater slapped Slick dead center in his nose with a ten-ounce ball peen hammer. Even after his nose was reconstructed to a somewhat normal appearance, Slick was never able to smell again. He was finally cured of his runny nose, but from that day on he sounded like he was in the grips of the worst cold known to man or beast.

Slick met Vidalia the day he graduated from high school and it was love at first sight. He had gone to the local poultry fertilizer processing plant to apply for a night job on the turkey carcass line, and saw Vidalia working her usual station near the exhaust fan. When Slick agreed to work next to Vidalia, the shift boss coughed and said he was hired as long as he wanted to be there. On his first day he worked up the nerve to ask her out to the drive-in, where they managed to have the whole two last rows to themselves, after a couple rowdy groups left cussing and yelling when one of them got sick. They were married that August, a nice outdoor wedding, and Slick's daddy Milton gave them five acres on the far side of his farm and said Slick could even have the pig yard over there to get started with. The moment Slick said "Ib doob", Vidalia was the happiest woman in the world.

Vidalia and Slick worked the night shift together for years, fed the pigs in the morning before they went to bed, and worked the farm in the evening before they went back to the plant. All in all they were fairly happy until the plant was assigned a new inspector from the county.

Generally when the county inspector came, the shift supervisor would keep him from Vidalia if at all possible. The last inspector had the same route for twelve years and had learned after the first visit that the last place he ever wanted to be was downwind of Vidalia Millpond. He also realized that processing picked turkey carcasses being prepared for fertilizer wasn't in his jurisdiction. The new inspector thought it her duty to visit every inch and every person in the plant so she could give it a clean bill of health, since the first part of it actually prepared chickens for fryers. There was a red line painted on the floor at the end of the chicken preparation line, and everyone agreed that everything after that was fertilizer processing and wasn't included in county inspections. The new inspector didn't give a fig about the red line, even though it was described in the license, she was going to see everything or she wasn't going to pass anything. Try as he could, the shift supervisor couldn't keep the inspector away from Vidalia. When the inspector got within thirty yards of Vidalia, even though the exhaust fan drew five thousand watts and was known to be able to suck unpicked turkey carcasses right off the meats hooks, she stopped dead in her tracks.

"Oh my Gosh! What is that awful smell??"

The shift boss put his hands in his pockets, mostly to overcome the urge to wipe the tears from his eyes, sniffed in the air like he was trying with great difficulty to detect whatever the inspector had noticed.

"What"-cough-"smell?"

"That smell! You can't smell anything?

Tears streamed down his cheeks and his nose began to weep. He had never been this close to Vidalia, but he was true to his people.

"Nope."-cough-"don't smell a thing."

The inspector brought a perfumed handkerchief over her nose, speaking through the fabric. "If that smell is coming from that woman, she has to go!"

"Lady, this part of the plant has nothing to do with food production."

"It's all the same building, so every inch has to pass inspection, and that,...thing...at the end of the line cannot possibly be allowed around food!"

The supervisor stalked off to his office for a quick call to the owner. He explained Vidalia's situation and then turned the phone over to the inspector. Certain the owner would convince the inspector to leave Vidalia alone, the supervisor paced outside his own office until she tapped on the window and beckoned him back in with a curling finger. The supervisor took the phone from the inspector with a smug smile of success, but lost it quickly in a falling face as the owner spoke.

"Bubba, you're right, but that inspector won't budge. Fact is, we can't afford the lawyers to take the issue to court. You're gonna have to let her go."

The inspector did not wait for a response, or even look at the supervisor. She simply walked away speaking into the air as she left.

"I'll be back in two weeks, after that thing is gone. Then you'll have your certificate."

The supervisor went back into his office for a moment and then returned to the processing room. Vidalia new something was going on, but could not hear all that was said, but was used to waiting for someone to yell instructions to her or pass them to her through Slick. The supervisor tried three times to walk close to her, but each time he had to back up, wheezing and coughing, until he returned to where he started. Vidalia held up her hands in question.

"What??'

After a long pause, Bubba raised a bullhorn and spoke to Vidalia across the remaining 75 yards between them.

"Got to let you go, Vidalia. I'm sorry but I got no choice in the matter." He explained the inspector's demand and the owner's position. "There ain't nothin we can do, child"

"I'm bein' fired 'cause I smell?? I work in a fertilizer factory, processin' half rotted turkey carcasses for fertilizer, an' I'm bein' fired cause I smell??"

Bubba reluctantly brought the bullhorn up to his lips. "More like 'stink', young'un."

Slick had had enough and grabbed Vidalia by the arm trying to pull her out of the processing room, and yelled back at Bubba.

"Thab ainb rightb Bubbab. Weed quitb!"

But Vidalia wouldn't budge. She crossed her arms in front of her, tapped her right shoe toe hard on the wood planking, and look from left to right. After a few moments she stopped tapping her toe and put her hands on her hips.

"You go on home, Slick. I'm not taking this!" She turned back to Bubba.

"I want a legal witness. I want an official legal witness to this here injustice. I want a Finton County deputy to come smell me and write it down that he agrees with the county inspector."

"You want a Finton County deputy to come smell you and verify that you stink?"

"Yep!"

"Now child, what good do you think that will do you."

"Cause I'm gonna sue every damned one of ya, 'cept you Bubba. You've always been kind to me in a distant sorta way, and I mean you no harm, but the owner and the county are about to reap the vengeance of Vidalia Millpond."

Moments later Bubba Greenwood found himself in the middle of the strangest phone call he ever made.

"That's right Sheriff, I need a deputy down to the fertilizer plant to assist in sorting out a labor dispute."

"And just what is the deputy supposed to sort out?"

"I need a deputy to smell Vidalia Millpond, write it up in an official report, and then be prepared to testify in court that she stinks."

"Bubba, you been drinking in the daytime again? Hell, you could throw a rock in any direction of Finton County and find someone who could answer that question." The Sheriff began to laugh at his own remark. Bubba had to wait a full four minutes before he could say anything else into the phone and be heard.

"I'm serious as a heart attack, Sheriff. This needs to be recorded legally, and this is what Vidalia is asking."

"Well alright, Bubba. I got a deputy been complaining he doesn't get out in the field enough since we got a computer. He'll be over there in 20 minutes."

Bubba stepped back out into the processing area and brought up the bull horn. "Vi' there'll be a deputy here in about twenty minutes. I know ya' always bring your lunch, so just sit down and have it while you wait." He turned toward the office then back to Vidalia. "Child, I got to turn that fan on. My sinuses are on fire." And with that he flipped the switch on the bare wood wall to restart the big exhaust fan behind Vidalia.

When the deputy arrived, Bubba was unhappy but not too surprised to find that the Sheriff had not told the deputy he was going to have to smell Vidalia.

The deputy stood there with long muscular arms hanging limp by his sides shaking his head 'no' in a slow exaggerated motion. "I am not going to smell Vidalia Millpond."

"You got to Mike. She has to have a legal witness, cause this whole thing is going to court. You got to get up close, take in a whiff, and then write down your findings."

"Hell no! Double hell no! A man do that and he'd throw up for a whole year!"

"Aw Mike, it won't be all that bad."

"Well you won't do it. I know full well you use a bull horn to talk to her. Slick is my second cousin. Besides, I remember she got on a Millersville Transit Company bus a couple years ago, when Slick was driving it on weekends while he was still in school. The bus company cleaning crew scrubbed that seat every day for six days and then finally had the maintenance man unbolt it, take it out back, and burn it!"

"You got no choice, Mike. You got to go smell that woman."

"Damnation."

The deputy stomped out of the office and headed down toward the end of the processing line. He walked hunched over like he was ready to dodge bullets, strumming his fingertips across his thumbs. He got within thirty yards of Vidalia when Bubba turned off the fan. The deputy took only two more steps until he dropped face down on to the floor and began rubbing discarded turkey parts onto his face to kill the smell. Bubba called out to him.

"That ain't close enough for that county inspector, Mike!"

The deputy combat-crawled back to the entrance and then got to his feet without speaking or looking at

Bubba, and left the plant for the parking lot. He hosed himself down with a surplus army fire hose plant workers used to rinse out the trucks. Dripping wet, he reached into the squad car and pulled out the microphone.

"Sheriff Lincoln, this is Mike in car three down at the fertilizer plant. You're gonna have to fire me and send someone else, 'cause I am not going to get close to Vidalia Millpond to smell her legally. And I'll tell you something else; you won't find anyone else in the department who will smell her either. Something else, too. This is going to court one way or another. I hope to heaven she doesn't do something to be in contempt of court. We just built that new jail, and we won't be able to put anybody in it ever again." Struggling to keep finding reasons for the Sheriff to change his mind, that deputy went on. "And if we don't smell her and write it down, you'll have to go into that courtroom with her to explain things to the judge."

The radio was quiet except for the scratchy static broken a few times when the Sheriff keyed his microphone to answer, but could not and he released it again. Mike removed his uniform and dropped in onto the dirt then kicked it over to a nearby trash pile, prepared to drive home in his skivvies rather than bring the uniform into his house. The Sheriff came back on the air.

"Go home, Mike. I need to call the judge."

The Sheriff called Judge Atkins and explained the situation about Vidalia Millpond, and how long such a trial in his courtroom could last, and how he would have to be there every day and so would Vidalia. In the end, all the judge said was "I'll get back to you Sheriff."

That afternoon the phone rang in the center hall of Red Oaks Farm, just off the Swamp Road in southern Finton County. The owner, Sarah Kozlowski, answered and received the call from circuit court Judge Averill Atkins.

"What can I do for you, Averill?"

"Sarah, does Stanley's brother still work for the Governor?"

"Yes he does."

"Sarah, I need a favor."

The next day the county inspector received a wonderful promotion to work for the governor in the state capital. They needed her so much that she had to leave her current position right then and be at the capital the next day.

The next day everything was almost back to normal at the processing plant. Except that Slick had sent a note by Vidalia, that he had quit.

"Sorry to lose him," Bubba said to Vidalia through the bull horn.

Several days later the receptionist in the business office at the front of the plant called Bubba to say the new county inspector was there.

"I don't guess this new one is going to want to smell the turkey line, is she?"

"Well, it's a he," the receptionist answered, "and yes, he said he needs to do just that."

Bubba hung up the phone and spoke to himself as he went out of his office into the processing area.

"Damn. I thought all this was fixed."

Soon the door to the processing area opened and in walked Slick Millpond. Bubba looked over Slick's shoulder for the inspector then back at Slick.

"Thought you quit."

"Ib dib."

"You can't see Vidalia now, we're waiting on the new county inspector."

Slick grinned, and placed his hand gently on Bubba's

shoulder.

"Wellb, I'mb hereb."

GEORGE, GRACIE AND CALVIN

I stopped off for a going-home beer at Al's Tavern in Tooey's Crossroads, after spending most of an August Sunday afternoon fishing on Lake Adolphus, and fell into a conversation at the bar with a grizzled old farmer I had not met before. His name was Berl and he loved to fish more than almost anything else in the world, but had a great sadness in his voice when he said he could never let himself do it again. He seemed reluctant to take the conversation on the subject any farther than that, so I bought him a beer and asked him why a fisherman could ever give that up. He nodded his thanks and drank down half the bottle in silence before he went on.

"I once caught a hundred and twenty-pound blue catfish right down there in Lake Adolphus."

After listening to the old wooden floor creak and the oscillating whirr from the ancient ceiling fan overhead for almost a full minute, I had to know more.

"What'd you use for bait?"

He gulped down the rest of the beer and turned to face me full on, the stubble on his face and the gold plating on a lower front tooth catching the sunlight coming in between the front window blinds. "An ornery 28-pound white Persian cat named George, and a three-pound gray city rat named Gracie."

I turned to the bartender, Big Al Tooey, who was drying glasses nearby, ordered a shot of Tennessee whiskey and lime for each of us, and then turned back to the old man.

"This, I gotta' hear."

"Well, it was during the drought of '78 and with most of the corn crop dead on the stalk, I did what I could to put food on the table by fishing for catfish down at the lake. The lake itself was a good three feet lower than usual and awfully muddy that year, and I had to go farther into the swamp than I'd ever been to find what few deep pools were left.

But wait, I need to tell you about George before I can ever tell about the catfish. I guess it really started the Summer of '67, right after I graduated from High School, when I got a mechanics job working for the Oldsmobile dealership up in Millersville, and took an apartment up there. The owner of the Olds place had a trailer park just outside of town and had converted a cinderblock garage there into three apartments. The old guy in the first apartment, Jimmy, managed the little building and the trailer park, and he let me in.

The furnished living room, dining room and kitchen were all parts of the same room, with the bedroom and the bathroom just off that. It met all my needs and with me working for the owner my rent was only twenty dollars a month, including utilities. I was going to be making a full hundred dollars a month, so this was going to be high living for me and any of my friends that came to visit. The people that had been in the apartment before me had vacated in a hurry without paying their last month's rent, and had left a pile of trash in the middle of the living room. On top of the trash pile, sitting there like a king on his throne was the biggest cat I had ever seen.

We had cats around my daddy's farm, but they were all short hair working mousers and half wild from being on their own. This cat was covered in thick long dirty white hair, had bright blue eyes, and was as fat as a pig. Jimmy said he was a Persian cat, and had stayed in the apartment with the last four renters.

"What's his name?"

"Different folks give him different names, but the last

fellah said he seemed to answer to 'George'."

I knelt down and looked in the cat's face and said "Hello George".

He blinked his eyes at me, stood up, peed on the trash pile in front of me and then trotted out the open front door. Well now, trot is not really a word I'd use with George. George was so fat he could never trot. It was more like a determined waddle, if you could imagine a four-legged snow goose.

Just as George went out the door, there was a movement in the trash pile, and then a large charcoal gray rat dashed from under the rubbish and out the door. I looked around for something to throw at the rat, but there was nothing close by and he was already gone.

"That's a big one! The fat ol'cat sure isn't earning his keep!"

Jimmy kept his hands in his pockets and smiled, flicking his chin in the direction of the door. "That'd be 'Gracie'. The last fellah told me about her. Said one day she just showed up with George like they were old friends, and George wouldn't come back in without her. He let her in and never had any trouble from her. Said she ate and drank what the cat did, even used the litter box, so they let her stay."

After I moved in, George and Gracie showed up at the door wanting in. I fed them outside for a few days, but finally gave in and brought a litter box into the bathroom. They took a little getting used to. At first I had to sleep with my bedroom door closed tight and them out in the living room, but after a while it just got normal, although I didn't go around telling folks I was living with a cat and a rat. The only trouble the rat ever got into was because of that little Chihuahua dog.

The woman in trailer number two lived alone, since her common-law husband ran off with one of the waitresses from the Sloppy Dog Diner. She was a bitter woman with nothing kind for anything or anybody except for that little Chihuahua dog she owned. She called it 'Baby' and carried it around most of the time like a play doll, but when it was out on it's own a lot of us would have loved to kill the little shit. It would nip at your heels and bark with that high pitched yap of its, and draw blood sometimes even though you were nowhere near its trailer. The little dog was so fast it always got away without a scratch.

One warm Sunday afternoon I left the front door propped open to let in a breeze, while I ate lunch at my dinner table that was hinged to the back wall. Baby got after Gracie, and every time Gracie would try to go out Baby would come charging at her and Gracie would dash back in the door. At first the dog didn't come in and Gracie would stop just a few feet inside the door, and then sit on her haunches squeaking back at it. As soon as the dog gave up yapping at Gracie and walked away, Gracie would go back out the door and then dash back in with Baby dead on her heels. Each time they did that Gracie came in a little farther and so did the dog.

Now George more or less lived his days on the little lamp table against the front wall between the end of the sofa and the front door. You couldn't always tell what part of George's body was moving in all that fat and fur. Sometimes it would look like he was facing one direction and then he'd open his eyes and raise his head and he would be facing the other way. Sometimes when he did move, it was almost like watching yeast dough rise and settle; a little faster than that, but not much.

So each time Gracie ran back into the apartment the dog followed her in a little farther until he was right beside the center on the lamp table. I had noticed George was shifting around, but didn't have a clear notion what he was doing until I noticed all four paws barely sticking out from under the fat, and they were all four side by side on the edge of the lamp table. I looked down at that yapping dog and then back at George when it happened.

At first it was like a sumo wrestler doing a wave. George slowly raised his head and front paws like a fat little boy yawning and trying to stretch. He didn't even look down at the dog; he just rolled his eyes back, held his paws up in surrender, and let gravity plop him down on that Chihuahua like a soggy throw pillow. George's rolls of fat and fur completely covered Baby and instantly muffled the dog's barking. George's head turned serenely from left to right with his eyes half open almost as if he was settling down for a nap. The only other part of his body I could see moving was the tips of his elbows, slowing moving in and out, in and out, like an old woman kneading dough, in and out. Gracie was nearby squeaking in rhythm to George's elbows. The dog's yapping had turned to yelping, and with each kneading of George's elbows the pitch of the yelp got higher and higher until it reached a frenzy.

When I figured George had done enough to satisfy the both of us, I threw an empty cracker box in his direction and yelled for him to let the dog go. George stood up and the dog was gone in a blurred flash out the door. I could see little spots of blood on George's belly fur as he climbed ponderously back up the sofa and onto his table. Gracie climbed up next to him and they settled into a nap.

Moments later there was a rush of people to the sound of shrieking coming from the woman that lived in trailer number two. I went to the door and saw a few folks gathering around her, she in her curlers and blood spotted housecoat, holding that little dog almost totally covered in different sized band-aids. It looked like she had used every band-aid that came in the twenty-five cent box. She was shrieking about her poor baby that had been attacked by a wild animal and was terrified it might come back for him. I glanced down at George, sound asleep on the table, and decided not to interfere with the community support the woman was getting, and went back to the table to finish my beer.

Later on, whenever I went fishing George and Gracie liked to come along in the boat and eat the throwbacks that were too far gone to live, and any leftover minnows I might have. That's why they were with me fishing for catfish that day in '67.

I had hooked something really big down deep and lost two brand new leaders with brass hooks trying to coax it up. At first I thought it was an old log, but then it moved a little farther away from the boat when the line broke. I thought then that maybe it was a big ol' turtle, and you could make a good soup with turtle, so I cast back in the same spot. The second time the line went taut almost as soon as the sinker took it to the bottom, and whatever it was started pulling the boat to the other side of the pool toward the far shore. I tried to reel it in, but it just kept moving away and taking us with it until the slip knot to the leader gave way and I lost the hook. I changed rods and tossed out the biggest fresh minnow in the bucket at the end of new thirty-pound test line, and waited for another bite. I could feel something big down there toying with the line; not pulling on the bait, but like it was just nosing around the line deciding what to do with it. That's when Gracie got into the bait bucket.

She was up on her hind feet, leaning over the rim of the bucket, grabbing with one paw, trying to scoop up a minnow onto the deck for a snack. She got under one of the slower minnows and popped him out of the water and into the air over the bucket. Before Gracie could grab him with both paws, he flipped onto the deck, and then double flipped again and bounced onto the gunnels strip with Gracie just inched behind him. Everything was in motion and there was no stopping either of them. The minnow flipped again into the air and Gracie sprang at him and then they both flew into the water. Out of the corner of my eye I could see something big coming to the surface of the water just as Gracie and the minnow went into it.

A dark hole opened in the water under the rat and as Gracie went down this huge mouth came up wide open. The fish jumped almost completely out of the water. It was the biggest catfish I had ever seen! Must have been four, maybe five feet long, mouth whiskers as long as my forearms and had to weigh at least a hundred pounds. It had a belly big enough to hold a piglet, and it fell back into the water, closing its mouth around poor old Gracie, and sending up a splash like a full-grown seal hitting the water. It sank tail first back into the brown water, taking Gracie with it. I could still her eyes shining in the darkness of its great mouth as the lips closed up and the head began to slip back under the water. Then I heard a shriek like a woman with her hair caught on fire, and George shot by my head in a burst of speed that would have been fast for a retriever, let alone a fat old white Persian cat.

George fixed himself to the catfish's face and was digging in with all four sets of claws, two above the mouth and two below, hissing and yeowling in a bobcat fit, and then they all sank below the surface, leaving me leaning over the edge of the boat in silence. A little wave washed over the spot where they all went in and the boat rocked a little, and I wasn't sure what I could do about any of it. I looked down into the water, you couldn't see more than a few inches, except if something big came just under the surface, but I couldn't see anything but water and muddy silt. The quiet over the swamp seemed to spread out from that spot as if everything was holding its breath and watching the spot with me. A full minute passed and I guessed I had lost them all. The ache in my back from leaning over sideways drove me upright and I had to twist sideways to take out the knot. I leaned back over the side of the boat to look at the still water again, but only saw my own reflection in the muddy water and the clear sky overhead.

Then the water burst up about fifteen feet away from me and that fish jumped clean out of the water like a sailfish in a Florida postcard, slapping his tail and twisting back and forth for all he was worth, and George was still on his face. George took in a rasping breath and picked up his hissing and yeowling in a sound that split the silence of the swamp and sent echoes of fighting cat screams to the far edges of the lake. The catfish flipped and turned and slapped himself against the surface of the water, but George kept on him, determined to dig himself a way down into that fish's belly after Gracie, or drown trying. They went down again, and this time longer than before, but the fish came back up still trying to get that damned cat off his face, shaking his head from side to side like a Brahma bull trying to throw a rider. Two more times the surface of the water exploded with the catfish jumping in the air and trying different ways to slap back onto the water to knock George off, but he held on and as soon as he got air in his lungs he picked up that cat war cry.

Finally, the catfish flung himself up onto the muddy bank and spit up everything he could get out of his mouth and stomach, between George's legs. There were several minnows and fair sized fish, a beer can, something with fur that was half digested, an old tennis shoe, and a very wet rat. As soon as Gracie crawled away from the catfish and got her breath back, she sat up on her haunches and started cussing out the fish in rat-speak. George heard Gracie and let go of the fish to go check on his friend. The catfish was cut up pretty bad in the face and lay on the bank too weak to work himself back into the water. I pulled the boat over to the bank and got out to look at the catfish.

He was huge. I grabbed him by the gills and lifted him up. I was strong back then and could lift more than my own weight. I judged him to weigh one hundred and twenty pounds at least. I checked on George and Gracie and then looked around to see if I could get the car close enough to drag the fish up the bank and then get him into the trunk. His skin was blue-gray, and one eye almost white with age, like my Aunt Maude's was. Thinking of my aunt made me wonder how old a catfish must be to get that big. I squatted down to look more closely at him as he struggled to pull in air with his gills from water that wasn't there.

"That's a magic fish," the voice said.

I looked up and across the pond to another mud bank where the voice came from and saw a full grown raccoon looking directly at me. He introduced himself, pointed a paw in my direction, and spoke again. "I said that's a magic fish. He's over a, uh, a thousand years old. You let him go and he'll grant you three wishes."

I could only stare at the raccoon, but I was joined by both George and Gracie who stared with me. At least they must have heard it too, I thought.

"You don't talk much, do ya?"

"How can you be talking?"

"Tongue, lips, lungs, same as you , Sport. Now what about that fish. You gonna' put Calvin back in the water and get your three wishes, or are you just gonna sit there and let him die – and miss your big break?"

"Magic Fish, hunh?"

"Yep. I caught him years ago. I let him go and he gave me the power to speak. We don't need money and stuff like that, but I've seen him give away tons of it to you two-leggers."

"I let him go and he grant's me three wishes?"

"Yep."

"He's a magic fish? A thousand years old."

"Yep."

"Why doesn't he tell me that himself?"

"Uh,…uh, he had a stroke, back in, uh, in 1897. He's made it so other animals could speak for him. It's my job now."

We stared across the pond in silence, until the fish thrashed again trying to work his way back down the muddy bank into the water again.

"Hey Sport, he's suffocating, put him back in the water!"

"What about my three wishes? When does he grant them?"

"After he's back in the water, Einstein."

"When do I make my wishes?"

"While you're putting him back in the water. Better get to it or you'll miss the whole rich and famous thing."

"I want the drought to end."

He pointed a paw at the catfish. "Don't tell me, tell him – while you're putting him back in the water!"

I started pushing against the scratched up face of the catfish and slowly slid him back down toward the water. "I want the drought to end. I want the Baltimore Orioles to win the World Series. I want to be rich."

As the old fish slid back into the water and began to revive in the shallows the raccoon called out a final time. "Oh, one other thing."

"What's that?"

"If you ever go fishing again, it will break the spell."

"When do the wishes come true?"

"Soon enough, but, uh…, sometimes it takes a little while."

The drought ended the following Spring, and as you

know, the Orioles took the Pennant two years later. I'm still waiting on that third wish and then I'm a rich man, but I still can't go fishing."

The tavern had become deathly quiet and I looked around the barroom to find everyone staring in my direction. At first I thought they were listening intently to the old man's story, but then I saw the mirth in their eyes and the barely suppressed grins spreading across their faces. I spun around on my bar stool to look at each of them, and it was more than they could resist. The entire bar erupted into a chorus of belly laughs and guffaws as they all had their joke on me. Red with embarrassment I turned back to the old man who had begun laughing, but I didn't see as much amusement in his eyes.

I leaned close to his face and asked him if he knew anyone named Donald out that way. He stopped laughing and only smiled at the familiar name.

BIG AL'S TATTOO

When I was still tending bar full time at Big Al's, she once told me, "Some people you know the first time you ever see them. Some will show up and smile and you know right then you'll be buddies for life. Then there are some people that walk into the room for the first time in their lives, and they just piss you off." The second way described how it always was between Al Tooey and Tater Millpond.

Al's brother Adam had told me that back when Al was still called Alexandra and hadn't been out of diapers more than a month or two, their Mommas put the kids down to play while the women shared coffee and gossip. Steam was still rising up from the coffee cups when both toddlers began to wail in the next room. They were found bruised and fussy, slapping each other in the face for no apparent reason, which set the tone between them for the rest of their lives.

In the first grade Tater pushed Alexandra down into a drainage ditch on the day her Momma had her wear her best jumper for school pictures, and of course that was before she'd had a chance to get her picture taken. In the second grade one of the Tucker boys taught Alexandra how to make a fist and throw a punch, so that year Tater lost two teeth and got that little scar on his upper lip. In the third grade Tater talked his younger brother Milford and Beetle McClanahan into helping him beat up Alexandra on her way home, saying she had called Beetle a sissy. Before she let them get away, Beetle had a black eye and split lip, Milford got his nose broken for the first time, and Tater lost another tooth. By the time they were in the sixth grade, when Alexandra had traded all her dolls for a pump BB gun and a hunting knife and told everyone to call her Al, and Tater got his first honorable mention in the police blotter for setting fire to the trash can behind the volunteer fire department, most of southern Finton County knew that you never put those two people together in the same room at the same time. And they never were again, that is until Big Al came back on leave from her first tour in Iraq.

Adam was running the Park 'N' Pump and renting the Tavern next door out to Tootie Hooker's nephew Thurmond. When Thurmond heard Al was coming home, he set up a special Happy Hour in her honor for that first Friday night and got it mentioned on the radio as part of the local news. Once the beer went around to wet everyone's whistle and some started switching to whiskey, Thurmond let it be known that if anyone would come up with another twenty dollars to cover his losses (not that he really had any) he'd extend the Happy Hour for another hour. Two fives and a Ten were almost immediately slapped down on the bar top accompanied by football stadium cheers from the other patrons. The Tavern was awash in good will, patriotism and alcohol, and groups kept pooling the cash from their wallets, so Thurmond wound up extending Happy Hour six more times; the last three times paid solely by Tater Millpond.

Al knew Tater was there, but paid little attention to him since he kept his distance. Tater had friends take his money to the bar to keep the Happy Hour going and to cover Al's tab for anything she wanted, but made no effort to let her know he was doing it. Al went to Iraq a green private in the Marines and came back a veteran sergeant with a chest full of ribbons, and had a thirst that took a lot to cover. By midnight Al had tried every mixed drink Thurmond knew how to put together under a name, and was ready to roll when Beetle suggested they try the new hippie bar north of Millersville. So Al and Beetle and four others piled into Beetle's GTO and headed North on 535, Tater among them, but Thurmond missed that.

Al woke up the next morning at the Tooey home place, the old house out behind the store that she and her brother had shared until she went into the Marines. The sun was high in the late morning sky and the simmering flame under the coffee pot had been turned off hours before. Al leaned against the kitchen counter wearing an olive drab sleeveless tee shirt and boxer shorts, drinking lukewarm coffee from the pot in one hand, and chasing it with half-and-half from the carton held in her other, when Adam walked in.

"What's that on your shoulder?"

"Semper Fi, Adam. You saw that before I went to Iraq."

"Not that one. I know it. The one below it."

"There isn't one below it." Her voice echoed inside the upturned half and half carton.

'Well something's there. My eyes aren't that bad."

Al looked down at her right arm. "What th'…" then quickly set the coffee and creamer down and stepped close to the small mirror hanging from the window frame over the kitchen sink. She twisted her arm around, pulling and pushing on her arm muscle to better see the figure tattooed on the side of her bicep, and brought the mirror over to give her a better view. "What the hell??!!"

She quick-stepped back to the bathroom for a better mirror and twisted her bicep into the overhead light and upper body mirror. "What the Hell??!!"

She came back to the kitchen, her mouth opening and closing and pieces of words or guttural single syllables stumbling over her tongue, looking at her brother for some answer to the unspoken question; her face growing redder by the moment. Shock and disbelief slowly shifted toward anger, then focused by Adam's next comment.

"You know what that looks like? It does, I mean, It is…"

"No way!!"

"Yes. It is. That tattoo is a drawing of…"

"The Hell it is!..."

"Tater Millpond!…It is…You've got a tattoo of Tater Millpond on your arm!"

"The Hell it is! The HELL it is!!"

" Bigger 'n shit, Sis."

" THE HELL IT IS!!"

Al began a sequence of curses and profanities that went non-stop while she burst out through the screen door charging toward her car, back into the house to get her pants, and then out to the car again, then back into the house to get her car keys, then out to the car again, then back into the house to retrieve her .357, and then out to her car again. She was still shouting curses when the orange Charger roared to life, rooster-tailing gravel all the way up to the second story of the house, pinging pebbles against the window glass. She shot down the driveway and past the store in a plume of red dust. The car launched out of that onto the pavement with shrill screeching tires, and headed north with its rear end still wobbling as it tried to go as fast as the big V-8 was pushing it.

Adam followed her out of the house the last time, and stood at the bottom of the back steps next to the driveway as she roared away, letting the red dust settle onto his white tee shirt like paprika snow, knowing where Al was going. He stood there shaking his head, picturing Al pounding Tater into mash with ham-sized fists - if she didn't just outright shoot him in the forehead as soon as he opened the door of his house.

"Tater's done it for sure, this time." The only thing

he could think to do was to call Tater. Then he called the Sheriff. Harley Poteat was in his sixties by then, but he was still in office and still the only man in Finton County that could talk to Al when her blood was up.

Three hours later Harley refilled his coffee mug and walked back into the squad room, settling into the wooden chair beside the desk with a muffled groan to the arthritis in his knee. He took a long draw of fresh coffee and began to set the mug onto the desk, until the desk began to bounce again. Four of his biggest deputies were arrayed and stacked spread eagle on top of Big Al, with the topmost deputy grabbing onto one of the desk legs with a death grip, trying to add more leverage to keep Al down. Al was almost pinned belly down under the pile, cursing and threatening the generations of each deputy by name, while hunching up every few seconds and making the pile of deputies, and the desk, buck like the mechanical horsey ride down in front of the Millersville Five and Dime.

The bottom-most deputy was pinned between Al's pushes up and the efforts of his brother officers pushing her back down. Mike Daniels had used well-practiced skills that had won him the cattle roping event at the Tri-County Rodeo three years running, and just barely managed to keep Big Al from killing Tater Millpond. Fresh boot heel marks painted two black parallel lines from the front door into the squad room. One of Mike's boots lay empty in a corner of the room and his nose had stopped bleeding, while the two whelps on his forehead and left cheek were turning a darker red. His shirttail was half out, his bootless foot about to lose its white sock, and his right shirt sleeve ripped from the cuff all the way up to the county seal patch on his shoulder, but he still held onto Al's right wrist with both hands.

Harley gently nudged Mike's side with the toe of his boot. "You doin' all right there, Deputy Daniels."

Mike spoke through clenched teeth over his knotted shoulder muscles. "No problems, Sheriff. As soon as this break is over I'll get back to my rounds."

Harley chuckled at the officer's bravado. "Good Man." Then he nudged Al's shoulder. "Al, aren't you done yet?"

Al began a description of what she was still prepared to do to the Sheriff if only just two of the deputies would get off the pile and wait their turn outside. Harley shook his head slowly, reached his hand down next to the exposed side of her head and finger-flipped her ear with an audible 'thap'.

"Oww!"

"Al, you got to give it up before someone gets hurt here. Fun's fun, but we got work to do, and you do not want to be put in jail for assault."

"The hell I don't. You give me a half hour with Tater Millpond, and I'll come back and lock myself in."

"You in that big a hurry to lose your chance to ever own that Tavern after you get out of the Marines?"

The desk stopped jumping and the room became still, except for the sound of four officers catching deep breaths.

"What's this got to do with my Tavern?"

"It's not yours yet. Al, I'd stand back to back with you against any ten men in the world, but sometimes you don't got the sense God gave a gopher! You get booked for assault and you become a Felon. As a felon, the county liquor board will block your application for a whiskey license quicker than you can say 'Gotcha Gert'. AND, without a liquor license, Big Al's Tavern would never exist. That place would just be a storage building for the Park'N'Pump. You better connect those dots in a hurry. This has gone on long enough."

Al lay motionless for several seconds, then relaxed her shoulders and rested the side of her chin down against the linoleum. Her warm breath fogged a little patch in front of her mouth as she exhaled her answer. "All right, Harley. I'm done."

Each layer of deputy dismounted and stood next to the desk stretching, shaking arms and legs to return the circulation, and adjusting their uniforms. Mike stood up and offered his hand to Al, who accepted it and rose with a half smile then looked away. Three of the deputies headed for the squad room doorway while Mike limped to the corner to retrieve his boot.

Harley shook his head. "We're not done here yet, folks. Al, you tussled with four officers duly deputized by me under the authority of Finton County and due your respect. We need to close the book on that, even if this isn't going before Judge Atkins."

Al held out her wrists for the handcuffs, prepared to accept Harley's application of justice, but he stood up beside her and palm slapped the back of her head as he would an errant schoolboy. "What have you got to say for yourself?"

Al flinched, looked into the eyes of each deputy one at a time, and apologized if she had been overly rough with any of them in particular. Everyone in the room nodded in acceptance, except Mike. He limped back in front of Al and pointed a finger in front of her face. "I paid forty dollars for that cattle rope you broke. I expect another just like it by the weekend."

Harley gripped Al's arm and escorted her to the front door of the Sheriff's office, and then tapped his fingertip lightly on her right shoulder. "On your way to the hardware store for that rope, you stop by Crazy Pete's Tattoo Parlor and see what he can do with Tater's portrait there."

Al blew out a sigh and left the building.

A couple nights later Adam stopped by the Tavern after he closed the store. Al was perched on a bar stool watching the evening crowd and leaning back with her elbows propped up on the bar. Adam leaned over to inspect the still-reddened artwork of her redrawn tattoo. "Who's that supposed to be?"

"What d'you mean 'who's that'? It's Abraham Lincoln, 16th president of these United States, and I'm proud to have him on my arm."

Adam squinted at Al's upper arm as she turned so the bar light could shine on it. "I don't know. That doesn't look like Abe Lincoln to me. The beard's way too shaggy and the face is a bit wide, too."

Adam turned to the man next to him and nudged him with his elbow. "Stumpy, have a look at Al's arm here and tell me who you think it looks like."

"Already saw it. Damned shame. And on the arm of a brave Marine like Al. It breaks my heart to see her brandishing the picture of a commie."

Both Al and Adam spoke as one "Commie??" Adam asked, "Who do you think it is?"

"Why it's that Fi-dell Castro from down in Cuba."

Adam swiveled around and squinted down at the tattoo again, then jerked up straight. "Damned if it isn't! That's exactly who it is."

Al twisted her shoulders around under a series of grunted mutters until she found a good angle in the light to see her own shoulder in the mirror behind the bar. She studied the tattoo for several seconds, changing the viewing angle a dozen times.

"Well,...well,...Hells Bells!"

Then she went into the back room and came out wearing a long sleeve red and black checkered flannel shirt Thurmond had left in there since hunting season. In a bar full of people wearing tee shirts and tank tops, the flannel shirt could not help but bring more attention to Al.

She was still standing there with her fists clenched

and mouth pressed into a thin line when Clifford Tibideaux came in and took a seat on the other side of Adam. He turned to Adam, while pointing a finger at Al's flannel shirt, then opened his mouth to ask the question.

Adam shook his head slowly. "If you want to live, don't say a word."

Al's leave ended the next day and she spent the next two days traveling to her new duty assignment. She reported for duty at a military base in California, where she was to teach marine recruits the art of hand-to-hand combat - her favorite sport. Her first weekend off, she visited a tattoo parlor out there and had another try at fixing what started out as Tater Millpond's portrait. Apparently, the next try resulted in a toss-up as to whether the modified tattoo looked like Jesus or George Harrison.

That Christmas she came home for a week's leave, and spent half of it spelling Thurmond tending bar at the Tavern. She always did love that place. When she was only ten she would put on those old skates that grabbed onto the bottom of regular shoes and then tighten them with a big key, and skate around on the wooden floors of the Tavern barroom until the late afternoon drinkers started coming in.

She always planned on running that place someday. The other half of her leave, she spent visiting the tattoo parlor up in Millersville and looking for Tater Millpond. She had decided that the beating she'd given him previously was insufficient for her troubles and intended to repeat the process with him at her first opportunity. Tater heard about it and spent that Christmas holed up in an old hotel in Louisville, Kentucky until Al's leave was up.

The last night of Al's leave she was tending bar again, and trading drinks with her favorites. Most everyone in the bar was in jackets and flannel shirts, except Al. She was wearing a U.S. Marines t-shirt with the sleeves cut off, showing off her new revised modified redrawn Tater-Abe-Fi~Dell-Jesus-George tattoo. There was almost a line formed up to the bar with folks brave, friendly or foolish enough to ask to see her tattoo, but Al seemed perfectly content to show it off.

Thurmond brought a fresh case of mixed liquor bottles from the back room to restock the shelves behind the bar, and Al said for him to have a look at her tattoo. Her face was flushed red from holiday shots and the hard day she had spent trying to convince Tater Millpond's friends to give him up. The Millersville Medical Clinic had worked overtime patching up a steady stream of Tater's acquaintances. When Al turned and pointed her thumb at the tattoo below the US marine logo on her left upper arm, Thurmond gave up a broad grin in appreciation. It was not only a good tattoo, with little indication of what it had once been, but the nature of it also suited Al to a Tee. It was the snarling head of a Kodiak bear - and no one could think it might be anything else.

Right after New Year's, Sheriff Poteat visited the Park'N'Pump to interview Adam Tooey regarding a string of altercations that took place at a hotel in Louisville. Reports described the vicious attack of a big boned woman on a man renting a room there. She had ripped a couple doors off their hinges and sent them sailing through a third story window, raining glass, and the doors, onto the roof of a Louisville police car. Witnesses said the man was chased through the rooms of the third floor shrieking like a mad woman and looking in wide-eyed terror back over his shoulder like a fleeing deer in hunting season. The hotel guest was found body-punched from forehead to shin bone and unconscious, draped over the third-floor banister in the stairwell. He was taken to the local hospital, but when they went to take his statement, he had come to and sneaked out from the doctors, the nurses, the police and his bill.

The only other thing the night clerk at the hotel could tell the police was that the woman was built like a pro-football lineman, and when she left the hotel one shirtsleeve was ripped, showing what the clerk thought was a tattoo of a bear. Of course Adam couldn't add a thing to what the Sheriff already knew, and Harley already knew that was going to be the case.

"Don't know what to tell you, Sheriff."

The sheriff looked at himself in the mirror behind the bar, and carefully straightened his Stetson.

"If you ever do think of who that might have been, you call me?"

"Sure will."

"Well, I got other things to be doing. Say 'Hi' to Al for me, the next time she's in town." Then he smiled at himself in the mirror and walked out the door.

ESTHER MADISON

After some time to get over the loss, and several bottles of Tennessee sour mash whiskey, Massey Ferguson Madison decided that between the two, Esther and the outhouse, he would have missed the outhouse more. In marriage, Esther was the orneriest woman God ever made.

On the far side of Lake Adolphus from the boat landing off the swamp road, there is a narrow gorge where the lake waters drift in to fill a little lagoon surrounded by dense forest. On a steep bank near the edge of the lagoon sits an old hunter's cabin that was re-sided in aluminum in the late fifties and then painted over brick red since then. Before the lake rose and flooded 600 acres of southern Finton County bottomland, the steep bank below the cabin was one side of a ravine cradling at its bottom a sweet spring water creek. The hunters had inherited the cabin and its surrounding lands from their daddies, who had bought the land for next to nothing at the end of WW2 after it had been timbered out to make PT boats. The forest returned almost quickly and the game never really left, so the hunting had been plentiful and satisfying for over fifty years. The hunters protested to the Finton County manager when the lake flooded into their ravine, drowning out sweet water creek, and sweeping away Massey Madison's wife Esther, who was in the camp's outhouse at the time the waters rushed in. The courts said it was all an act of God and Finton County had no legal responsibility in the matter.

With the help of local folks, who had fishing boats stored on their farm property, which was now lakefront, the Sweet Water Creek Hunting Club outhouse was recovered, but no sign of Esther was ever found.

In her younger years Esther had a trail of suitors pining away for her. She had the face and shape of a movie star, and an unmatched set of beautiful eyes; the left was emerald green and the right was opal blue. Of all the men in Finton County Esther could have chosen, Massey Madison was never even a remote consideration, until the day he won a trip for two to Bermuda in a legion raffle. That weekend, Esther climbed into his bed and performed acts he had only dreamed about when he was thirteen and still sneaking peaks at the girly magazines down at the drugstore. They had only dated once before and it didn't seem to work out since they went home early from the movies, but when he won that raffle he offered Esther the dream she had always held, and she was determined to have it. They were married on the Miami dock in front of the cruise ship and left that same afternoon for Bermuda.

Massey came back a week later with a tan, 34 new magazines he had bought to read while Esther pranced up and down the beach in a bikini, and a bitch that wanted a divorce as soon as it could be arranged. No one in Massey's family had ever got divorced, so he pledged his life to make their marriage worthwhile for Esther, and she pledged to make it a living hell. Esther was way ahead on meeting her pledge when the lake waters pulled the outhouse from the gorge and sent it to a marshy bank a mile and a half north.

In the Spring, after the new sign was nailed up identifying the area as Sweet Water Lagoon Hunting and Fishing Club, Massey was walking the low edge of the lagoon when he spotted a huge five-foot snapping turtle eating a deer carcass in the shallows. It stopped eating and looked at Massey with something like a smile at the corners of its mouth. The turtle had a head the size of a basketball, with one eye emerald green and the other opal blue. It tilted its massive head down and gulped up the stag's testicles, then eyeing Massey, it dragged the carcass down into deep waters. Massey knew for sure three things that day: (1) it was the biggest snapping turtle in the world; (2) they couldn't let kids swim in the lagoon until the turtle was gone; and (3) Esther was back.

During perch season the fishermen staying at the cabin had to be really watchful of their catches kept alive on stringers in the lake water. More than once an angry and disappointed fisherman pulled up the mangled remnants of a steel wire stringer with an entire dozen perch and bullheads gone to memory with only a few strands of skin left to show what had been there. Once, three fishermen took a rowboat out over the deepest part of the lagoon, but when the fishing turned poor, the man in back said he'd push off from that big rock so they could find another spot. When he pushed the oar against the rock, the rock turned out to be Esther, and her huge head came up and bit off the end of the oar. The aluminum boat sustained three penetrating bites to the hull before they could get it back to shore. The damage looked just like a giant had taken an opener to the back of the boat like the edge of a beer can.

Visitors to the cabin started carrying large caliber handguns in case they saw Esther, but she was too smart to be caught out of the water. The hardness of her shell was able to shun off even a .44 magnum in a few feet of water. Nothing they tried had an effect toward either killing Esther or driving her out of the lagoon. They even invited a state natural resource officer and a biologist from Millersville Community College to help them, but on the days of those visits she was nowhere to be seen, and the experts left the lagoon shaking their heads at the ruse. Massey knew she had figured them out and had spent the day hiding, unseen and watching the visitors stumble around the edges of the lagoon looking for her. She ruled the lagoon the way she had ruled Massey's life – through pure meanness and obstinance.

Massey came to the conclusion that she had come back because she never got that divorce, and that if he finally gave it to her she would go away. He didn't care if that would give her spirit rest; he just wanted the snapper out of the lagoon. So, Massey went to the courthouse and filed for divorce from his dead wife.

It seemed to be going along the way he had hoped until the clerk asked him to take the papers to his wife's lawyer and have her sign them, then return them to the courthouse.

Massey shook his head at the clerk, "I can't get her to sign these papers. She can't sign no more."

"Mr. Madison, then she'll need her lawyer to sign for her, or someone other than you, who has her power of attorney."

"She doesn't have anyone with power of attorney."

"Well Mr. Madison, she may have done that without telling you. I'll check with the court records office." Before Massey could say anything else the clerk called another office and asked about Esther Madison. A frown spread over his face as the person at the other end spoke, and then covered the mouthpiece with his hand as he spoke to Massey again. "Mr. Madison, county records say your wife is dead."

"Yeah, that's right."

"…and you want to divorce her?"

"Yeah, that's right too."

The room fell silent except for the overhead ceiling fan, whirring just below a heavily painted ornate tin ceiling several feet above.

"Sir, if your wife is dead, you don't need a divorce."

"Oh, yes I do"

"Sir, she has no legal rights and no legal standing because she is dead. What good would a divorce do now?"

"I need her to leave the lagoon out at Sweet Water Lagoon Hunting Club."

"Your wife is alive and living at the lagoon of Sweet Water Lagoon Hunting Club?"

"No, she's living 'in' the lagoon at Sweet Water Lagoon Hunting Club."

Once again a curtain of silence descended in the room except for the old fan.

"Your wife is alive and living 'in' the lagoon?"

Massey's frustration boiled to the surface. "No. She ain't alive like you wanna think. She's dead and come back as a giant damned snapping turtle, and I need her ass out of the lagoon! She wanted a divorce for thirty-five years and I never gave it to her, so I figure she's back for the goddamned divorce and I want to give it to the nag!"

The scowl on the clerk's face deepened.

"Did Tater Millpond send you over here?"

Being accused of collusion with a widely known local rowdy only added to Massey's rising anger. "No! I need to divorce my dead wife!"

"I'm sorry sir, but you're going to have to leave or I'll have to call Deputy Tibideaux to escort you out of the courthouse."

Massey huffed out of the courthouse with the realization that the only way to settle with Esther was for him to deal with her himself. He stopped off at his father's house and rummaged through his attic until he found his grandfather's Sharps model 1874 buffalo rifle. He loaded up his old Dodge pickup with ammunition, food, and beer to last him a few weeks, then moved into the hunting cabin at Sweet Water.

He spent the next several days chumming the water

in front of the cabin with fish heads, old meat, half rotten carcasses he found in the woods, and even a deer he shot out of season, trying to lure Esther to the surface. She'd come up now and then to taunt him, but before he could draw a bead on her head she'd slip under the surface while the water exploded above her where the Sharp's bullet struck. She feasted on everything the surrounding countryside had to offer and he wasted ammunition as the air above the lagoon exploded in clouds of gunpowder, until even the leaves on the maples surrounding the lagoon smelled of sulfur and nitrate, and the water of the lagoon itself reeked of dead flesh.

Early the morning of the tenth day he was down to a single round of ammunition. He had managed to catch a fat five-pound catfish at sunrise, and sat there on the bank looking at the lagoon, wondering what he could do to lure her close. Smiling at a new thought, he went back to the cabin and retrieved his hunting license and the title to his truck, rolled them up tight and shoved them down the throat of the catfish, with just the edges still sticking out of its mouth. Then he picked up the Sharps in his other hand and walked around to the shallow side of the lagoon. He left the Sharps on the bank behind him and waded out into the water waist deep.

"Esther! Esther! Here's your damned divorce! I got the papers in this catfish. Esther, come on in! You can finally have your divorce!"

The surface of the lagoon was still as glass that morning with not a ripple from wind or fish's fin. Then far down the lagoon near the gorge, a dark shape neared the surface and came slowly in his direction. He waved the catfish back and forth just above the surface of the water and watched the dark form take the shape of a huge round disk gliding toward him. He glanced back at the bank to make sure he was within a few steps of the

Sharps.

At thirty feet out the dark disk of her massive shell went deep and he lost sight of her. He stepped cautiously back toward the shore still holding the catfish out in front of him until the water was only knee deep and over yellow sandy bottom, so he could see into the water better. Ten feet in front of him the water slid gently off her head without making so much as a single ripple and she opened her mouth for the fish. He waved it back and forth along the surface, letting its aroma seep into the water.

"Come get it girl." He took another step back closer to the bank.

She opened her mouth wider, but did not come any closer to him.

He held the fish out at her, shaking it gently in his hand. She closed her mouth and looked directly into his eyes, then at the surrounding bank, and then back at him. She eyed the catfish, then him, then tilted her head to the side thinking about the fish. Then she shook her head no.

"Come on girl. Come get this thing. Come get the catfish and the divorce. It's all here, signed and legal."

Esther's big head rose completely out of the water as she stretched her neck from the shell. Her head was over twice the size of the man's standing in front of her, but still she hesitated. He waved the fish again and she shook her head no a second time, then backed up in the water about a foot.

"No! Don't go. Here! Take this thing!" And without thinking, he took a short step in her direction and leaned far out over the water. She opened her mouth wide but did not come closer. He stepped farther out into the water and she backed up again, just a few more inches into deeper water. She looked him in his eyes and he did not see the slight upward curve at the corners of her gaping mouth.

She let him come closer with the fish, but did not move away, and he stepped close enough to drop the fish into her mouth. He figured he still had enough time to dash for the Sharps as she would take the first possessive bite on the fish, and he turned his head to look back at the Sharps. As soon as he turned his head, she pushed off with her hind feet and extended her head as far as her neck could stretch. Before he could even begin to turn back, her huge mouth engulfed the catfish and his hand in a bone-crushing grind taking off his hand at the wrist.

"You hag!" He screamed and dashed back for the Sharps in blinding pain, reaching out for it with his other hand and yanked the Sharps from the bank. He cocked the hammer and released the first of the Sharps two triggers as he swung back toward her. He tried to place the barrel into the crook of his damaged forearm but missed and the heavy steel barrel began to dip down toward the water. Then the water in front of him exploded, at first thought he feared he had wasted his only remaining bullet into the lagoon, but then saw her gigantic shell coming at him. Her head came up and her jaws opened again, showing the mangled catfish next to her arm-thick tongue with much more room yet to fill. Her snout slipped up in front of his crotch and her lower jaw went deep between his legs, as the vice began to close. The hooked tip of her lower jaw sank into the flesh behind his scrotum while the snout tip began to crush his zipper high in the front. He pushed his right shoulder as hard as he could and barely managed to bring the rifle barrel to the top of her head. The pressure was building on his crotch to a blood blister exploding force when the Sharps bullet and gunpowder flame erupted down through the top of her head, sending bone and brain matter onto the bottom of the lagoon. Her jaws stopped in mid-motion and her feet began an automatic reflex motion, pushing her back into deep water and taking him with her. He pushed up with his legs and shoved the barrel of the Sharps into her snout and pried himself loose from her mouth, but could not retrieve the rifle. The giant turtle, with the Sharps still stuck in her mouth, slid beneath the surface into darker water and vanished slowly from view. Madison pulled his belt from his trousers and made a tourniquet around his wrist, then climbed slowly onto the bank and made his way back to the cabin.

Not long after that, Deputy Tibideaux came by the cabin to check on the man, as he had each day since the courthouse clerk called him. Madison was sitting on the steep bank next to the deep side of the lagoon, with a tight tourniquet around his wrist and his hand gone. His pants were down around his ankles and the man was massaging his badly bruised privates with butter in his remaining hand; just staring out at the water.

"Good God, Mr. Madison! What the hell happened out here??"

The man looked up at the deputy and smiled weakly. "I lost my Granddaddy's rifle, my hunting license, the title to my truck, my left hand, and almost lost my nuts. I guess as divorces go, it was about what you'd expect."

RUFUS'S OUTHOUSE

It was common knowledge in Finton County that once Harry S. Truman asked to use Rufus Broadway's outhouse but was turned away. I never thought it was actually true, but it was a funny thing to bring up around election time. Then when Rufus was brought down to Big Al's Tavern from the old folks' home by his great grand nephew for a shot of Tennessee Whiskey on his 92nd Birthday, I got a chance to hear the whole story from the man himself.

Rufus came home to Millersville from the Pacific after W-W-2, a changed man looking for nothing more than peace and quiet, but found little of either. When the movie theater re-opened and the town got its first radio station, he decided the whole place was going to Hell in a handbasket, and moved out to his great Uncle Ivy's second place down on Greenwood Road. Uncle Ivy's first place was destroyed by a tornado in 1907, leaving nothing but his outhouse at the edge of a beautiful little glen. Rufus always liked his Uncle's second house, never having seen the first, but when the time of need came he would make the quarter-mile trek to the old outhouse. It always just felt right to him.

In southern Finton County back then, two dirt roads kissed up against State Route 535 at Tooey's Crossroads. The Swamp Road ran east past Tooey's General Store out toward Camp Finton, and the Greenwood Road ran west through old farm country and then just sort of faded away in a low-lying rocky ridge known as Indian Rocks. Ivy had died during the great depression, and his place had stood empty since then, as did most of the neighboring farms. Rufus moved into a little forty-acre farm in the center of over twelve hundred acres without another living soul, which suited him right down to his bones.

The following Summer a Trailways bus roared to a dust cloud stop in front of Tooey's General Store and discharged a little dark-haired woman in a neat gray dress and feathered hat, carrying only a single small suitcase. She marched into the shade under Tooey's great old porch and perched herself on the front edge of the bench with her back rifle barrel straight, and sat there almost motionless for over two hours with her gaze fixed on Greenwood Road. The owner of the store, Abner Tooey, sent his little pudgy daughter Alexandra out to the woman with a glass of cool water, hoping to lure her in for some shopping while she waited, but she only sipped the water and returned the glass quickly to the girl without even looking at her. Little Alexandra, who even then liked to be called Al, told her brother Adam that the woman said "Donkey"; nothing else, just "Donkey". A young veteran who had come back to complain that his beer bottles were only two-thirds full, said he thought she was German. When Rufus pulled up in his new Kaiser *Henry-J* and took the woman back down the Greenwood Road to Ivy's Farm, four noses were pushed against the window from inside the store watching them go.

The veteran nodded to himself. "Yep. German. Rufus got hisself a mail order bride."

Abner went back to the counter and made a note to order some pumpernickel flour, which came on Thursday. On Friday Rufus and his new wife visited the store, holding hands as they walked up and down the narrow aisles. They said very little, but bought all four bags of pumpernickel flour, ten pounds of bologna, two cases of beer, seven pairs of nylons, and a new dress – Abner ran a catalog ordering counter in the back of the store where the old post office used to be. Abner figured Rufus must have been getting some kind of disability check, because all through the Winter he came back the last Friday of each month, and each month they bought just about the same things. By February they were no longer holding hands and she was three dress sizes larger. By March Rufus came by himself, bought the usual larder, ordered two of the next larger size of dresses, and sat out on the store's front porch drinking beer until almost sunset.

One rainy June morning that Summer, Rufus and his wife were sitting in their *Henry-J* under the big oak next to Tooey's store when the Trailway's bus pulled into the parking lot. Abner watched from the porch as Rufus wrestled six large suitcases out of the car and helped push his bloated wife up the stairs onto the bus. Neither of them looked back as the bus pulled on to the paved road, flinging red mud daubs onto the concrete and headed north toward Millersville. Rufus walked into the store and bought a morning beer and a cigar. He slipped the cigar into his shirt pocket, then ambled onto the porch and sat down on the bench.

Abner stood inside the screen door nearby, leaning against the jamb. "She going on a visit back home? Looked like she might say awhile."

Rufus sipped from the brown bottle and then pointed it in the direction of the highway. "She went home for good. I hear they got a cold war going on back over there. She'll be good at it."

"Not cut out for country life, was she?"

"Didn't like my outhouse. Said she'd have inside plumbing or go back to the old country."

"Wha'd you say."

"Told her I'd bring her down here when she was ready." He drained the beer bottle and dropped it into the oil-drum trash can as he went down the porch steps, hunched over in the momentary downpour, and then got into his car. He was humming 'Happy Days are Here Again' as he drove back down Greenwood Road, and the sun pushed through the clouds painting Indian Rocks in yellow light.

That evening, when Rufus made his evening walk to his outhouse by the glen, he made a horrible discovery. While he was finding ways to pack his wife's suitcases into the car that morning, she had made a final trip to the outhouse herself – and had left a farewell message. She had taken the lantern that hung on the wall inside the outhouse for the occasional late evening return, and smashed it against the wall, splashing it with kerosene. She took a wooden match from the box perched on the stud brace near the lantern nail and lit the kerosene. The overcast dawn sky above the outhouse glowed orange and gold as flames began to eat the old outhouse, and she walked away without looking back. The house blocked the view of the firelight above the trees to the south, so Rufus only sat quietly in the car until she finally made her way onto the front seat next to him, smiling at the windshield. A light rain began to fall as he had driven to the bus stop at Tooey's Crossroads.

There in the light of the setting sun, Rufus stood motionless, looking at the burned structure. The roof was completely gone. Charred remains of the door planks lay jumbled on the ground, and the walls were burned down level with the seat. That's where the rain had stopped the fire. A rumble reminded him why he was there, and noticing the seat still fully intact, he mounted the open air throne. He spent his time looking at the charred edges of the wall, and then the trees at the edge of the glen. He admired the old pin oak spreading grandly over his head, and the sycamores standing guard at the far end of the glen, and the hues of the setting sun bathing the tall grasses growing in the glen. Then he decided his wife had given him two blessings that day: She had left, and she had given him a perfect seat to watch one of the most beautiful spots in the whole world. He forgave her for what she did, and thanked her for what she did, and filled his heart with the glen. He forgave the Japanese, and the Germans, and even the revenuers who had beat up Uncle Ivy in 1928. When he returned to the house, walking up the slope in the moonlight since the lantern was gone, he was free of hatred, worry, resentment, lunch, and maybe some slightly tainted smoked ham from breakfast. He was at peace, and he only wished there was a way for everyone to feel the same harmony in their lives. He would become evangelical – in a whiskey sort of way.

Tooey's Tavern, there next to the General Store, became Rufus's first pulpit. The Tavern was run by Tootie Hooker, who claimed to be the grandson of a famous Confederate colonel (but who in fact had been a mere captain under Abner's great Uncle Alphonse, whose statue stood in the field across the road from the General Store). Rufus started coming over to the Tavern on Tuesday nights, which were generally slow, and shared his newly found philosophy with the other customers – which Tootie didn't care for one way or another – but the whiskey sales went up once Rufus got into his stride, and that Tootie cared for a great deal. Tootie noticed that once Rufus switched from beer to whiskey the rhetoric got hotter and the whiskey sales among the patrons doubled, so he started pouring Rufus a free shot of Tennessee Whiskey as soon as he walked in.

"Things are not so complicated that you can't figure out the right way to handle them." Rufus would say. "You need some true peace and quiet to reflect on what bothers you, and then come to a way to let it go – or think of a way to work through it without hurting people."

There would almost always be a murmur of agreement rolling through the congregation at the bar, but if Tootie didn't hear one coming he'd add in his own "Damn right." or "Hell yes." to stimulate the crowd's response. A quiet bar sold little whiskey. That was quickly becoming Tootie's new motto.

"You got to get right next to the harmony, brothers." Rufus said. "You got to remove the walls around you and let loose what's bottled up inside you."

All over southern Finton County, outhouse doors began to stay open when the interior was in use, so the occupant could stay close to the harmony of nature. Little camping potties began to dot rural farmland at the owner's favorite places, allowing trousers and inhibitions to drop away so troubled folks could find the peace described by brother Rufus. Short, highly sanded hand-carved benches with 10-inch holes in the center began to show up in Woodcraft stores.

One industrious believer that had a metal shop just outside Millersville, came up with a folding stool with the appropriate hole that could be back-packed or easily carried to that special tree site or meaningful meadow. The trouble with that was, not everyone had enough private land with special communing spots to meet the needs of the converts. So, fallow fields edged by old wide-branched trees and not far from the roads, which in the past saw the occasional picnickers, were now visited by Rufus' followers. It was a phenomenon destined to be discovered by battalions of ladies auxiliaries, and the County Sheriff's office. Sheriff Harley Poteet wadded up the arrest paper and threw it back at Deputy Wilson. "NO! We are not charging this man with 'Unlawful Shitting"! Gilbert, you don't have the sense God gave a gopher! It's got to be 'Indecent Exposure', 'cause the county doesn't have any laws about where a man can drop a load. It wasn't near a state road, so we can't use a state law. And it wasn't in a town limit, so we can't use a hygiene ordinance."

The reception area was in pandemonium behind the railing as the deputies and clerks tried to process the charges, while eleven men sat serenely on waiting benches, forgiving everyone around them, and deputies brought in four more.

Harley swirled his coffee, trying to get the cheap powdered lightener to break up from the clabbered clumps that had formed on top. His first re-election campaign had not gone well for Harley so far. That new fellah had moved in from outside of Little Rock, said he'd been a sheriff there over ten years and wanted to be the new one here in Finton County. The ladies of the county were swooning all over him, and now they were mad at Harley over all these indecencies. "This is all I need." He said into his coffee mug.

At the end of a long confusing day, Sheriff Poteet looked at the stack of no less than 22 arrests made since the beginning of the day shift. All of them had been made due to indecent exposure while communing with nature on other people's land and/or within plain view of a public county thoroughfare. All of them also had another thing in common: Rufus Broadway. Harley slammed the ledger closed, ending the Tuesday police blotter, and headed for the parking lot behind the county municipal building. As he turned the ignition key, kicking the Ford V-8 to life, and slid the gear lever into reverse, Rufus walked into Tooey's Tavern, and Tootie poured him a shot of Tennessee whiskey. Harley turned left onto Main Street and shot past the Millersville Second National Bank. He was going considerably over 55 mph when he passed that speed limit sign at the end of town, where South Main Street once again becomes State Route 535, thumping over tar seals hot-drizzled into aged concrete cracks, heading to Tooey's Crossroads.

Philosophy and whiskey were flowing in general agreement around the bar of Tooey's Tavern when Harley walked in. Tootie saw the big man and nodded, but most everybody else kept their attention on the slender soft-spoken farmer in faded denim overalls and a three-day stubble. He'd offer some simple truths and sip from his shot glass, and then wait to see what anyone else might have to say. It wasn't anything like Harley had expected. This guy wasn't trying to smooth talk anyone, and he wasn't trying to stir up any trouble.

Seeing Tootie's eyes dart to the back of the bar from time to time, Rufus turned to see who had come in behind him, and seeing the Sheriff he smiled and nodded hello.

The sheriff eyed him a second before he spoke. "You think a guy has a right to go do his business anywhere he pleases? Like right out in the open where passing women can see? Do you?"

Rufus laughed out loud at the thought. "'Course not." He slapped his leg in simple appreciation of the joke and turned to hear another comment there at the bar.

Harley sat at a table near the bar and watched the group for about half an hour, until Rufus said it was time for him to go. He paid his tab, said goodnight to everyone at the bar, and headed for the door, but then stopped beside Harley. "Sheriff, you seem real tense and bothered. I'm going across the parking lot to the General Store and just sit on the porch for a little bit. You're welcome to join me."

They talked for quite a while and Rufus told him all about his Uncle Ivy's outhouse and the gift his wife had left him. Harley was determined to find out something about this man he could latch on to and put him in jail over, or do something legal, but no such information came out. Fight it as much as he could, he could feel himself beginning to like Rufus and see the plain simple sense of what he said. They talked for hours and watched everyone else go home. Said goodnight to Abner after he closed the store, leaving the porch light on for them. Saw Tootie turn the lights out and lock up the tavern, and wave as he got into his car and went home. Harley and Rufus talked the quiet talk of men who had seen a few things in life, and listened to the crickets and the katydids.

It was almost a surprise when the sky lightened up over the eastern treetops and dawn was coming. Rufus invited Harley over to his place for coffee, and Harley accepted saying "Coffee sounded real good."

As soon as Harley had cream and sugar in his coffee, Rufus pointed out the door with his spoon. "Harley, you need to take that cup of coffee with you and follow that path going by the garage, and take it down the hill to where it leads you."

Harley sipped his coffee from an old chipped navy mug, smiled at Rufus, and then looked down the path. It had been a long night. "You know, Rufus, I believe I will."

"You just take your time, Harley."

Almost an hour later Harley came up the back steps and set the empty coffee mug on the counter by the sink. "Rufus, how 'bout remindin' our friends to find their inner peace, out of public view and on land where they're invited."

"That's a reasonable thing, Harley."

When word got around about the concerns of the ladies' auxiliaries and the un-asked landowners, Rufus' friends down at the bar appreciated how the Sheriff had approached the issue. When the ladies learned that in a single night the Sheriff had successfully addressed their concerns, they all agreed he had handled it wonderfully.

Harley won his re-election by the largest margin in Finton County history. And soon two or three people a day were stopping by Tooey's General Store, asking how to get to Rufus Broadway's farm.

Rufus was actually happy to have the company when the people began to show up at his farm. He gave them what simple truths had come to him under the pin oak and a little philosophy on what it all meant to him. He gave them a little cod liver oil, and then directions to the half burnt outhouse.

Early on a father brought his distraught daughter whose wedding was only a few days off, accompanied by her eight very protective brothers, while the girl's mother waited in the van. It didn't seem too clear what all was bothering her, but Rufus could tell she was consternated. Four of her brothers thought her betrothed was a wonderful fellow, while the other four thought he was sneaky. The father wasn't sure one way or the other, but thought a visit to Rufus' would help her come to a decision and relieve some of the tension she was carrying.

The daughter professed to love the young man she was soon to marry, but admitted to moments when she wondered if he was really the man she thought he was, which had led to some recent nervous overeating without sufficient relief. The brothers fanned out across Rufus' farm to ensure their sister had 12 acres or so all to herself, and the father set down in the kitchen with Rufus while the young lady went down the path to the pin oak. An hour later she came through the back door into the kitchen a serene young woman free of troubles. The father offered Rufus some money, but of course he would not take it.

Two Tuesdays later Rufus was in Tooey's Tavern while Tootie told him all about the evening the girl's father came in and bought the bar a round of drinks. The girl had decided not to marry the young man, who apparently flew into a foul-mouthed rage over the rejection at the family home. On the way out he fell into a scuffle with the oldest brother that led to a fist fight out near the road. Officer Tibideaux happened by to break up the fight and put both their names in his report, which wound up on the Police Blotter section of the weekly newspaper, *The Finton Bugle*. That particular edition *of The Bugle* was read by a cousin of a young woman who lived over in Harper County, and whose husband had run off from her, taking a good bit of company money from her father's office with him. Shortly later, the Sheriff from Harper County had called Hurley Poteat, who then collected the young man in the back of his squad car and delivered him to the waiting arms of his wife's family on Monday. Then the man told everyone in the bar his daughter would have had a disaster had he not taken her to see Rufus Broadway.

Soon a dozen people a day were stopping by Tooey's General Store, asking how to get to Rufus Broadway's farm. Not wanting to miss an opportunity, Abner began selling maps to Rufus' place for a dollar. That Spring, Greenwood Road saw its first traffic jam, and the Finton County Roads Department had to send a load of gravel to stiffen up the dirt road into Rufus' farm.

It's curious how people behave differently when they're part of a group, compared to their actions when they come alone. One visitor decided it would be understood if he sat on a chair in the shade of the porch, while he waited for Rufus to come back up to the house, and the next decided it would be all right to take his mother in so she could sit in the front room. The next person thought getting some water from the kitchen wouldn't cause a problem, since he was already sitting in the front room as well. By the time Rufus returned from the pin oak that morning, his front yard was a muddy parking lot full of cars, and his house was full of strangers making themselves at home in every room. As he walked into the kitchen a heavyset man standing by the stove turned toward the door saying "If you're after coffee, you're out of luck, Bub. This is the last of it, at least 'til that Rufus guy gets here."

Rufus nearly lost his temper and let the screen door slam itself shut. "Well, that 'Rufus Guy' is here, and you folks need to back up out of his house, because I'm Rufus." Rufus asked them all to leave, except for the elderly woman sitting in his parlor with her son. After that he began herding the people with widespread arms, until the last one filed through the yard gate and made their way to their car. Rufus was standing at the gate looking at the mess in the yard when another car came down the dirt road and pulled up in front of him. He started to shake his head 'No' but realized it was an Army sedan, so he just watched in curiosity as the driver dashed around to open the back door. A trim little man in a short uniform jacket got out. He had left his hat in the car and stood bareheaded, almost bald, smiling at Rufus as pleasant a smile as he had ever seen. The stars on the man's shoulders almost sparkled in the sunlight.

"What can I do for ya', Gen'rl?"

"I'm not quite sure. Are you Mr. Broadway?"

Behind the smile Rufus sensed a little sadness and couldn't help but warm to the man, so he invited him in for some coffee – knowing where the rest of it was. Rufus invited the driver as well, but he insisted he should stay out in the parlor, so Rufus brought his coffee out to him there and then sat in the kitchen with the other man. The general had been to parties and dinners all over the country and was trying to decide if he should go into politics next, and he was troubled by both activities. His driver had heard about Rufus and told the general.

The general cradled the old mug in his hands and

looked down into the coffee as he spoke. "Not sure if this is a thing I ought to be doing, but a lot of people say I should."

"I know what it is like to have a head full of thoughts and a face full of people. Sometimes they can both get to be too much. Rufus pointed out the back door with his spoon. "What you need to do is take your coffee with you, follow that path going by the garage, and take it down the hill to where it leads you." It'll give you some peace and quiet, so you can sit and sort things out."

Rufus turned from washing the dirty dishes left behind by all the strangers when the general returned. He came in, removed his jacket and rolled up his sleeves, then stood next to Rufus and began washing dishes. Rufus rinsed and dried them as the General washed. Neither said a word, but Rufus knew the man was at peace inside. After the dishes were done the General left with his driver. Rufus decided he needed a few days of peace himself and went out to the garage to find a piece of plywood. He had some barn paint in an old can that was still good, and a brush that was only hard halfway down, so he painted "Closed" on it. When the paint dried Rufus took the sign, a hammer, and a few nails and walked down to the gate at the road. As he nailed the sign to a tree next to the gate, two long black sedans pulled off the road next to him. A window of the first car came down and a man in a brown fedora spoke to Rufus. "We have someone needs to come in there. Do you know this Rufus?"

"I am this Rufus."

The man looked at the sign. "You don't want to be closed right now, Rufus. You want to be open now."

"I'm closed. I'm not seeing anybody for a while. I'm just peopled out."

The man got out of the sedan and stood nearby while Rufus finished nailing up the sign. The man spun on the heels of his highly shined shoes and walked back to the second sedan. The back window came down and the man spoke to the inside of the sedan for a moment, then he stepped back and opened the door. Harry S. Truman got out of the car and walked toward Rufus. He stood on the other side of the fence on the side of the road.

"Rufus, I'm Harry."

Rufus recognized the voice from the radio and spun around. Harry extended his hand and Rufus took it.

Harry held his hand in a tight grip. "You gonna' open up for me, and do whatever you do?"

Rufus smiled at Harry, but slowly shook his head. "All I do is help people get things out. I've heard you speak. I don't expect you hold much of anything back."

Harry laughed and winked at Rufus. "Well that's the damned truth." He chuckled and shook his head, then let go of Rufus' hand. He returned to his sedan and the man in the brown hat closed the door for him as both car engines started at the same time. The other man quickly returned to the front sedan and both cars pulled back onto the road. The back window rolled down and Harry leaned toward it so Rufus could see him. "Don't forget to vote, Rufus." He waved as the window came back up.

Rufus went back to his peace and quiet, to his thoughts, and to his pin oak. He never did take down the closed sign, and he stopped going down to Tooey's Tavern. He decided he had said all he had to say. Rumors spread that he was dead, but he still came to Tooey's General Store on Saturdays for a beer, so that one went away. Then the rumor spread that the outhouse finally burned to the ground, and he never said it hadn't, so that one stayed and got told as part of the story.

After he had told all of the story he cared to, the old man said he was storied out and ready to go, but the nephew's car battery had gone dead, so I said I'd take them both back in the Jeep. The nephew said Rufus wanted to be taken by his old place before he went back, it was all part of his birthday trip, and I said I'd be glad to do that, too. The old gate still worked and as I pulled it back on its hinges in the headlight, I could see a faded old closed sign wrapped inside the briars next to the roadway. We lit an oil lamp in the kitchen so Rufus could look around, the electricity had been turned off for years, and he talked us into making a fire in the old wood stove in the kitchen so he could have some coffee. The nephew had brought the makings in a sack, and set it all out on the dusty table. We found cups in the cabinets and wiped them out with paper towels after we rinsed them with water from the iron pump.

Rufus stared at me in the lamplight as I sipped on my coffee. He took a plastic spoon from his cup and pointed it at the old ripped screen back door. "Pug, you need to take that cup of coffee with you and follow that path going by the garage, and take it down the hill to where it leads you."

I traded looks with the nephew. He smiled back, "It's still there."

The moon was bright and it was easy to find my way. It was almost bright enough to read a newspaper. I found the pin oak and the seat, but pulled out the flashlight I had taken from my Jeep to make sure I wasn't about to share space and time with a critter of some sort.

The seat was comfortable and the coffee effective, and I looked up at the moon through the pin oak leaves. It was so easy to think through things. I was born in a place like Finton County, and had spent my whole life up to now trying to get away from it, but all along I was coming back to it. The last failed job and drinking spree had landed me in the Finton County Jail, and work release had even brought me to Tooey's Crossroads like it was my home all along.

Later on, after I had taken Rufus back to the old folk's home and helped the nephew jump-start his car, I drove back to the cabin in the moonlight. I wasn't ready for bed, so I took a small Whiskey out on the porch to watch the moon settle over the abandoned field that was my front yard. In the moonlight I could even distinguish the individual trees that lined the field. There at the far corner was a huge pin oak.

"Well, I know what I'm puttin' there," I said to the night.

BUFORD HUDDLE LEDBEDDER

Buford Huddle Ledbedder was born in southern Finton
County, but spent most of his childhood elsewhere while
his Momma and Daddy followed the circus, between
their rare visits to his Grandma Ida. In his late teens, he
stayed behind with a kindly family after the circus had
played three days outside Elmira, New York. He
finished school and went on to become a New York
State Policeman, thinking very little of Finton County
until his retirement. His folks had returned to Tooey's
Crossroads after the wanderlust had been satisfied and
spent the rest of their days on a 20-acre farm that was
bequeathed to Buford when they moved on to that great
circus in the sky.

In the quiet solitude of his bachelor apartment one
Saturday after his retirement, he came across the deed to
the old farm while looking for the spare keys to his
Harley. Saturday slipped into Sunday as he kept coming
back to look at the deed again, studying the outlines of
the farm while sirens and truck horns blared from the
nearby highway. By Thursday he had sold or given away
most of his things, except for what was stuffed into the
leather bags strapped to his Harley, and set out on
Highway 15 South for his return to Finton County.

The following Saturday evening as the sun set over
the big oak tree at the intersection of the Millersville
highway and Swamp Road, Buford parked his Harley in
the gravel lot between Big Al's Tavern and the Park "n"
Pump, and walked stiff-legged into the tavern. Al was on
her knees cleaning and pulling up old stock from under
the bar, and raised her head to look at the customer while

Buford used his gloves to slap road dust off his leather jacket and riding pants. Her chin jutted onto the bar like that was all there was to her, and she spoke to him with a frown.

"You can just take all that dust back outside, mister. Don't be messing up the tavern."

Taller than most men and used to being taken seriously, Buford gave her a sour look.

"Don't you worry about it Sweetie. Just get this man a beer – in a clean glass."

Al slowly stood up from behind the bar, in her sleeveless Marine T-shirt the muscles of her shoulders and forearms rippled as the fingers of both hands curled into fists resting on her hips. She then leaned over the bar looking Buford level in his eyes only inches from his face, but did not say another word.

Buford met her stare in the silence under the old ceiling fans whirring slowly overhead, and allowed a small smile.

"Yes Ma'am."

Then went back outside to finish his dusting. When he returned to the bar there was a frosty glass mug filled with draft beer waiting for him, and Al had returned to her chore. Al's voice echoed from under the bar.

"Where ya' headed"

"Here."

"You had a lot of road dust on you. You must have ridden far just to come to my tavern."

Buford turned on the stool to look around the tavern, resting his elbows behind him and leaned back against the bar, speaking over his shoulder.

"Not your tavern. I mean here, Tooey's Crossroads."

Al stood back up and stretched the tightness out of her back, then drew herself a draft beer.

"From where?"

Buford swiveled around to answer her.

"Elmira, New York."

Al spoke into her mug as she drank.

"Now you're a long way from home."

Buford shook his head.

"No. This is home now, I guess. I'm going to stay at my folk's old place, if I can find it. I inherited it after they passed away several years ago."

Al wiped her hands with a bar rag and put them on her hips.

"Who were they?"

"Speed and Leunie Ledbedder"

Al's mouth dropped open.

"Good God a'mighty. You're one of Ida Ledbedders grandkids."

Ida Ledbedder had dedicated her early days to American patriotism, and after spending several enjoyable years as a close personal friend of the U.S. Seventh Fleet in Norfolk, came home to Millersville with a small fortune. In the years since, she had renovated the old Millersville gentlemen's club – once owned by Finton County luminary Mauzy Broadway, then sold it for another fortune, and had gone through six energetic husbands like doses of Epsom salts, burying them each one after the other in a row in Union Rest cemetery.

She had given Finton County eleven children, 32 grandchildren, and no less than 54 great grandchildren. Her offspring alone could decide county elections if Ida ever had a particular favorite among the candidates – or a grudge. Now in her early eighties, Ida had taken to terrorizing the rural roads of Finton County with the ear-splitting roar of a 1964 Harley Davidson road hog, with previous sets of her dentures super-glued to the front fender, and her walker strapped to the back one.

Al snatched down an out of date advertisement flyer taped to the mirror and flipped the blank side up on the bar.

"Well I sure don't want to be on the wrong side of any of Ida Ledbedder's kin. Let me draw you a map from here. It's not far, and you'll be right next to a friend of mine that works here part-time. His place is just on the other side of yours."

Moments later in the growing darkness Buford's Harley gingerly weaved its way along a rutted dirt lane off the Swamp Road, its headlight beam slicing left and right through the black shadows among the trees. The engine thrumped slowly, letting each big cylinder fire and cough in turn as the engine barely pushed the Harley into a small clearing behind a meager cabin. Yellow light filled a small side window with shutters pinned back against the timbers. A thin flashlight beam jumped out from the front porch, sweeping the side yard to settle on Buford.

"Whatcha need?" I said.

Buford turned his headlight toward the flashlight and almost blinded me.

"I'm looking for the Ledbedder place."

"Well you didn't find it. Where's it supposed to be?"

"If I knew that friend, I wouldn't be in your damned back yard."

I chuckled and stepped off the porch and walked back toward the motorcycle, shading my eyes from the bright light.

"You're not one of those Hell's Angels fellahs are you?"

"No. I'm a retired cop, and trying to find the place my folks had before they passed away a while back." Then he turned the headlight away from me.

"Well, I've only been here a year or so myself, so I don't know who used to be where. But I was told the place next to mine has been empty for years. Don't know it by any name, though. You sure you're on the right road?"

Buford killed the engine, but left the headlight on and heeled the kickstand down, then pulled out a folded flyer and held it in front of the light.

"There was a tall strong-boned woman up at that last bar who drew this map. Said the Ledbedder property was next to a friend of hers."

"Well, the strong-boned woman was Big Al Tooey, Alexandra to her family or others with a death wish. As to her friend, I'm proud to be called that. I'm Pug Greenwood." I shook hands with the man. He had a firm grip equal to Al's; full of muscles and power, and you could tell they had to work at it not to crush a hand when they shook one.

"You passed the gate about a half mile back. It would be hard to see even at high noon, let alone evening. It's all grown over with inch-thick briars, and hateful things they are too. You won't get in there tonight. There's a motel about five miles back up the Millersville road, just before you get to Union Rest. They'll answer the doorbell until 9:30, but after that old Abercrombie takes his hearing aid battery out to recharge and then wouldn't be able to hear an atom bomb go off."

Buford looked around the little flat upper field that ran from behind the cabin back to the tree line.

"If you don't mind, I've got a tent and sleeping bag on the back of the bike. I'd like to just camp here and get at the place first thing in the morning."

I nodded in the darkness, then realized what I had done hadn't given him an answer.

"Sure. If Al pointed you this way, I'm O.K. with that. You had supper yet?"

He put his hands on his hips and looked back at his motorcycle.

"Well, I had a pretty good lunch, and there's some jerky in one of my saddlebags."

"You eat venison?"

"I guess."

I started walking back toward the cabin.

"Well, you will if you have supper with me. I'm heating it up now. I'll set us plates on the porch table in a couple minutes. There's a faucet at the front of the little water tower on the other side of the cabin, if you want to wash off before supper."

So me and my new neighbor sat out on the porch eating black bean venison chili, and washed it down with some of Adam Tooey's recapped watered-down beer. Later, while we were sipping whiskey he stuck one finger out from his glass and pointed to my fire pit in front of the cabin.

"I like campfires. After I fix a decent sized fire pit at my place – after I find my place – I'll have you over and do a nice campfire."

We talked about things in general and he told me about his trip down from New York and his meeting with Al, and we finished our glasses. Then he said, "I once lived with two women."

Now that was an eye-opening story if I had ever heard one, but some things a man just ought not to pass along, so you're just going to have to hear that one from Buford himself.

The next morning after first coffee, Buford borrowed my wood ax and a beat up old machete I'd found along the highway and re-sharpened. He set off back up the cabin road to his property gate, and I drove off to the crossroads.

I had promised Adam Tooey I'd go in for a couple hours and straighten up his storeroom at the Park 'N' Pump. As always, when Adam asked for a couple hours I'd wind up working six and get paid for two. But, I had learned that he expected me to steal something, because he would have, and he would deduct it from my pay whether I did or not. So, I stole four cases of his watered down beer and a bag of ice, and let him get by with only paying me for two hours work at eight dollars an hour, which he didn't report, but that was OK because I didn't either. All in all it wasn't a bad system once a person got it figured out.

When I got back up the road to the cabin as far as Ledbedder's gate, it was all cleared and wide open, and he was building something out of logs in the clearing in front of the old home place. I had known there was a house back in there, but couldn't see much beyond the road until that day. I decided to pull in and share some of Adam's beer with Buford and see how he was doing.

I heard him singing before I saw him. He walked out of the nearby stand of trees carrying a six-foot log on each shoulder, singing that old Green Beret song from the sixties, but he stopped dead quiet when he saw me.

"You got a fine voice Buford. You ever sing for money?"

His face turned red and he almost looked angry, but it passed quickly and he smiled at me.

"Oh, hell no. Auntie Maude, the lady that took me in, always said I should go out for the Glee Club, or chorus, or something like that, but I never had time for that kind of sissy stuff. I played every sport the school had, except basketball – that was hunting season."

He dropped the logs onto a pile growing next to a log frame he had put together that was almost waist high.

"Whatcha building there, Buford? A smokehouse?"

He laughed and shook his head, then rubbed the sweat off his forehead with the back of his forearm. I handed him a beer which he took with a grateful grin and drained half the bottle before he said anything else. He looked down at the bottle in his hand and chuckled.

"Don't believe I've had a beer before with a duct tape label, and the name written on it in magic marker."

"What's yours say?"

"Tooey Blue Ribbon."

I looked down at mine.

"Mine says Tooey Highlife – it's a local thing. So, what is this thing you're building?

"Like I said last night, I like campfires."

And then he stood back to admire the stack.

I looked at the squared stack of logs, and then up into the tree branches, guessing he had about sixty feet of clearance overhead before it would come to the lowest branch of the old oak.

"That's going to be a good sized campfire, Buford."

He drained the bottle and tossed it into the log stack, nodding his head as he turned back to the woods and speaking over his shoulder as he went.

"Yep, it will be when I'm through, but it's only halfway now."

I heard his feet thump through the dead leaves back in the trees as he headed down into the little ravine sloping toward the creek in back, and then he began singing that song again. To me it sounded even better than the original. The man had a voice that would make an Irish Tenor green with envy. I had never heard an opera, but if it was any good I'd be willing to bet it would sound like Buford.

He yelled up from the ravine, he voice echoing between the trees. "Come back at sundown. We'll have a fire."

Back at the cabin I put some of Adam's beer in an old cooler I'd found with one hinge broken and one still holding, added the bag of ice I had taken from the Park 'N' Pump, and started fixing super. In warm weather I took the camp stove off the counter in the cabin and set it on the porch table. So I was sitting next to the table reading last week's Sunday paper in the fading light and occasionally stirring the chili when I heard a motorcycle come on to the property.

I figured it was Buford, but it was an old woman barely able to reach the ape-hanger handlebars riding a rusty old motorcycle puffing blue oil smoke. She shut it off, but the engine kept coughing and firing off by itself for several more seconds until a short flame banged out of the exhaust pipe followed by another larger puff of black smoke and the engine clanked to a stop. She kicked down the stand and swiveled around on her seat to unstrap a walker from the back fender, then plunked it down on the low side of the cycle. She grabbed the walker and slid off the motorcycle to stand behind the frame, the hand grips at the same level as her elbows. She moved slowly, lifting the walker over the weeds and shuffling toward my cabin.

I stepped down off the porch and walked toward her.

"Can I give you a hand ma'am?"

She looked up at me, the brim of her black WWII German-style motorcycle helmet resting on top of her glasses, her eyes big behind the thick lenses, her face small, deeply wrinkled and framed in white hair bristling out in random wire clumps from underneath the helmet. The name Ida was hand painted in pink on the front of the helmet above the brim. Her voice was gravely and hard, like someone who was used to yelling, but couldn't anymore.

"Only if you want your ass kicked, young man. Where the hell is Buford?"

"His place is back up the way you came, Miss Ida. He's building a campfire for tonight, and I'm going up there in the Jeep after the chili is done. You're welcome to come along with me if you want."

She stopped and took off her helmet, strapping it to her walker.

"You got any beer?"

"Yes ma'am."

She worked her way to the porch, her head bobbing up then down as she watched each step carefully before she took it. When she finally got to the single step that led up to my porch, I extended my hand to help her up, but she slapped it hard.

"Get the hell out of my way. Go get my beer."

Once up on the porch, she settled into the old rocking chair with a grunt, and almost snatched from my hands the chilled beer I brought up out of the cooler, gulping half the bottle before stopping to take a breath. She frowned and held the bottle up close to her glasses to read the duct tape label.

"What the hell is this shit? Tooey Light?? Is that no good Adam Tooey still cheating people with watered down beer? How much did you pay that fool for this swamp piss?"

"Well, actually, Miss Ida, I stole it."

"Good for you, but you still got cheated." She belched two syllables and then tossed the half-empty bottle into the yard where it bounced once before hitting against the tire of my Jeep. "You got anything else besides that sewage flush?"

"Well, I do have some Tennessee Whiskey,…"

"That's it! Let's have a glass of that!" and she slid her tongue along her wrinkled lips that wrapped inward back over her gums.

Almost as soon as she had taken her first gulp of whiskey we heard Buford's amazing voice trumpeting through the woods singing Queen's "We are the Champions", and then the woods in that direction were filled with sun-bright yellow light. Ida followed me into the Jeep while I packed the chili and we drove back up the road to Buford's place, where the shadow of the old house was projected up onto the trees by the blazing campfire like a drive-in movie. The light was almost too intense to look into. We couldn't see any details of

Buford except his outline, where he stood shirtless in front of white-hot ten-foot flames with his arms held out at shoulder level welcoming us.

"I really love a campfire, don't you?"

The ancient oak limbs sixty feet above the fire swayed like saplings in the heat wind rushing up toward the sky. The fire roared and the surfaces of the logs built head high were already painted in red embers. The sparks were jumping off the logs into the upward rush where they formed a red geyser going up about thirty feet and then arching out into the cooler air to settle back down toward the hard packed ground. The heat on my face from twenty feet away was painful and I had to back away from the fire.

Ida held her forearm up in front of her face and squinted into the firelight under it, looking at Buford.

"You got shit for brains? You're gonna burn this damned place down!"

"Grandma Ida!!" Buford leaped toward her and lifted the little woman up into his arms and danced a circle with her.

"Put me the hell down, you idiot!"

He brought her closer to the porch where I had retreated, and set her gently on the planks.

He grinned from ear to ear showing two large rows of perfect white teeth.

"Don't you just love a campfire? Maybe I should add a little more wood. What do you think?" But before either of us could answer he trotted over to the wood pile and shouldered two six-foot logs as thick as his thighs and hand-tossed them onto the fire. Embers showered into the air. Then he spun around again with his arms outstretched like a circus performer, and began to sing again.

Ida looked up at me.

"You two been drinking today already?"

"Just one of Tooey's watered down beers earlier, unless he found something else over here."

She settled into an old ladder-backed chair on the porch and smiled out at Buford. "The child can sure sing. We need to get him into a choir somewhere."

I set up the chili and crackers on an old unplugged freezer lying on the porch, and brought some plastic bowls and the cooler from the Jeep. Buford joined us and we watched the fire from the porch and ate venison chili and crackers, and drank Adam Tooey's weak beer until everything was gone. Then Ida stood before us with a great smile on her face and held her arms out the way Buford had, and produced a long ragged fart that echoed among the trees beyond the fire and sounded like shave-and-a-haircut-two-bits, folded her one arm in front of her stomach and the other behind her while bending over giving us a schoolboy bow and then returned to her chair.

Next Buford got down on one knee next to his grandmother and gently took her hand in his and sang "Lady of Spain" better than any I had ever heard do that song. In the crackling glow of the fire she turned her head away from us and sniffed in the darkness.

"Damned sinuses."

Buford returned to his log pile and fed all the remaining logs into the fire, and tossed in all the empty beer bottles, and then we sat there together on the porch watching the bottles melt, and sipping the rest of my Tennessee whiskey.

"NO! You're not getting mine, you little ragged-assed furball!"

I turned and saw Donald holding his communion cup up to Ida, who was holding her own glass up out of his reach and shaking her head at him. I leaned over and poured a little out of my glass into his cup as Buford watched from the edge of the porch.

"Much obliged."

Buford's head rose up on the top of his neck. "Did it just speak?"

Donald spoke from within his cup. "Been doing it a while."

Buford stood up and stepped toward the raccoon.

"No! I don't believe that for a second."

Donald ignored Buford and offered his cup up to me again.

I looked at my glass, the empty bottle sitting on the freezer, and Buford's glass, and then pointed at Buford.

"Ask him, he's got a lot more than me."

Donald sighed a heavy sigh and turned toward Buford rolling his eyes back like a pouty teenage girl, and held his cup up to Buford. Buford leaned away from the raccoon and covered his glass with his other hand, his eyes large and full in the firelight. Donald held up his cup higher.

I shook my head. "Donald, you're just gonna have to talk to him."

Donald hissed out of his nose and grumbled "Well shit fire in a bucket. May I please have some of your whiskey?"

Buford smiled his toothy grin and leaned down close to Donald. "You're a cute little fellah. How are they making it look like you can talk?"

"The same way they made it look like that old woman farted a song, I guess. You gonna share or not?"

"This I gotta see." Buford poured a few drops from his glass into the plastic communion cup.

Donald looked pitifully into his cup. The bottom was barely covered.

"Oh come on! Don't be so damned stingy!"

Buford laughed to himself and looked carefully at both me and Ida to see if our lips moved, then filled the rest of Donald's cup.

"That's better." Then Donald settled down on his haunches, sighed, looked out at the fire and then back at Buford.

"Nice campfire - if you want to burn down the damned woods." And sipped his drink.

Buford looked from me to Ida, then back at Donald.

"He can really talk!"

"Who?" I asked

"Him! That raccoon! He can really talk!"

Ida turned toward us.

"What raccoon?"

Buford laughed and pointed at the shadowed planks between us, but Donald had taken his drink to go, and was no longer on the porch. Buford searched around the porch, the house, and the nearby woods, but found no trace of the raccoon. Neither Ida nor I showed a smile.

Buford was still looking for Donald when I drove Ida back to the cabin and her motorcycle. Before she cranked the starter she reached up with a small gloved hand and gently slapped my cheek.

"You'll do. Keep an eye on him 'til I can get him linked up with your cousin Dot."

Doris Greenwood had gone through hard times in her church back when she was called "Crazy Dot" by some of the other members, when she had started the Evangelical Sisterhood in a presumed state of grace much closer to God than she really was. Since then she had settled back down as a relatively satisfied member of the church choir. She was also another strong-boned woman close to the size of Buford, and had a voice that could fill an empty warehouse like a door slam, if she felt the spirit move her. It was Ida's intention to go move Dot's spirit.

The following Sunday the entire gathered congregation of the Union Rest Third Baptist Church fell to gaping mouthed funeral silence when the front doors opened in the middle of the first reading of the selected gospel and in walked Buford Ledbedder and his Grandma Ida. The curiosity over the identity of the big man was overshadowed by the awe and shock that Ida Ledbedder had come to church for the first time since she was baptized, which was years before anyone in that church had even been born or would have thought that it ever happened, and she was wearing a black lace cuffed dress with a white corsage pinned on it.

They slowly walked down the aisle, the only sound being the muted scuff of bright green tennis balls stuck on the bottoms of the walker legs, and Ida looking casually from side to side with a steely smile freezing the watchers where they sat. When they got to the second row Ida jabbed her walker into the knees of the heavyset woman on the end, who quickly shoved herself and her three kids to the far end of the pew to give room for Ida and Buford to sit.

The preacher finally found his voice again, remembered where he was in the gospel, and finished reading in a rush so he could go sit down. Then in the dead silence he got back up and stepped to the podium, looking back at the hymns listed on the wall for the day's service.

"We will now, uh, sing Hymn 206, uh, 'Lord Lifted Me'."

Papers and books and dresses shifted, and voices cleared in ragged starts. One or two voices started to sing, but quickly faded to mute in the heavy quiet that they could not push off themselves. With a snort of determination that no one was going to interfere with HER church, Dot stood up back straight and hymnal splayed open in both hands before her, took in a deep breath and belted out the song, filling the rafters above. The rest of the choir and the congregation stood slowly and disorganized, and joined in weakly with the singing.

Ida snatched the hymnal from the terrified woman next to her and planted the open book in Buford's hands. He looked at the book and the operatic woman in the choir, smiled, took in a deep breath and joined in.

The volume and the harmony between those two magnificent voices intertwined, wrapped the whole congregation in its arms and rattled the windows and tin roof of the church, making the old brass bell in the belfry hum. Everyone else fell silent and stood there while Dot and Buford took that song to levels and emotion only angels could have known about. Their eyes locked onto each other and the space between them reverberated, pulsing the podium and shaking the lily in the little glass vase sitting on its top. Ida smiled and slipped a hand down into her matching lace covered purse and withdrew a silver flask, spun open the chained cap with a practiced motion of her thumb, held the flask up in salute to the preacher, then downed its contents in quick gulps. Her work was done.

Buford soon became a member of that choir, and the early Sunday morning quiet at the cabin would rumble to the eager sound of his Harley taking him to church. Dot and Buford convinced the choir and the preacher to consider adding different kinds of songs to the selections during the Wednesday night service, and by that Fall if a person wanted to park within the little gravel lot next to the church, they had to come early. By the time the service started, the lot was full, and cars were lined along the grassy shoulder on both sides of the Millersville Highway. As it got close to Christmas, Sheriff Poteat had to send a deputy to Union Rest on Wednesday nights to direct the traffic coming out of the service and filling the road. The choir willingly became the musical back-up to the duo of Dot and Buford, and the janitor had to turn the heat up and then open the windows to the Winter air just before Dot and Buford were to hit common notes to keep the old stained glass from cracking. Interlaced with old traditional protestant hymns, came selections from Rock and Roll groups going back fifty years or just a couple, but Buford's favorites were from Queen.

Finally, in the quiet lull after Christmas, the preacher gave in and allowed the choir full reign to hold a talent contest in lieu of one of the Wednesday night services. Anyone in the congregation was allowed to dig up and bring out whatever skill, talent or ability they thought they once had and share it upon the attendees brave enough to come – no holds barred. That Wednesday finally came for the contestants in early February with a full complement of parked cars along the highway.

After a painful series of exhibitions including baton tossings that flew dangerously into the audience, mind-numbing poetry, arthritic-knee dancing, rusty squeaking saxophones from ancient high school band days, and badly played out-of-tune guitars accompanied by songs sounding like the wailings of wounded wild animals, it was finally time for the act everyone had come to see. Dot had pulled all the old lime green robes from her days with the sisterhood, and dressed herself, the choir and Buford all the same.

Slowly the green-robed group mounted the steps at the front of the sanctuary. The audience erupted into applause that went on a full minute. Dot stepped to the center while the applause continued, the janitor turned off all the lights in the sanctuary except the one hanging by a long chain over where Dot stood. Dot tapped her foot in aggravation, placed her hands on her hips and yelled one word.

"Sit!"

Three hundred rear ends slapped down on unpadded wooden pews in a single act that shook the church foundation, rattled the windows, and jiggled the light chain over Dot, and pushed the single light into a gentle sway. As light and shadows slowly swept over Dot's face, she smiled and spoke in a hushed tone.

"Buford Huddle Ledbedder."

The audience sprang to their feet again with another roar of applause. Dot nodded to the janitor to turn off the last light, but the applause continued until the rasping voice of Ida Ledbedder shouted out in the darkness.

"Sit the hell down! You won't hear a damned thing until you get quiet!"

With a rustling in the darkness everyone who had one, found a seat. Steps were heard on the raised preaching platform, then complete silence settled over everyone. The choir piano sounded, simple dancing keys and chords began and ran gently across the keyboard. The single light came back on. Buford stood centered under it with his hands folded in front of himself, his head bowed while he sang looking down. The words gently drifted through the sanctuary. Smiles appeared on face after face as they recognized the song and realized the treat they were about to enjoy. He was singing Queen's "Bohemian Rhapsody". Soft applause swept across the audience and then quickly faded so no one would miss a note. The piano was supported by recorded music and the choir came in as the song began to surge. Note after note, word after word, line after line, it came forward perfectly. And then the song erupted, the music filled the room, Buford's voice rang out and filled the church and the yard outside. He flung open his robe and let it drop to the floor, shirtless and wearing tight metallic gold pants he spread his arms while reaching notes that only the very best could touch. Then Dot stepped next to him and sung the same words, notes and pitch, as if they were both only a single voice.

The janitor cranked up the thermostat and began opening the windows, each shove of the window frame timed to match a drum beat in the background of the song. On through the entire song, all of its sections and beats Dot and Buford sang together as one voice, never wavering from the musical union. Windows cracked. Light bulbs exploded. The janitor threw open the doors to let out some of the pressure off the rest of the windows. Lighters clicked hundreds of little flames in the audience. The wind rushed in toward the pulpit, swirling around Dot and Buford and putting out most of the lighters. Then the sparks of the lighters flared again, sweeping through the audience like little waves of light dancing with the wind and the music.

In the middle of the last verse the preacher ran forward, waving his hands and yelling at everyone.

"Stop! Stop! This is the devil!! How dare you sing such a song in the presence of God! Get out! All of you get out! This is wicked!"

Joined by the church elders the audience was swept out the doors and the remaining lights turned back on. Old man Abercrombie snatched up Buford's robe and shoved it into his hands.

"Cover yourself! What were you thinking?"

The preacher was yelling at everyone, spittle on his lips, when he turned to Dot.

"Get out of here! Now and forever! Don't you ever come back into my church again!"

They were escorted from the church, the elders standing on the doorsteps with folded arms barring anyone from coming back in.

After that I didn't see much of Buford at his place, and he never built another bonfire that I saw. In early April he walked through the woods between our places and came up on the porch to tell me that he and Dot were getting married and were going to start their own revival. They had the wedding up at Indian Rocks in May at that circle of old stones. Dot was stubborn about changing her name, and had said if she had to take his, then Buford would have to take hers, so they decided just to keep the ones they had. I was happy to see how many of the good friends I had found in Finton County were there. Sarah Kozlowski brought her homemade barbecue for the guests afterward and I took up a ladle to help her serve. She told me she had offered the hardware store that she and her husband once had, to the new couple to start their own mission. And the couple would be taking up living in Rufus Broadway's old place up the Greenwood Road since that was not far from the old store.

Now, across the railroad tracks, on the other side of the Millersville Highway at Tooey's Crossroads, the old empty store on that corner has become the New Evangelical Musical Ministry. On Wednesday nights Adam Tooey tries to sell religious trinkets at the Park 'N' Pump, but does do a brisk business in pirated Queen tapes; and the jukebox at Big Al's Tavern is unplugged while Al and me serve drinks to people sitting on the hoods of their cars in the parking lot listening to Dot and Buford sing.

It's quiet at my cabin again, and the briars are growing thick on the gate to the Ledbedder home place. The other night I had an urge for a campfire and built one in the fire pit in front of the cabin. I sat there in my old canvas chair watching the flames when I heard a little scratchy voice clear its throat down beside me, and I spoke to it without turning my gaze from the flames.

"Not tonight, Donald. I'm just watching the fire."

He settled down on his haunches with a grumpy sigh. While we watched the yellow light dance, and felt the warmth feather across our faces, between the occasional pop of firewood I heard him humming, "We are the Champions."

CLIFFORD TIBIDEAUX

Heat waves rippled up off the blacktop road ahead as I drove the Jeep north toward Millersville. The July noon sun was baking Finton County, and the tree leaves hung limp from the branches in steamy air along the side of the road, only rarely disturbed by the faintest breeze. Adam Tooey pulled a sweat matted T-shirt away from his chest to let the sixty-mile an hour wind rush over him from the open window. He pointed out at two huge oak trees set in a small meadow off the road next to an old yarn factory.

"If ol' Clifford Tibideaux was still a deputy, he'd a been sitting right behind those oaks and would be pulling you over for speeding."

I pulled back my right foot just enough to let the Wrangler drift back to forty-five, and grinned over at Adam. His eyes were still on the massive oaks and I could see he was looking back at another old memory.

"Clifford Tibideaux and Tater Millpond were bosom buddies through elementary to high school. They used to race their ol' jalopies on this very road when it was still loose gravel. Clifford went off to the Army, became an MP, and then took a job as a county deputy when he came back. Tater just stayed home and kept getting into deeper and deeper trouble."

"Wasn't he the deputy that once put a snow plow on a squad car?"

Adam slapped his leg and grinned back at me. "He did worse than that, but he always did like to tinker with things. That probably wouldn't have got him in so much trouble with the sheriff, except for his run-ins with Tater.

Clifford was assigned to squad car 17, because he

was the newest deputy in the department and Number 17 was the oldest car they had. It was still a black and white years after the county had decided to paint their sheriff's cars brown over tan. The only reason they even kept it running was so they could assign it to new deputies. Paint was flaking off the hood, the right front fender was a dented blue junkyard replacement, the rooftop flasher was a big red bubble light, and the engine had a governor on it to keep it under 60 miles an hour. The first day of traffic patrol he was assigned to watch the southbound Millersville road there at Union Rest. As soon as he left the Sheriff's office, the desk sergeant, Fred Hobart, who was Tater Millpond's cousin on his mother's side, called Tater and let him know Clifford would be out there.

Number 17 wasn't under those oaks more than fifteen minutes before Tater drove up the road in a supercharged muscle car and then came to a complete stop on the road right in front of Clifford. He blew his horn three times then popped the clutch sending his car screeching north in a cloud of gray-blue rubber smoke, making his tires yelp each time he shifted gears. Clifford revved the engine on Number 17 and shot onto the road in a spray of sand and gravel and a short screech of his own when he grabbed onto the blacktop, and radioed a 'Hot Pursuit' to the dispatcher. Tater was already a half mile ahead when Clifford hit the switch to the siren. About the same time Clifford hit sixty, the siren blared out with the ice cream man melody, chiming little metal bell sounds to the tune of '*Pop Goes the Weasel*', and when it got to 'Pop', the governor kicked in. Clifford stomped on the gas pedal and beat on the steering wheel and the dash, but it did no good, and he tooled along at 59 and a half miles an hour, while Tater soared beyond the horizon of the Millersville road two miles ahead.

The entire day shift was standing around the

dispatcher, biting their fingers to keep the background noise down, while the dispatcher grilled Clifford on the status of his Hot Pursuit. When Clifford tramped into the office later on that morning to tell them at least he had video of Tater's car from his dash camera, he discovered in a fit of laughter around the squad room television that the lens of the camera had been pointed at the squad car driver. The sheriff managed to keep his composure just long enough to give Clifford a mild rebuke for excessive use of force against the steering wheel and the dash. Clifford smiled good-naturedly, but made a secret vow to correct all the things on his squad car.

Clifford spent the entire next weekend down at his Uncle Clarence's auto shop reworking the limitations on old Number 17 and was out at Union Rest just as soon as the Monday morning roll call was over. Just as quick, the dispatcher called Tater. Clifford wasn't under the oak trees more than five minutes when Tater coasted to the spot on the highway directly in front of the yarn factory. Tater honked his horn three times and popped his clutch. His car's rear end was surrounded in grey-blue smoke again and the air filled with the sound of screeching competition tires. At the same time, Clifford popped the clutch on Number 17 and the shade trees were completely cloaked in an exploding cloud of sandy dust that spread all the way out to the highway itself. By the time Tater saw the cloud billow out from the meadow, Number 17 shot out from it onto the road in front of him and blocked his patch. Both cars locked brakes and slid to within less than an inch of each other.

Quiet settled back over the road and the clouds drifted away showing the two cars nose to nose, each throbbing with low rumbles of V-8 Hemis barely contained by their mounts. Clifford got out from his squad car and ambled slowly over to Tater's window.

Tater gave a sheepish smile and looked up at Clifford.

"Aw Cliffie, you ain't gonna give ol' Tater a ticket, now are you?"

Clifford gave a toothy grin and gently slapped Tater's shoulder with his ticket book.

"You bet your ass I am."

From then on it was a constant series of competitions and dirty tricks between Tater and Clifford. That Winter Finton County had its first snowfall in eight years, dumping nine inches on the roads and highways around Millersville. The only county driver that knew how to hook up and operate the snow plow that attached to the trash truck was in the hospital having his gallbladder out, so the county manager asked the sheriff to assign a deputy to plow the roads. The Sheriff didn't even hesitate to answer when he said he'd send Tibideaux right over, and the dispatcher didn't even hesitate to call Tater's house. By the time Clifford had the snow plow mounted on the trash truck, Tater had his chains on and was chugging into town.

Everywhere Clifford went with the snow plow Tater, would dash in front of him, just missing the blade by inches and forcing Clifford to swerve to miss him. Clifford was having trouble enough gauging distances from the cab of the Mitsubishi Fuso to the outer edge of the blade without Tater dashing out in front of him at the last second. Twice when Clifford swerved, he forgot to raise the blade and he ran it into the curb, leaving chunks of concrete in the little snow banks he left behind. After taking out a parking meter in front of the Dollar Duz It, Tater left him alone for a while and Clifford thought maybe he had gone home.

Later, while plowing the parking lot between the second national bank and the courthouse, Tater was back and shot out from the alley next to the Sheriff's office heading for Clifford. Determined not to be harassed by Tater any more, rather than swerve away from him Clifford gunned his engine and headed straight at him. Tater twirled around on the packed snow and began sliding sideways away from the trash truck. His anger up and a need for revenge building by the second,

Clifford gassed the engine again and raised the blade up about two feet off the road. Just as the blade reached for Tater's car, he caught traction with his chains and managed to move out of the way, but Clifford's momentum would not let him stop. Just beyond where Tater had just been, Clifford could see a brand new silver Volvo parked at the courthouse directly in front of his truck. He could only sigh with regret when he read the personalized license plate of Judge Averill Atkins as the snow blade cut into the trunk. Almost like a slow-motion movie, even as the blade was slicing up the judge's car, Clifford could see a face in the window of the courthouse watching in horror and then turning to red rage – the judge himself.

Clifford could only hold on and ride the truck until its inertia was spent into the judge's Volvo. When everything finally came to a halt, the snow blade was buried in the back seats of the Volvo, the car was up over the curb with the front end smashed against the brick wall of the courthouse, and the judge was standing in the window just above his ruined car pointing his finger directly at Clifford. Clifford could only shake his head and hold up his arms in universal surrender.

"Well, Shit."

Later on Clifford looked back at the aftermath of destroying the judge's car as a kind of job security, when the Sheriff said the County was going to dock four hundred dollars a month from his salary until the car was paid for. The other deputies looked on it at as a gift as well, since night duty rotations were halted as Clifford became permanently assigned to the hours of darkness. The only really bad outcome, other than Judge Atkins' threat to give Clifford the gas chamber if he ever came before him for so much as a traffic ticket, was that the snowplow attachment had to be blowtorched off the trash truck and the sheriff ordered Clifford to weld it on to the front of Number 17. In place of the dash mounted video he had to install the hydraulic controls to the plow.

It rarely snowed in Finton County, but when it did, Clifford dearly hated it, and some folks would get up out of bed just to watch Number 17 plow the roads.

When both the transmission and the rear end both blew out on Number 17 and the mechanics couldn't fix it, the county manager said they had to junk the car. So, the Sheriff finally brought Clifford off permanent night duty and assigned him to running a tractor, cutting weeds along the county roads. They let him have a radar gun and a police radio, with instructions to call in when he clocked a speeder and someone else would go after them.

When Tater found out about Clifford's new duty assignment, he would stop by the station to visit with his cousin, while his brother would speed by Clifford doing 90mph in his car. Tater would be standing there in the dispatch room when Clifford called in to say Tater was speeding again, and the dispatcher would tell him Tater was standing right there in front of him. So, the deputies just stopped paying attention to Clifford's calls, and he stopped making them.

People would drive by Clifford along the road and wave and laugh. He had painted the tractor brown over tan and put the Sheriff's Department logo on the side of the tank. He even had a red light mounted to the roll bar over the driver's seat and wore his deputy's crash helmet and dark sunglasses, but he was not a happy man.

The tractor slowly changed as Clifford spent

weekends with it down at his Uncle's shop. Clifford knew that sooner or later Tater would get bold enough to drop himself right in Clifford's lap, and he waited his days for that moment.

It was in the middle of the Spring cutting season, while Clifford was trimming the roadside along the Millersville road just north of Union Rest, when Tater sailed past. Clifford knew he was speeding but had long ago given up even putting the radar gun on him. He knew no one would come. He also knew that whatever was to be done would have to be done by himself. Clifford watched Tater shoot farther up the road, and then the Dodge's taillights came on and Tater's hood dipped down as he turned around. Clifford smiled to himself and quickly checked his controls. Tater rolled back down the road until he was even with Clifford and did a Y-turn in the middle of the road, then just drifted along next to Clifford smiling up at him and shaking his head.

Tater shouted something at Clifford, but he could not be heard over the two engines. Tater shook his head again laughing at Clifford's plight and then popped his clutch just enough to squeal his tires and send his car a couple hundred yards back up the road. His tail lights came on and then he backed down the road to Clifford again. Tater stayed even with Clifford calling out taunts to him.

Clifford resisted the urge to look over at Tater while he cut a few more yards and then calmly looked over at Tater and gave him the finger. That was all it took.

Tater yelled out over the engine noise, "Catch me this time, Asshole!!" and revved his engine to five thousand RPMs before letting out the clutch. The Dodge and the Kubota tractor were both swallowed in a massive cloud of gray-blue smoke. The Dodge fishtailed side to side on screeching tires, painting the road with a black double

S, and then launched itself up the Millersville road, hitting 60 mph in less than four seconds.

Clifford tugged on his seat belt to make sure it was tight, and then flipped the switch that jettisoned the mowing deck behind him. Climbing the tractor onto the pavement, he hit a second switch that settled the tractor nose down with a menacing hydraulic hiss to just six inches off the surface. As Tater's Dodge mounted the first rise in the road a half mile ahead, the Jaguar V-12 replacing the stodgy original Kubota diesel engine roared into life, blowing exhaust cut out pipe covers in a high arc thirty yards into the trees on either side of the road. Bright orange flames shot out five feet on both sides. The oversized rear tires squealed like a monster unleashed, sending black smoke up into the air and rocketing the Kubota in a Kamikaze dash up the Millersville road, hitting 60 mph in 1.9 seconds, and screaming after Tater Millpond like a banshee going after a lost soul.

Tater wasn't sure what it was he could see coming at him in his rearview mirror, but he knew anything that could gain on him like that when he was already hitting 90 mph would bring him nothing but trouble. He drove the gas pedal to the floor and his head was pinned against the neck rest as the Dodge leaped ahead. The speedometer needle passed through one hundred miles an hour without the slightest hesitation, and the engine roared like a jet. The distance between the two vehicles began to increase again.

Clifford was finding it harder and harder to control the misfit Kubota, but he let go of the steering wheel with his right hand just long enough to hit a red button on the dash. He was almost yanked from his seat as the flood of compressed nitrous oxide poured into the cylinders, and the Kubota launched ahead screaming through the asphalt heated air barely touching the highway and twirling the speedometer needle around past the hundred mph mark a second time. The Kubota shrieked passed Tater's Dodge like a missile, cresting the rise in the highway, covered the two miles to the next one in a heartbeat, and then sank from view over the horizon.

Seconds later Tater crested the second rise to find the Kubota facing him, and Clifford grinning over the barrel of his riot gun, pointed directly at Tater's windshield. Heavy blue smoke from burned oil puffed out of the Dodge's exhaust pipes as Tater killed the engine and drifted to a clanking stop in front of Clifford.

Clifford motioned with the riot gun.

"Get out of the car and lay on the road!"

Tater got out and walked amiably toward Clifford. He started to speak, but stopped at the sound of Clifford pumping a shotgun shell into the chamber.

"Lay down on the road!"

"Dammit Clifford,…"

"Now!"

Tater reluctantly settled onto the road and lay on his stomach with his arms outstretched. He was no stranger to this procedure. Clifford unbuckled from the Kubota, stepped down onto the highway, and then handcuffed Tater's wrists behind his back.

Inside the open door of the Dodge, in plain view, were cases of cigarettes. Unable to wait until the cigarettes were delivered to have a smoke for himself, Tater had opened the top case and pulled out a pack, leaving the flap open to show that not a single tax stamp was on any of them.

Seeing the cargo, and noticing the absence of tax stamps, Clifford walked back to Tater lying on the road, and nudged him gently with the tip of his boot.

"Tater, I'm really going to enjoy this."

Tater turned his head away from the deputy.

"Aw, kiss my ass."

When Clifford towed the burned out Dodge into town behind the Kubota, he had Tater strapped belly down across the hood like a deer season trophy. Tater's only words when later that month Judge Atkins gave him 18 months at the county farm, were directed only at Clifford.

"This ain't over by a long shot, Cliffie."

Clifford grinned back at him.

"Be sure and tell your friends down at the farm that you couldn't even outrun a tractor."

Clifford kept his grin, but Judge Atkins only scowled back at him.

"Get your ass out of my courtroom, Tibideaux."

Some people carry a grudge for a long time.

CRAZY DOT

Before she was Crazy Dot, Doris Greenwood always wanted to be a Nun, but being a born into it hardshell Southern Baptist, she could never reach her dream from there. She was however, a third generation member of the Ladies Auxiliary to the Southern Finton County Militia Reserve Historical Association. So it was no surprise to anyone else in Finton County when Doris formed the Sisterhood of Baptismal Evangelists at the Union Rest Second Baptist Church, and dressed them all in key lime green habits.

The unusual just seemed somehow ordinary around Dot. She once won a magazine contest sponsored by the Eternal Life Battery Company. Her prize was a reproduction of a 1930 radio that played Janis Joplin (not Scott) when it was tapped or somebody clapped their hands across the room. Afraid to keep it at home, and not knowing any other place to keep things hid away, she put it in the church basement behind the kitchen until she could find a way to give it to someone that didn't know her. But before she could do that, the prize box got pushed back behind new boxes of old choir robes, when the church choir bought new ones, and it fell between the walls, wedging against the old sewage pipes. The sanctuary of the church, originally built within an old boarding school, was expanded years before, moving the choir loft over what was once the shower room, and rebuilding the podium over a capped off toilet drain. From then on, whenever the preacher slapped his hands on the podium the vibrations set off the 1930's reproduction radio and Janis Joplin's voice would rise up through the podium singing "Oh Lord won't you buy me a Mercedes Benz!"

Each Fall the Union Rest Second Baptist Church held its annual food drive for the needy. One year it was held during the same week as the Annual Finton High School "Beans for Basketball" Superdunk as well as the Annual Southern Finton County Militia Reserve Historical Association Charity Cotillion, so the food drive did poorly compared to previous years. The preacher proclaimed the results of the church's efforts "hind tit" and suggested the elders pick a better week in the future. The Seniors Sunday School Class, which normally found something useful to do with the results of the food drive, held little hope for success that year and so bequeathed the effort to the newly formed Baptismal Sisterhood.

Monday night Dot brought the ladies of the sisterhood together to survey the larder. They had three loaves of frozen bread, 1 pound of bacon, 28 cans of tomato paste nearing the expiration date, 10 pounds of Spanish onions, and 132 cans of assorted kale, mustard greens, and spinach, also nearing their expiration dates. The owner of the Route 17 Got-It-All Grocery was a member of the Church, and had been almost the sole contributor, except for the bacon that had come from Dot's mother. The sisterhood got down all the cookbooks in the basement kitchen and put on a pot of coffee in determination to serve the needy one way or another.

The basement fell into silence except for the rustle of starched green habits, sighs among the ladies, sips of coffee and flips of cookbook pages. After a long interval of sips-and-flips, Margaret Flowers thumped the open pages of her assigned cookbook with the flat of her hand and said to everyone, "This is it!" With her chin up and her finger pointing to the lower half of page 136 in the 1957 edition of *Greens, Greens, Good For the Heart,* she announced,

"This recipe requires exactly the food we have been given."

Dot forced away the frown that had settled over her face, gave the inside of her lower lip a quick chew, and then fixed her full attention on Margaret's beaming face in unspoken question. Margaret met Dot's gaze with supreme confidence.

"It's called Spinach Casserole. And we should have enough to serve two helpings to every man in the Finton County Jail."

So, Dot called the Jail, said the church would like to donate dinner to the inmates one evening, and was invited to come down that Thursday.

Dot gave Margaret a nod, letting her know the Jail had accepted.

"Margaret, honey, you do know that Spinach Casserole is an acquired taste, don't you?"

Margaret gave a wide-eyed shrug.

"Who doesn't like greens and toast?"

Thursday afternoon the sisterhood met in the church's basement and collected enough flat pans, bread pans and casserole dishes to hold it all. Margaret chopped and fried the bacon until it was crisp in the bottom of a large cooking pot. Dot chopped up the onions and tossed them in with the bacon bits and grease. As soon as the onions were caramelized, the tomato paste was mixed with just enough hot water and then poured into the pot, sending a hissing plume of tomato paste cloud up over the stove. The pans and dishes were ladled half way up with the mixed canned greens, and then covered with the tomato-paste-onion-bacon-sauce. The bread was layered over the tops of all the pans and dishes, and then it all went into the ovens for 45 minutes. When it was all cooked, the ladies took assigned covered dishes out to their cars for the drive over to the jail.

The sisters were welcomed into the guest area of the jail by two county police officers taking their rotation as guards, who quickly backed away toward the nearest window as the aroma of the casseroles filled the little room. Years of police training were put to the test as Officer Mike smiled warmly and thanked the sisterhood for their good deed. With only the slightest hint of stress in his voice he asked,

"What wholesome meal have you ladies fixed for our inmates tonight?"

Margaret stepped forward.

"Spinach Casserole. Have you ever had that before, Officer?"

"Ye-yes,…ma'am."

"Well there's plenty there. Should be enough for everyone to have two helpings."

Mike thrummed the tips of his fingers against the seams of his pants and turned toward his partner.

"Ted, who's got kitchen duty tonight?"

"That'd be Tater Millpond. He's got two more weeks 'til he's finished off what the Judge gave him for speeding and harassing Officer Tibideaux last Winter."

Mike turned back toward the sisters with a beaming smile filling his face.

"I just can't tell you ladies how much we appreciate your kindness. We'll have one of the inmates come collect this wonderful food and serve it out.

"Oh, well be happy to serve it, Officer."

"No ma'am, we best let the inmates do that."

Dot stepped in front of Margaret.

"We came to serve it. We cooked it. We brought it. We're going to serve it."

"No Ma'am, we can't let you ladies do that."

Nose to nose with the officer, Dot placed her hands on her hips, holding a plastic ladle in each hand.

"I said, we're going to serve it. Now, tell us where to set it up."

Mike placed his hands on his hips and shifted his feet slightly apart.

"I said 'no', and that's the end of it."

Dot did not move.

"Mister, we're doing God's work. Don't get in God's way. We're not going to tell you again."

Silence settled among the people standing in the room. Slowly Mike shook his head.

"Doris, go home."

Dot stood in front of Mike while first one then another sister tried to take her hand and lead her from the room, but she would not move. When the door opened and Tater Millpond walked in, Dot finally stepped away from Mike, but then stopped to point an angry finger at the officer's face.

"You will suffer for this."

Tater looked around the room, then settled on Ted.

"Smells like someone has already suffered. You shoulda told me to bring a mop. What happened?"

Ted pointed to the dishes on the visitor's table.

"Take those dishes to the dining hall. That's supper."

Tater watched as the lime green robed sisters filed from the room.

"Are they the Klan?"

Mike flipped his hand at the dishes.

"Just serve that stuff out, Tater. It's supper tonight"

Tater leaned over the table and cautiously lifted aluminum foil from a corner of one casserole dish, and then jerked his head to upright. "Jeez…"

"Tater, just take that and serve it to the men."

"No way. I'm not serving that."

"You want to be uncooperative? You want to lose your good behavior status and do another six months? Or do you want to serve that stuff and then get out of here in two weeks?"

"Somebody'll beat my ass over this."

"That ain't my problem, Tater. Two weeks or six months. Your choice."

"Well, ...Hells Bells!"

On the third Thursday of each month the bug sprayer came to treat the dining hall and the inmates usually had supper in their cells that evening. Tater Millpond traveled the cell walks pushing the serving cart stacked high with plastic trays and fully stocked with spinach casserole, served two helpings to every man in the jail, and did it in record time. At the end of his duty, all the casserole had been served out and he didn't have to eat any of it. He did, however, get kicked seven times, got splattered with spinach casserole on the back of the head twice, had a plastic tray slung at him, endured every curse and damnation he'd ever heard, and had two death threats from guys he figured might be able to deliver on them.

All the way back to the church, Dot was in a fit and fury over being run out of the county jail before she could serve that spinach casserole. Margaret tried to hold a prayer meeting in the basement when they got back, just to calm Dot down, but she only got worse. Finally, after Dot said she was ready to call down brimstone and damnation on the county police, the ladies had had enough and started turning in their habits. Crazy Dot was still slamming pots and pans and fussing with the air in front of her in the kitchen, when Margaret gently folded the pile of lime green robes and left them on a dining table, then quietly slipped up the steps out of the basement. Dot argued with the air all the way home, and didn't come out of her lather until Friday evening when she heard about the jailbreak.

The county jail had been modernized to an extent in 1964, when each cell had received its own government surplus porcelain commode. The funds and plans to modify the jail was provided through the will of Montreat Millpond, who died that year and had spent much of his early adult life there before he became rich during prohibition. Miles of terra cotta pipes had been laid to connect all the commodes to the county sewer system that had to be extended from where it stopped in 1943 under the old school that was now the Union Rest Second Baptist Church. The old private school had paid for the sewer to be run out there to service 40 active young people and a staff of 10 in civilized hygiene.

One by one the porcelain commodes received the double helpings of spinach casserole, some portions before and some portions after human processing. Apparently the bacon grease and onions added to the intense physiological reaction triggered by the canned greens and experienced by most of the inmates. Also apparently, or at least possibly, the year of the expiration on the canned greens and the canned tomato paste may have been altered by an ink pen, although that was never formally proved in a court of law. In a matter of minutes after supper, 93 commodes were being flushed again and again in an effort to wash away the product of the Baptismal Sisterhood and the bowel contents of the entire inmate occupancy of the Finton County Jail - except for Tater.

The pressure in the southern end of the county water system dropped dramatically, triggering three county water towers to begin refilling. The vacuum effect in the sewage system as most of the water in southern Finton County tried to rush down the county jail drain pipes, was followed by a tremendous pressure buildup as the three county towers dumped a tsunami into the cold water pipes of the commodes. One by one, commodes began to explode and spray the cells with cold water and whatever remnants were left behind from the last flush.

Each exploding commode carried the momentum of the previous one and each explosion grew larger and more damaging. Men dove behind their mattresses for cover. The main cell hall sounded like it was being carpet bombed as the explosions worked their way down the hall that ended with an outside wall. When the explosions finally stopped, and the great flood of spinach, human content, and a thousand gallons of water surged on through the drain pipes, inmates crawled out from under mattresses and crept slowly through doorless jambs into the hall to look around. All gazes gradually turned toward the end of the hall, where a gap had opened in the wall big enough to ride through on a circus elephant, and the inmates could see the field out behind the jail and the highway lights a half mile beyond. Without a word between them, first one then another walked briskly down the hall and out through the gap, to begin loping across the field toward the highway in the growing dark. Finally only two remained standing in the hallway. They turned to look at each other.

"Two weeks," said Tater.

"Six days," said Cornelius Hooker.

They were both sitting in their cells when the guards managed to unlock the warped entry doors and make their way down the corridor.

Sirens blared. Spotlights beamed out from the rear tower outside and panned back and forth across the field. Mike and Ted looked out at the field as other officers dashed across the field after the escapees, shotguns held at port and keys jangling.

Tater walked to the inside edge of his ruined cell doorway and looked out at Mike.

"You should never have made me serve that nasty ass casserole."

Mike kept watching the activity in the field.

"Shut up, Tater."

When Dot heard about the prison break, and about fifty rumors describing apocalyptic destruction at the jail, her anger settled deep into her and was capped by vindication like icing on a bakery made birthday cake. She called the preacher to ask if she could say a word or two in witness to the congregation, and he agreed, saying it would give him a chance to catch his breath and rest his throat a moment. She became almost serene as she began planning what to say at the service Sunday morning.

Dot skipped the Adult Women's Sunday School class and was already sitting in the front row next to the aisle when Elder Abercrombie opened the sanctuary for service. She smiled pleasantly as the service progressed from congregational news through two hymns, the offering, and the beginning rumbles of the preacher's sermon for the day. Lost in her thoughts of the coming moment of glory she had heard very little of the service and the preacher had to call her up twice before someone in the second row nudged her from behind. She stood bolt upright and cast her smile over her shoulder at the multitude of sinners she was about to call to accounting, and then turned for the podium. As the Preacher sat down mopping his forehead with a fresh white linen handkerchief, Dot planted herself behind the podium and gripped its edges with her hands. Like the old song, she started out low and soft, planting the seeds of service, duty, and loyalty in the ears of the congregation, to a wave of knowing nods and sleepy smiles. Then she began to call on the thunder in her heart and listed the failures and abandonment by her former sisterhood followed by a life long list of hurts, embarrassments, and long-simmering snubs that had dwelled in her mind for decades. A rumbling noise started to come up through the foundation of the sanctuary. People began trading stares with each other and shifting in their seats as Dot grew more and more tumultuous. Little taps were heard against the underside of the flooring as tiny pieces of old terra cotta popped away from the old drain under the podium and hit against the subflooring. Finally, the preacher decided Dot had ranted far beyond what folks could tolerate and stood up to resume his own sermon.

Knowing her moment was coming to an end, Dot hollered out that they would all remember this day and tremble at their punishment, and she raised her hands up to the ceiling. Ignoring the increasing rumbles from the basement and the shaking floor beneath her feet, Dot slammed her hands down on the podium with all her might and opened her mouth for her last damnation, but no one heard it. The jittery voice of Janis Joplin rose up through the podium singing "Oh Lord, won't you buy me a Mercedes-Benz", and the floor under the podium began to rise.

The rumble in the basement grew louder, accompanied by firecracker pops of shattering terra cotta and violent snaps among the oak floorboards. Then the entire podium platform lurched into the air, spewed upward atop a giant green gelatinous geyser three feet wide, exploding from the sewage pipes. The platform opened a ten-foot wide hole in the roof, roaring through like a launched missile. Instantly the spray from the geyser covered the entire congregation in a shiny green film with a horrific aroma beyond description. People climbed and crawled over the pews and each other, struggling for the doors and pouring out of the sanctuary doors, chased by tsunami waves of the green muck exploding out of the sewer pipes and bringing with it every ounce from the county jail. The podium platform shot a hundred feet into the air with Dot and the Preacher still standing next to the podium and holding on to each other in death grips. The platform arched over the Sunday School building and crashed floor first and dead center on the roof of the Preacher's new Cadillac.

Dot and the Preacher opened their eyes, realizing they had lived, and stepped down off the podium in dumbfounded amazement into a scene reminiscent of the Great Blitz in London during W-W-II. The church roof was holed and the steeple gone. Muck was gushing down the church steps. Green-painted people were running and limping in all directions, trying to decide what to do and trying not to touch themselves, and the air was filled with a stench like no one had ever smelled. In the middle of all the slime-covered catastrophe stood the preacher in his unsoiled white suit crying over his new Cadillac, and Crazy Dot in her spotless starched lime green habit looking at it all. Folks say she laughed for three days.

It took the insurance company three tries to get an inspector to stay on the site long enough to document the damage. It was decided just to bulldoze the entire building and start over, but when the ground was cleared the lingering stench still made the site unusable, so the church was rebuilt on the far side of the graveyard. By the end of that Summer there was a christening of the new Union Rest Third Baptist Church, but nothing ever did grow at the old site. Not long after, the army sent a man from the Chemical Corp to study the bald spot near the Millersville highway going through Union Rest, and to collect the recipe for that spinach casserole, but no one ever heard anything more about that. An aging Viet Nam vet once got drunk down at Big Al's Tavern and said the army added cumin to Dot's spinach casserole recipe, and that's how they got agent orange, but that was probably just talk.

Just the same, everyone there agreed it would be best not to say anything about it to Dot.

BIG DOG

On the far side of Lake Adolphus, just beyond the site of old Confederate Camp Finton, a man built a log house up on the ridge. He bought fifty acres from old man Hooker that straddled the ridge with twenty-five acres on each side, and had a right of way snaking down the woods on the south slope to a dirt road across from Sweet Water Lagoon Hunting and Fishing Club. No one but Hooker and the courthouse knew his name for sure, and the man made no effort to meet or speak with anyone. He lived alone on the ridge and was rarely seen.

One weekend after fishing all Saturday afternoon at Sweet Water, then playing cards and drinking all night with Clifford Tibideaux, Slick Millpond, and Stumpy Madison, Big Al walked stiff-legged out into the early morning light and decided she'd explore the barely cut trail up to the ridge across the road. The mist over the lagoon below and the fog in her head cleared at almost the same rate while Al pumped her legs up the slope, keeping straight on even when the trail switched back and forth to ascend toward the ridge. She pushed her way through a stand of short cypress and came upon two figures walking slowly along the trail to her right. The skylight was behind the two figures and Al could only barely see their forms. Similar in height, one wore a poncho and an old western slouch hat pushed low over his face, while the other seemed to have a fur hat with large ear flaps. As she shaded her eyes from the bright skylight with the flat of her hand, she was amazed to see that the second figure was actually a dog standing flatfooted at over six feet tall. Al backed up a few steps toward the cypress.

"Jesus!"

"Nope. You lost?"

"Just walking around, getting some exercise."

"You usually get your exercise on other people's property"

"No. What the hell kind of dog is that?"

"Mine."

The dog's huge head swiveled to look intently at each speaker in turn, pendulous jowls slinging spittle in an arc with each turn.

"What do you call him?"

"Dog. He doesn't seem to respond 'Cat' or 'Coon'."

"That's his name?"

"Name's 'Big Dog'. Thought that'd do."

"I've never seen such a b-"

"You go on down, now"

Al kept to her spot, wanting to ask another question, but the man turned to the dog and quietly spoke one word. "Fetch."

Big Dog stepped forward on camel sized paws and came swiftly at Big Al, who automatically ducked her head. Big Dog clamped on the nape of her jacket and lifted Al from the ground, then looked back toward the man in the poncho.

"Put Away."

With that the dog trotted down the slope and dropped Al on the dirt road. There was a single note whistle from up the slope and the dog dashed away through the trees as graceful and quiet as a white-tailed deer.

Al rose from the dirt road brushing sand and pine needles from her jacket. Her back was covered in drool. Al was six-foot-three, and at two hundred thirty pounds had been one of the Marines' best hand-to-hand combat instructors until she retired fours years earlier. Anger boiled in her gut.

"That was a big damned dog."

As she flipped her hand through her short hair to shed more of the sand from it, she realized her favorite Marine cap must have been knocked off up on the slope. Even as she had the thought, the dog reappeared from the trees and stood nose to nose with her, the cap in its mouth, and its arm-thick tail wagging like a puppy. She snatched the cap from its jowls and it gave her a playful "woof", then disappeared back into the woods. She stood there holding the cap out in front of her as great dollops of drool slipped off the saturated cap and plopped onto the sand in front of her boots.

At sunrise the following morning, the south slope of the ridge awoke from the night's sleep to the roar of an ancient bulldozer began making its way along the switchback trail leading down from the log house. The man in the poncho operated the old bulldozer with a rhythm and familiarity of long experience, pushing down small trees and grading the roadway. Big Dog trotted along behind the aging equipment, content to go wherever the man went. On the third switchback the dozer sputtered, sent a huge cloud of jet black smoke from its rusty exhaust stack, and then with a short jerk fell silent.

The man worked knobs and levers and buttons and pedals for several minutes, but the old CAT would not be revived. Accompanied by a small string of quietly uttered profanities, the man worked his way down off the bulldozer and back up the trail to a garage behind his log house. Moments later he returned with a long section of serious logging chain and attached it to the monster box blade at the front of the CAT. Satisfied the chain would hold, he gave a short whistle and Big Dog dashed to his side eager for something to do. The man gave two loose wraps of the logging chain around Big Dog's muscular neck, and left him sitting there in front of the box blade while he climbed back up into the operator's seat.

The man spoke only just loud enough for the dog to hear him.

"Fetch home."

With a jerk, the dozer began to inch forward and the tracks began rolling over the drive wheels as Big Dog dug his paws into the hillside and pulled the stalled CAT up the slope; Big Dog clearly enjoying the exercise. The man-made minor course corrections by pulling on track brake levers, but Big Dog knew where to go and how best to get there. Halfway back to the garage, the man saw a shape trotting along the ridgeline he had not seen in years. A large female moose loped along the crest of the ridge, making her way in the general direction of the distant mountains.

Big Dog spotted the moose and began to whimper, wanting to go play with it, and the CAT began to dash up the slope. Big Dog's whine turned into a yelp as he tried to get the moose to come in his direction. The moose saw Big Dog and decided this was not a place to linger, so she picked up her pace, keeping Big Dog in her rear pointed eye, snorted a moose-like rejection grunt and dashed for thicker woods. Loose dirt and mud was flung off the front end of the tracks as Big Dog drug the CAT to a sliding stop in front of the garage, with the man pulling back on both brake levers to keep the CAT from smashing into the building.

Big Dog whined and yelped and tugged at the chain to be released for playtime with the moose, but the man would not unhook the logging chain.

"No! Sit! Last time you ran off after something that big, you drug back that half-crazed black bear. Damned thing charged down into the basement and wouldn't come out."

Big Dog's yelping and whining grew louder as he jumped up and down against the restraint of the logging chain.

"You heard me. I said 'No' and that's the end of it. You remember we had to tranquilize that bear and drag her up out of my basement with this very CAT. She was terrified of you. It still smells like bear shit down there! Now, SIT! "

Big Dog dropped his rump flat on the ground with a heavy 'thump', sending a cloud of dust out around him, and continued to whine and give puppy yelps in the direction of the departing moose, minding the man but still dragging his sitting half around by his front paws within the reach of the logging chain. The man went into the garage and retrieved another length of logging chain attached to a 12 x 12 post in the corner of the garage. He placed two loops around Big Dog's neck and then released the chain to the CAT. Big Dog bounded to the end of the logging chain and began howling after the moose as it disappeared into the woods. The man went into the back of the garage and came back with two old wool blankets, frayed and worn at the edges. He dropped them in a loose pile near the 12 x 12 post.

"Here. You lay down on these. You're sleeping here until you calm down."

The dog did not calm down and remained agitated through sundown. He continued to howl off and on at the tree line where he last saw that moose. In the fading light, the man brought out a six-quart steel bowl filled with dog food and set it next to the five-gallon pot holding Big Dog's fresh water. Around ten o'clock that night the dog finally went quiet and the man turned in to bed.

Shortly after sunrise the following morning the man slipped on his poncho and carried his coffee cup down with him from the house to go check on his dog. The dog was gone. The logging chain was gone. The 12 x 12 post was gone. The garage was gone. He stood there sipping his coffee through the steam rising from his tin cup, and looking at the fourteen-foot wide trail gouged into the topsoil from the garage foundation to the far tree line where the moose had gone.

"Damned Dog."

After taking his cup back to the house and retrieving his slouch hat, the man tracked the garage trail into the tree line. Cedar and pine saplings had been crushed down leaving a cleared roadway a hundred yards into the woods, to where the road turned and went out of sight. In the center of the raw roadway were Big Dog's huge paw prints dug deep into the soil. After about three miles along the ridge the trail turned down the north slope and went into taller trees.

Two hundred yards down from the ridge sat the garage wedged against two ancient oak trees, each over three feet wide and no more than five feet apart. Between the trees, arched out like a pulled wishbone, the remaining section of the sprung and splintered 12 x 12 post pointed in the direction of Big Dog's paw prints and the swish slap marks of the freed end of the logging chain. The man knew it was useless to try to track the dog now without the garage to slow him down. He shook his head and turned back toward his house.

"Damned Dog."

Stories and rumors came back down from the mountains, brought by truckers winding their way down to State Route 535, so they could be at Tooey's Crossroads for lunch. Crazed, panic-stricken moose were seen dashing across roads without concern for truck traffic, running from something in the dark woods. Occasionally the moose were seen fleeing the woods, with a giant dog in hot pursuit. One moose was thought to have actually thrown herself in front of a charging logging truck just to escape the attention of that dog. After a while the sightings stopped, but many of the stories continued, embellished after second or third beers at watering holes near overnight truck stops, and retold as local stories hundreds of miles away.

Each morning the man took his morning coffee and hiked up to the double oaks on the far north ridge. He sat on a time-worn granite boulder next to the misplaced garage, the lichen covering the boulder worn away in the spot he routinely occupied. One morning in late Summer he was almost near the bottom of his cup and ready to go back to the house, when Big Dog slowly emerged from the trees. Every part of the dog's body that could hang low was doing it. The dog's ribs rippled under his thinned dusty fur, his big head was barely up off the ground drifting side to side as he walked, and his eyes were swollen and dark. Still dragging behind him was thirty-eight feet of logging chain. Big Dog almost stumbled up to the man and placed his watermelon-sized head in the man's lap.

The man rubbed the dog's head and gently scratched behind his ears.

"You Done?"

"Woof."

The man stood up and walked to the back of the garage and pointed at the rear 12 x 12 center post. Big Dog slowly limped to where the man stood and then sat in front of the post, looking back up at the man with bleary saddened eyes.

"Don't look at me like that. You drug it up here."

The man set his coffee cup on the ground, then looped and hooked the logging chain around the post. He picked up his cup and began his walk back along the ridge. He spoke over his shoulder as he went down.

"Fetch home."

The next morning when the man brought out Big Dog's breakfast, the garage was back, although with some adjustments yet to be made. Big Dog was curled up on the old tattered wool blankets just inside the garage, still in a deep sleep, and the logging chain had been returned to its bin. Standing there examining the garage and deciding which aspect to fix first, the man heard brash music thumping through the woods. His first thought was the hunting club had pulled another all night card party and was just letting out, but the music came more from the west than the south, so he began walking toward it to investigate.

A hundred yards into the woods, and still well inside his property line, he found a four-tent campsite in a clearing. Beer cans, plastic wrappers, molded Styrofoam and cardboard boxes were tossed around the campsite. The boxes were freshly ripped open and labeled for tents, sleeping bags, air mattresses, folding chairs and a gas cooking stove. Still, the music was not coming from the campsite.

The man followed the noise deeper into the woods until he came to the edge of his property and the decaying split locust wood rails that had once been the State Property boundary to old Camp Finton. The boom box source of the rapper song blasting the morning air sat on a small grassy knoll in the center of four dig sites of flinging dirt. Men busied themselves jabbing the ground and tossing shovelfuls of red dirt in all directions. Even the boom box had received a spray of red dirt. The man spoke to the closest digger.

"This is state property."

The man looked up with a start and then looked around at the others for support.

"You a Park Ranger?"

"No."

"We ain't bothering you. Why don't you just go away?"

"Oh, you're bothering me. You're filling the air with that racket. You're digging up a state monument.

You're camping on my land and turning the whole area into a garbage dump. I'm real bothered."

The broad-shouldered digger snickered, looking around to see he had the full attention of his friends, and stepped out of his hole, holding out the new shovel blade toward the man.

Almost silently and instantly the digger found his nose pressed against Big Dog's, with the dog looking intently into his eyes. There was a low rumble that sounded like a down-shifting logging truck in the far distance, but it was coming from deep in Big Dog's chest.

The man spoke again.

"You boys want to tell me what th'Hell you're up to?"

"M-m-map."

"Buried gold stashed at Camp Finton in the final days of the war?"

"Y-y-yes"

"You get it from the store that sold you the camping equipment?"

Glances of understanding flashed among three of the diggers, while the first remained as still as a marble statue in front of Big Dog.

The man chuckled to himself and shook his head.

"I hear he's done that before."

The man turned and headed back toward his cabin, speaking over his shoulder as he went.

"You boys clean up good before you leave this morning, and don't dawdle. The dog hasn't had his breakfast yet."

He gave a short whistle, but Big Dog did not move. Spittle dripped from his jowls onto the digger's new plaid shirt, and the spreading moisture stain joined the one that had already begun below his beltline. Sensing the dog had not responded, the man stopped in the dry leaves at the edge of the trees and looked back at the digger.

"I think the dog would be a little more comfortable about leaving if you'd just drop that shovel."

The shovel fell to the ground and Big Dog slowly turned away to follow the man home. Twenty minutes later the holes at Camp Finton were filled, the campsite cleared, and quiet returned to the woods at the ridge. After another cup of coffee while Big Dog finished his breakfast, the man decided he should go visit the Park'N'Pump over at Tooey's Crossroads.

It was almost noon when the man's old '69 Jeep Gladiator chugged to a stop in front of the Park'N'Pump. Sitting at an angle in front of the old wooden steps to the porch was a brand new red Super Cab 4x4, with all four doors left wide open and the keys still jangling from the switched off ignition The cargo bed was a jumbled mass of hastily collected camping gear and shovels. There was yelling coming from behind the store out toward the swamp, so the man made his way around the highway side of the building and eased around the back corner to see what was going on.

The digger that had stood nose to nose with Big Dog back at Camp Finton had a neck lock around the poor old Adam Tooey from behind, and held a serious sized Bowie knife up in front of the old man's cheek with the blade edge angled at his throat. They were both standing next to the dumpster facing Big Al who was holding the business end of a pump action riot gun barely 12 inches away from the digger's face. Behind the dumpster stood the other three diggers, nervously trading glances with each other.

The man muttered to himself.

"Well this ain't good."

He pointed at the three nervous diggers and spoke to the dog.

"Fetch here."

Big Dog moved almost silently with a lightning cut-out maneuver that would have made a sheepherder proud of his Border Collie. The man pulled on the collar of the first wide-eyed digger and brought him close to his face so he could whisper.

"You boys wanna stay alive?"

The three men nodded in quick response. The man pointed to the huge oak on the highway side of the store and spoke to the men.

"Go Sit."

Relieved to be out of it, the men half stumbled to the tree and sat down with their backs against the trunk, releasing strained breaths in ragged sighs. The man then pointed at the digger holding the shopkeeper and spoke to the dog again.

"Nose."

The digger was alerted by a flicker in Big Al's eyes as she quickly looked to his left and then brought her focus back to the barrel sight of the riot gun. He wished with all his heart he had not taken this stupid stance when the muscular woman dashed across from the Tavern next door carrying the shotgun. He needed to find a safe reason for both of them to back away from this insane situation. Heavy warm breath on the left side of his neck brought the reason. Without turning his head or moving the knife he pulled his eyes as far left as he could and saw the pupils of Big Dog just as its nose delicately touched against his cheek. His shoulders sagged.

"Aw shit."

He then dropped the knife and held up his hands.

Adam spun around and kicked him in his shins and then dashed behind Al. Al spoke to Adam.

"Go call the Sheriff."

Adams hesitated and then scampered in through the

back door of the store. Al lowered the barrel of her riot gun, but still kept it in the direction of the digger. At the same time the man stepped around the corner so Al could see him, and know he was not one of the digger's friends. She acknowledged the man with a curt nod and then asked,

"Where's the others?"

"Sitting against the big oak, and glad to be out of it. They're no trouble."

"We'll let the deputies decide that."

She turned a frown on the digger.

"What was this all about?"

"That old fart sold us a map to an old Confederate fort, and then several hundred dollars worth of cheap camping equipment, and we weren't up there more than a few hours till we got run off."

Big Al's muscular belly jerked several times as she chuckled.

"I can't believe you guys fell for that old map routine. Say, I'll bet you were the ones Pug told me about spent most of the night at the Tavern drinking and planning to go 'look for something' in the woods."

Al herded the men around to the front of the store, where Adam met them on the front porch.

"Just have them sit there on the bench, I know they'll stay."

He gave each would-be gold hunter a keen look into their eyes that was answered by four sullen nods of submission. Adam then placed his hands on the shoulders of Al and the man.

"Let me pay you for coming to my rescue with a couple beers. On the house."

Al chuckled.

"Now that's a first."

Not only did he bring them both beers, but it was two national brand first-time-opened bottles. Al was impressed. The man looked back toward the front screen door.

"What about them?"

Adam chuckled and picked up a nearly empty large tube of Superglue.

"I spread this all over the bench seat."

Al chuckled again and shook her head at her brother. Adam pulled down a large piece of beef jerky and pointed it at Big Dog standing nearby. The man took the jerky and gave it to the dog who consumed it in two chomps.

Then the air filled with the roar of a supercharged V-8 and the front of the store was peppered with a hail of gravel. Al and the man dashed to the porch to see the front lot completely filled with a dust cloud and the men gone from the bench. Left behind, solidly glued to the top of the bench were four new pairs of Wrangler jeans, with one pair still holding onto a tiny bit of flesh in the middle of the glue puddle. Adam still had not come onto the porch.

Al spoke back through the screen door.

"Adam, you didn't call the cops, did you?"

There was a long pause before he answered.

"No."

"How much you take'm for?"

"Altogether?"

"Yes. Altogether"

There was a pause before he slowly answered.

"Eleven hundred dollars."

"Eleven hundred dollars??!!"

He gave another short pause, then answered.

"Yeah, and I just added that superglue to their credit cards."

Al rolled her eyes up at the porch ceiling in response to her older brother's brazen nature and let out a long breath. The man shook his head and chuckled softly as he stepped off the porch, pushing his slouch hat down on his head, and walked out to his old Jeep pick-up while the dog trotted behind him. He started the engine and leaned to the other side to flip open the door for Big Dog, who filled the right side of the cab once he was completely in. The man waved a crooked finger at Al without looking back as he drove off.

Al called the sheriff herself from the Tavern, omitting the parts concerning Adam's business practices, but they never caught up with the red Supercab. All they ever got on the case was a statement from a clerk up at the Miller Mart, saying a big man from out of town came in that afternoon wearing just his skivvies and charged four extra-large pairs of jeans and some large padded bandages, but she didn't see what he drove. She said he limped a little, and was in a real sour mood.

THE GHOST AT INDIAN ROCKS

At Tooey's Crossroads, the Greenwood Road drops off from the old railroad tracks on the other side of the Millersville highway to run west past an old abandoned hardware store, out through lightly populated farm country, and then just sort of fades away at a low-lying rocky ridge known as Indian Rocks. There aren't many stories told about how Indian Rocks got its name. It seems the place has just always been called that. But if the Ghost at Indian Rocks comes up, spoken in quiet tones on late evening Summer porches while the lightning bugs are still busy, or around tinking iron stoves in snug Winter parlors, there will be a different story from each person that tells it. Even so, they almost always start with the same line.

"He was the color of a heavy harvest moon, the color of pumpkin."

Malcolm Ironwater had grown up on the road, the only son of migrant farm workers. His father had always told him he was descended from an Indian warrior chief, but never could really say which tribe. One early Spring Malcolm's family found themselves in southern Finton County working the farms around Indian Rocks. His sister, Odie, had blossomed into a pretty young woman and had captured the heart of the older Broadway boy, whose father was a hard-working but kindly widower. Odie and Ivy were married up at Indian Rocks, surrounded by families from the local farms and officiated by the circuit preacher that came out that way twice a month. Old man Broadway welcomed Odie, and since his younger son Julius was already leaving in the Fall to go to sea with his cousin down in

New Orleans, Malcolm could stay on too, if he wanted.

The Ironwaters found plenty of work through the Summer and into the Fall. They were among the well-wishers at the Broadway place when Julius went off to New Orleans, and found a good warm place for the Winter on a nearby farm. Malcolm had grown into a strong young man, and his daddy said it was time for him to watch over his sister – at least for a while, so he stayed on at the Broadway place when his parents moved on in the Spring.

Through the Spring and Summer, when he wasn't working one of the local fields, Malcolm would find himself up at Indian Rocks, drawn there, belonged there. The rocks formed more of a crown on the hilltop, than a ridge line, enclosing almost four acres in a ring of granite stones five and six feet high. Even when the wind howled in the late Autumn, if the sun was out at all, the climate was almost pleasant within the rocks. That may have been why a curious little blue plant clung to life near the base of the rocks inside the ring. One Sunday afternoon Malcolm lay propped against one of the granite boulders watching a warm Autumn sun settle over the granite brothers on the far side of the field. He had a blade of field grass dangling from his lip when a mischievous wisp of wind snatched the grass from his lip and tossed it up into the air in front of him. Without thinking, he reached down and plucked the next plant and brought it up to his mouth as a replacement, but rather than field grass he had plucked one of those curious little blue flowers that only grew within the circle of rocks. As soon as he bit down on the fragile little stem his mouth was filled with sweetness better than hard candy, and he reached up to pull the plant out to look at it.

Malcolm looked up at his fingertips, but they did not hold the little plant, and his hand was surrounded by a field of stars. He sat up in the moonlight, lost in the confusion of going from a sunny afternoon to midnight in what seemed only an instant. He was bone cold, sore from head to foot, and completely naked in the moonlight. Something was tied tightly around his head, and he pulled it down to find his own handkerchief knotted as a bandanna, and a turkey wing feather stuck through the knot. He jumped to his feet and spun around, finding his clothes thrown in all directions. A bright moon, high in its arc overhead, covered the field in bright silver light, and he quickly discovered that his body was covered in a fine yellow powder – the color of a harvest moon, the color of pumpkin. His shadow beneath him was merely a dark oval with arms, as he sprinted around the field brushing off the powder, collecting his clothes and getting into them.

It was then, hopping on one leg to pull up his trousers that his memory opened up a dream that seemed as much real as dream, even though he knew it had to be a dream. He was an Indian chief leading a war party over a low rocky ridge white people would someday call Indian Rocks. Rising to meet his tribe was the chief of another leading his braves up the other side of the ridge, and then there was a terrible struggle of tomahawks and fighting knives. There was a scream in his dream memory, a war cry, and he remembered next standing alone on the ridge in his war paint, placing an eagle feather into his bandanna.

He stood there in the moonlight, stilled for the moment, with one leg in his trousers and one leg out, trying to figure out what happened, then let out a 'whoop' that echoed within the rocks. Malcolm believed he'd had an Indian epiphany; a message from his Indian spirit world, so he ran back to the Broadway farm and charged into his sister's room, barely missing being shot by his sister's husband.

"Odie!! I've had a vision! We need to return to our roots! We're really Indians!!"

The room erupted in a flash of orange light and a terrific explosion.

Slapping Ivy's face and pushing her husband's shotgun away from the direction of her excited brother, Odie peered through the gun-smoked darkness while Ivy cursed his brother-in-law.

"Malcolm, you crazy fool! I almost killed you!"

With the spark of a kitchen match flaring to life, Ivy lit the oil lamp next to the bed.

Odie fanned coiling smoke from in front of her face, and slapped Ivy's backside.

"Malcolm, what's all this fuss about?"

"I saw our heritage, Odie. We are Indians! We need to move out on to the ridge, where we belong!"

"We need to do what??!!"

But, there was no answer, Malcolm had left the doorway and run out to his room, and the darkness beyond the lamp lit doorway was filled by old man Broadway. He leaned in and saw the blast hole in the wall next to the door.

"What the Hell happened in here? Did you just shoot at Malcolm?"

Ivy ducked more slaps from Odie, who had come off the bed so she could reach the side of his head, and tried to answer his father while his wife rained slaps around his face and shoulders.

"I don't know for sure what happened! The door burst open in the dark and I grabbed the shotgun. It was just sort of reflex. I thought maybe we were being robbed…"

"Of what?…" mumbled the old man.

"Quit, Odie!!"

Odie screamed at Ivy.

"You idiot!"

She delivered more slaps with both hands like a pair of frantic bats, while Ivy ducked and ran into the closet with Odie right on him. Ivy managed to push Odie out of the closet and slam the door behind her, and she screamed at him again, pummeling the door with her fists and kicking it with her bare feet.

"You Idiot! You almost shot my brother."

Old man Broadway shook his head and gave a small smile in the moonlight.

"Family squabbles. I sure did miss'em."

Then he went back to bed.

Odie turned the key on the bedroom closet, locking her errant husband in it, gave one more kick to the closet door, then put out the lamp and flung herself back into bed. She gave her husband's pillow several slaps and then kicked it off the bed out into the center of the room. Then she slapped his side of the blankets in a single thwump and flung herself down onto her own pillow. The house finally returned to silence and darkness, with bright moonbeams slipping through opened curtains to lay on the floor. Occasionally the silence would be broken by Ivy's timid muffled voice coming from among the heavy coats and dresses hanging in the closet, seeping out under the door.

"Odie. Sweetheart. Baby. Please unlock the door. Odie?"

Malcolm rushed around his room picking up one item after another to take with him back to Indian Rocks, then tossing it back after deciding it was far too white for an Indian. He had finally settled on two wool blankets and his harvesting knife when he was overcome by exhaustion creeping into his euphoria. He laid his head on his pillow and covered himself with the two blankets and fell into a deep sleep.

It was sun-up when he stumbled through the house, following the trail of coffee aroma drifting out from the kitchen, and flopped onto the ladder back chair at the end of the kitchen table, staring down at the red and white checker pattern on the table top. Odie's hand slipped into his view and set a cup of coffee in front of him, and then slapped the back of his head as hard as she could. Malcolm reached up to his head.

"Oooww!"

"Darned fool! Ivy almost killed you last night!"

Malcolm spoke into his cup, his head throbbing worse than the Summer before when he found that jar of his father's moonshine.

"He missed by a mile."

"Yeah, well, Ivy and Father Broadway are already out in the barn, but Ivy and me ain't speaking this morning. And it's all your fault.

"I had a dream, Odie, I - Oooww!"

Odie had slapped the back of his head again.

"I don't want to hear no more about it!"

Malcolm left the table, pulling his coat off the peg by the back door as he headed for the barn. The old man smiled and spoke good morning to him, but Ivy had no smiles for his brother-in-law that particular morning.

"Millings' already done, no thanks to you."

Ivy twisted his back and stretched his shoulders, trying to work out the kinks from spending half of the night squat-sleeping in the closet.

"We still got the rest of that hay to put up in the loft. Reckon you can manage that?"

Malcolm tossed his hand at Ivy and went for the stacked hay bales outside. Flipping up the old canvas cover that kept the dew off them, he hooked the first one onto the pulley rope hanging down from the loft door. The sun came up warm and bright, and the sweat from working the hay bales blanched away his headache and too, most of the memory from his Indian dream – but not all.

After supper, Malcolm was still determined to make good on his vision, so hiked back up to Indian Rocks in the moonlight. He brought a lantern from the barn and a few kitchen matches. In the shadow of the big rocks he lit the lantern and began crawling along the inner bases of the boulders, looking for the little blue flower. At the foot of the sixth rock he found one, and popped the whole flower into his mouth. Settling with his back against the rock, he leaned his head back, looked up at the stars, and chewed up the little flower. In the distance he began to hear a rumble, at first barely audible over the whisper of night winds dancing across the tops of the rocks, then louder and closer.

"Buffalo" he said into the night.

"Buffalo are coming."

Then he shut his eyes to meet his Indian self again. The rumble came again, louder and, and, within his own stomach. His bowels cramped and the rumbling spiraled across his abdomen, gurgling and moaning, warning him he should already be heading for the closest outhouse as fast as his legs could carry him. He realized his imminent peril and stood up, looking around the rocks for the quickest way beyond them and down the ridge. He only managed to get over the first rock and down into a shallow depression on the moon shadow side, and get his trousers out of harm's way when it hit. In an almost endless series of cramping waves that little blue flower proceeded to empty every molecule Malcolm's insides contained. Between moans and groans, he watched the lesser stars in the sky slowly rotate around the North Star, and watched the moon rise and then settle in its nightly arc.

Dawn found Malcolm stumbling hollow across the back yard behind the Broadway house as Ivy popped open the back door, heading for the barn.

"At least you're up at a decent hour. C'mon, we got

post holes to dig today."

Malcolm moaned and turned toward the barn, his left foot still partially numb after squatting for six hours, his arms dangling with his fingers dancing wildly at the ends of his cocked hands, and his neck in a crick at an odd angle tilting his head to the right. He stumbled in jerks and stops like a scarecrow trying to come to life, stepping flat-footed as much to either side as to his front, barely making headway toward the barn.

That night after everyone had gone to bed, mostly recovered from the previous night, Malcolm took his blankets, a tent, and whatever else he could carry and moved up to Indian Rocks. On the west side of the granite ring, one boulder had fallen in over the centuries and created a little crook that offered shelter on three sides. Malcolm set up his tent in the crook and made a campfire on the open side. Clearing away the grass for the fire pit he discovered a yellow chalk deposit running under the fallen boulder and out beyond on the other side.

The chalk was yellow, the color of light pumpkin, the color of a heavy harvest moon. Malcolm had also liberated a half-full bottle of Whiskey from a hidie-hole in the back of the barn that Julius had told him about, and sat next to his fire, taking swigs from the bottle, deciding his first steps to take as an Indian. After several increasingly larger sips from the bottle, he stripped down to his birthday suit, cinched up a loincloth made from a piece of old canvas and tied at the waist by a worn leather strap.

He squatted down over the chalk deposit, scraped up a small mound of the yellow dust with his hunting knife, and covered himself with it from head to toe. Then he went looking for those little blue flowers, smarter from his previous night, he would only eat the stem and shun the flower petals. It was the night the legend was born.

Malcolm's next vision was about the buffalo. A tremendous buffalo herd drove through his valley below on their annual migration to the plains, and he led his people on a great spear hunt. He cut saplings and tied rock shards in their split ends for spear tips, instructing his people in the ancient stone tool art. Filing down from the ridge he moved bravely toward the thundering river of bison as it penetrated his land through the narrow valley opening. The hard packed ground shook with the force of thousands of buffalo stampeding through the gap. With a blood-curdling war cry he launched himself at the edges of the herd, and without thought to his own safety, he dashed to within inches of each beast, driving the spear tip into its hide. It was the greatest hunt his people had ever experienced and they chanted his name as they hurled their spears into the herd.

"Mal-colm! Mal-colm! Mal-colm!"

Except that, there had been no buffalo in Finton County for hundreds of years. And, Malcolm was actually mostly naked, covered in pumpkin-colored powder, running by himself along the Millersville highway in the middle of the night, and throwing sticks at angry passing transfer truckers and the occasional horrified late night sedan driver making his way home to Millersville.

Altogether, Malcolm's buffalo hunt resulted in four serious paint scratches, two punctured radiators, and a cracked side window on a Studebaker. He arose the following morning, oblivious to the flurry of strange stories circulating local towns, and hungry for fresh bison meat, but had to settle for a piece of the smoked bacon he had liberated from the farm the night before.

Luckily for Malcolm, he was able to snare a few rabbits and with the unnoticed donations from nearby corn fields, he managed to remain in the local wilderness living his self-constructed Indian life for a while. Also lucky for Malcolm, there was not yet enough facts in the bizarre stories about his nighttime activities to generate a good reason to send a deputy looking for him. At first his sister sent her husband to find him, but Malcolm sent him back with the threat of scalping, so Odie decided to leave him be for the time being. He kept to himself and created what he thought were Indian tools, and followed what he thought were Indian ways, knowing only what he had read in dime novels or heard from campfire stories growing up. Being only rarely found, his blue-flower visions were only occasional and generally not nearly as noticeable as his great buffalo hunt. That is, until the blue-flower visions began lasting into the daytime.

That's when he proclaimed his tribe the Maliqroische and held a great war council, at which time he/they decided that the white people squatting on Indian land in the valley had to be driven out. So, he declared war on southern Finton County. He stole a bicycle, telling himself that it was his war pony, and put barn paint handprints on its fenders. He made a long headdress of turkey, vulture and chicken feathers that hung down his back, with a raccoon tail dangling from the end on one side and a found fox tail on the other. He then fashioned a war shield by tying a piece of cast-off quilt around a metal trash can lid.

Malcolm's battle campaign to rid the valley of intruders began with Bessie Lackey's garage, just south of Union Rest, which he had decided was the northernmost cavalry outpost in Maliqroische territory. One midnight, with the blue flower stem snugged down between his cheek and gum, he pierced the quiet night with a shrieking war cry and began raining spear sticks at the garage, managing to break out one of the little side windows. He lit a torch made of a short green wood pole with corn husks tied in a bundle at its tip, and tossed it up at the broken open window. The torch missed and bounced off the garage wall sending sparks up into the air and setting fire to several vulture feathers in Malcolm's headdress.

It was to the vision of a pumpkin-colored night demon dressed in a flaming Indian war bonnet, riding a bicycle around her back yard and trying to set fire to her garage, that the widow clawed herself out from a deep sleep and pleasant dream about her high school sweetheart. She stumbled from her bedroom into the den where she kept the old .45 single action Colt left behind by her long-departed husband, and grabbing it up in her right hand pulled back the curtains with her left.

There to her amazement, she saw Malcolm pedaling as hard as he could straight for the garage/fort on another torch run, determined to lob the thing through the window. Deciding in an instant that the replacement cost for a window pane in her sewing room was far less than replacing her Chevy Bel Air, she gripped the Colt handle in both hands and thumbed back the hammer, then jerked the trigger.

The room exploded in a flash and boom, and the window pane disintegrated into a shower of glass needles that followed the bullet out toward Malcolm. The biggest turkey feathers at the front of Malcolm's headdress immediately vaporized into an expanding cloud of feather dust and the garage wall in front of him erupted in splinters a mere half heartbeat before the sonic boom slapped his ears. Just as Malcolm deduced that he was being shot at, the matter was reinforced by another .45 caliber bullet exploding from the nearby house and ricocheting off the handlebar a hair's breadth from his hand, throwing a narrow puff of air across the hairs on the back of his hand and leaving a new notch in the rusting chrome.

Even the effects of the blue flower couldn't overcome his instant sense of self-preservation. Malcolm dropped his torch and war shield beside the driveway, stuck his butt high in the air to give leverage to his legs, and pedaled for his life to get away from there. The dew in the grass behind him put out the torch on the ground and the wind in his bonnet put out the vulture feathers, leaving it to stream out behind him in the enfolding darkness like a gap-toothed drunkard's smile.

Not letting the defeat at Fort Union Rest deter the Maliqroische quest to rid the valley of white men, Malcolm continued the campaign with another series of raids closer to Indian Rocks. He managed to come up with two blue flower stems the following evening and took his trusty steed to the other side of Greenwood Road with a plan to set free the wild mustangs being held by the white-eyes at the training farm for the Finton County Fox and Hound Club. Indians learn and adapt to the enemy he had told himself, and so he was determined that this raid would be silent, without war cries, to minimize the chance of unwanted gunfire in his direction. He was the ultimate silent warrior, except that the front gate was locked and the farm was encircled in about three miles of barbed wire. He had to lift his bicycle over the gate, but the tires snubbed the top rail and the bicycle fell to the packed ground in a noisy metallic clatter, and he got his headdress caught in the chain sprocket when he got over to pick up the bike, trapping the foxtail in the chain links and pulling it loose from the line of turkey feathers.

He started a fire in the outhouse behind the main pen and then pedaled over to set loose the herd of mustangs, which were in actuality no less than eight packs of hunting beagles in training. He set them loose in a tornado of barks and yelps and howls. His plan then was to let the herd run free to the front gate while he would sneak out the back of the farm, quietly slipping over the fence at some remote corner while the herd trampled down the front gate.

However, as the mega-pack was dashing down the road where they had come into the farm, and Malcolm began pedaling across the back field into the dark, the last beagle in the mob happened to notice the fox tail caught in the bicycle chain links and yielded to his training. The dog let out a long howling tally-ho beagle yodel that filled the night and stopped the pack dead still. The metallic rattle of Malcolm's bicycle fenders as he jiggled over weed clumps in the field, was followed by the solitary wailing of the youngest beagle and soon joined by the rest of the fox hunting mob that turned from its dash to freedom to race in the direction of the foxtail.

The barn lights came on as the farmer and his sons finished their dash from the house and lined up along the fence below the night training lights, each carrying a well used 12-gauge pump shotgun, and began to fill the air low over the field with thunder and number 4 shot. Only Malcolm's position as the lead of seventy-eight excited beagles in hot pursuit, protected him from flat trajectory back-of-the-head shots the farmers did not take for fear of hurting one of the dogs. When the thunder ceased and quiet returned to the farm, the beagles trotted back into the light in small groups, one carrying in its mouth a foxtail, another a raccoon tail, another had a mouthful of feathers, another a piece of bicycle tire and one had a dirty strip of canvas with a worn strap of leather still knotted in one corner.

Malcolm buried the remains of his bicycle among the wet leaves in the woods beyond the beagle farm, and limped cross country back toward Indian Rocks. A single vulture feather remained stuck in his disheveled hair, its end singed by fire, and his only bodily cover was the layer of pumpkin yellow chalk dust. A bright harvest moon lit his way and he walked disgusted without regard to Indian stealth or keeping from view. Several people saw the ghost that night, putting out the trash or locking up the barn or garage for the night. Dispirited, he made his way to the Broadway farm only just barely beyond the grip of the blue flower and his Indian visions, but still close enough to reality to know he was naked, cold and hungry, in a new falling late Autumn rain.

A few weeks later his sister and her husband drove Malcolm to a sanitarium over in Abercrombie County, where he stayed for about a year until the doctors had talked all the Indian nonsense out of his head and got his medications balanced. When he got out he went by to see his sister who gave him some money for a new start. He said he was going out to Oklahoma where the air was dry and he could clean his brain out. Said he knew he wasn't a Maliqroische Indian, that there wasn't any such thing, and for them not to worry anymore.

That Saturday he boarded a plane to Tulsa, but when it landed he stayed on it. He stayed on the plane until it reached its final destination in San Francisco, California, where he signed on as a coal shoveler for a cargo ship headed to Australia. As it left port he was tossing ten-pound shovel loads of anthracite coal into the furnace and stopped to wipe the sweat off his forehead. He was satisfied that he had finally figured it all out. He wasn't an Indian after all. He was the spirit of the Aborigine people, and he was going home to the great Outback to set them all free. He patted his shirt pocket absentmindedly, feeling the little bottle of pills he was no longer taking, and thinking about the speck-sized seeds sprinkled in among the capsules, and the little blue flowers they would become in the red Australian soil.

EFFRIM DICKELS

Effrim Dickels was fresh out of college when he came home in the mid-seventies to become the other half of the news staff on the county's only radio station. His first assignment was to cover the tractor pulling contest down at the fairgrounds, and he was interviewing the first place driver when the third place tractor plowed through the stack of hay bales behind them. When the rescue team dug Effrim out of the straw, they found nothing broken, but Effrim was out cold and stayed that way for six days. He woke up wide-eyed and hungry at the regional hospital over in Buford County, and when they asked him if he could say his name, he said it was Walter Cronkite, sounding just like him. That afternoon he dressed himself, picked up a complimentary tube of hemorrhoid cream off the nightstand, and holding the tube like a microphone walked out of the hospital saying aloud his evening newscast that included everything he saw and every thought he had. He has continued that newscast every waking moment since.

I first saw Effrim while I was still on work release at the Park'N'Pump and Big Al's Tavern, when Mike Daniels dropped Effrim off at Tooey's Crossroads just as we opened the Park'N'Pump. Mike was off duty and on his way to fish for Crappie down on Lake Adolphus when he pulled his rebuilt Bronco onto the oil-soaked packed dirt drive in front of the Park'N'Pump's two gasoline pumps. When the pumps were new, one was labeled 'Leaded' and the other was labeled 'Unleaded', but thanks to a gray duct tape patch on pump 2, they both now said Unleaded. If you had out of state plates and were paying cash, the owner, Adam Tooey, would

tell you the pump you had just used was High Test –
whichever you had used, but in fact both were Regular.
Since Mike was a Deputy Sheriff, Adam was quick to
snatch down the High Test price card off his counter
before Mike went in to pay.

I heard him tell Adam, "Brought you a visitor."

When Mike pulled away with his aluminum john
boat bouncing in its trailer behind the Bronco, there
stood Effrim. They didn't dare give Effrim a driver's
license, but he got around fine with people giving him
lifts. He never asked directly, since he only reported his
news and never spoke to anyone since his accident, but
he would report on his newscast that Mr. So-and-so had
"offered to provide 'this reporter' transportation to the
scene of a late-breaking story". He stepped around the
pumps, a unique vision at the crossroads on a bright
sunny morning. Effrim had to be in his early fifties by
then. Still in the gentle care of his only sister, and
receiving support checks from the state and a settlement
from the radio station insurance, he wanted for very
little. Yet he still wore the same clothes he wore before
the accident, whenever they were out of the wash or
returned from patching. He owned a bright orange and a
bright yellow leisure suit, and on this day the yellow one
was so bright in the sunshine I had to squint my eyelids
just to look at him. The coat long since lost the reach or
willingness to wrap itself over his belly, and just hung
from the strained seams around his arms in stretched
folds. His Day-Glo orange shirt had its collar outside
the leisure jacket and its tips hanging over the padded
shoulders. The front shirt fabric scalloped from button
to button, forming thin points at the frilled buttonholes,
and appeared only an instant away from jettisoning eye-
piercing button fragments. His once thick red curly hair
had been at the height of hair fashion and called an Afro
at the time of his accident, but had now fallen away from

his hairless crown and remained thin ringed around his skull just above his ears, dusty auburn speckled with early gray. His beige suede platform shoes had long lost their rust-colored soles and were now built up layers of black neoprene, patiently glued on by a kindly shoe repairman named Bert up at Union Rest.

Effrim drew the tube of hemorrhoid cream from his shirt pocket, and began his commentary as he ambled toward the porch of the Park'N'Pump, and me.

Local people have gathered on the veranda of the town hall to welcome this reporter and share the excitement the community feels, now that New Calabash Films has announced it will shoot the final scenes of the sequel to 'Swamp Detective' in this very location.

I stepped back into the store as Adam was slipping the cash drawer back into the register for the day. "You need to see this, Adam."

Adam didn't even look up. "He wearing the orange suit or the yellow one?"

"Yellow."

"That'd be Effrim Dickels. I've told you about him."

I gave Adam a nod he didn't see, "Said there was going to be a movie made out here," but he did not respond, and then I stepped back over to the screen door, just as Effrim came in.

A quaint store with a generous front porch, welcoming well-worn chairs to pass a quiet morning, and the fragrance of fresh coffee drifting out through an ancient screen door. Just another wholesome Summer morning at Tooey's Crossroads.

Adam looked up over the rims of his drug store reading glasses as he counted the bills in the cash drawer to ensure he had lost none during the night since he counted them last. "Help yourself to the coffee Effrim. Use the yellow cup." Adam turned his head only slightly toward me with the same gaze. "He's a third cousin on my Daddy's side, I think. Comes by here two or three times a year." Then he nodded toward the coffee pot stand and the little shelf above it. "Those are his."

There were two rounded cups I had looked at many times. The handles appeared to be afterthoughts. Each painted with the classic smiley face of two dots above an upward curving line and the name of a kids cereal below the face. One cup was lemon yellow and the other was candy orange. Effrim took down the yellow one and filled it halfway with fresh coffee and held the cap end of the tube close to his face as he slurped, sounding similar to the last water twisting down the drain of a running garbage disposal. With both elbows held straight out from his shoulders he looked like a giant stumpy-winged canary trying to glide.

Now folks, that's the sound of great coffee going down warm and welcome at Adam Tooey's Park'N'Pump here on location this morning at Tooey's Crossroads in southern Finton County. We'll return with more news after this important announcement from our sponsor.

Effrim then set his coffee cup and tube of hemorrhoid cream down on the edge of the coffee stand and slipped out back to the restroom. I was setting bottled drinks into the half barrel ice tub by the checkout counter when he returned. As he retrieved his cup and tube, Adam snapped his fingers to get Effrim's attention, and pointed down at his unzipped fly, where a corner of the orange shirt tail still hung down the front of his lemon slacks like a sickly tongue.

An old Jeep Gladiator pulled up into the Tavern's parking lot next door and out stepped Stumpy Madison from the passenger side. I recognized the man driving the Jeep. He was the one that built a log house up on the ridge above the Sweet Water Hunting and Fishing Club over on the other side of Lake Adolphus, and so I looked around for his dog. I never did know the man's name, he never gave it when I was around, and I never met anyone else he had given it to, but I knew the dog's name. Big Dog. He was a Mastiff, bigger than a large Shetland pony and just shy of the shoulder height of a small quarter horse. I was always relieved that it was good-humored. As the man killed the engine and stepped out of the driver's side, Big Dog stepped down gracefully from the truck bed and fell into step behind him. It was eerie to watch an animal that big move that quickly with almost no sound.

Stumpy was birth named Massey Ferguson Madison – his Daddy had owned a tractor franchise when he was born – and it seemed to Mr. Madison like a fair thing to do at the time, but Massey never begrudged his father for his name. He said he came off much better than his father, who had been named Malfourth Ezekiel. No one in the family ever had a chance to figure that one out, because Massey's grandfather had been shot by revenuers just a few days after Malfourth was born. Stumpy got his nickname name after he suffered a mishap over at the Hunting Club and lost his left hand the year the lake flooded.

The man gave a soft-spoken command to the dog who promptly set his tail down on the porch just outside the door, and the man came in giving a nod to Adam and me before going to look at the hunting magazines. Stumpy went over to the upright glass front freezer and pulled out two morning beers and set them on the counter and then pulled down four large meat sticks from the display by the cash register.

Adam gave a half smile. "Nice Breakfast."

"Hell Adam, we been up since four a.m. This is lunch for us. We got some beautiful trout out on the lake this morning."

Stumpy took a bite from one of the foot-long meat

sticks and pointed the remainder at the man.

"He wanted to stop by and give some of them to Al. Said he thought she would appreciate natural food."

"Didn't know they knew one another."

"He says they ran into each other on his property a while back."

"You going to stick around and watch the movie crew set up?"

"What movie crew? Where? What movie?"

"New Calabash Films. Here. Sequel to Swamp Detective"

"Swamp Detective?? I really liked that movie. Saw it three times up at the Roxy in Millersville."

Stumpy turned back to the man and raised his voice to him.

"They're going to make a sequel to Swamp Detective! And shoot it right here at Tooey's Crossroads."

The man stared back.

"Don't go to movies. Don't have a television. Don't need that stuff. Got plenty else to do without it."

Adam grinned and looked back at Stumpy.

"Right chatty today. Most I ever heard him say."

" 'Bout as much as he said all morning fishing, but that was spread out over four hours."

The screen door screeched wide open and then slammed shut behind Sarah Kozlowski.

"The chili ladle fell down in the chili when I set the bucket down to open that door. Pug, how 'bout finding me a pair of tongs to fish it out?"

Then she toted the daily pails of chili and Cole slaw into the back kitchen and started setting up for the lunch rush.

Adam called after her.

"You're a little bit early today, Sarah."

"The Hell I am, Adam Tooey. You're running behind

again."

Adam looked over at the Beer Clock above the standup freezer and noticed it was ten thirty.

"We are running behind. Pug get the grills on. Those truckers start getting hungry by eleven."

Two other arrivals put two more cars in the parking lot between the Park'N'Pump and the Tavern and brought four more people into the store. They were all excited about the film crew coming. Had heard it from friends and came over to watch. Adam sold them the rest of the coffee and the rest of yesterday's donuts.

By eleven o'clock there were nine cars in the parking lot on one side, about thirty people milling about the store, and the first logging truck came to a dust cloud stop in the bus stop area by the big oak on the other side next to the highway. Two truckers got out of the cab and made a beeline for the side window where Adam and Sarah served hamburger deluxe baskets with chili cheese fries from 11 A.M. until 2 p.m., or until the chili and Cole slaw ran out. Adam's hamburgers were just common fare without Sarah's chili and Coleslaw. All of Finton County knew that. Within minutes of those first two, the line was fifteen people deep outside the window. I was frying burgers, Adam was deep frying and dumping French fries, and Sarah was dropping ladles of her magic onto everything before it disappeared from the window sill. The tens and fives floated down into the plastic bucket just below the sill. We all three fell into a well-practiced rhythm.

Sarah stuck her chin over her shoulder toward Adam.

"Good thing you told me to make extra, all this stuff is going fast."

"Fast and furious, Sarah. Fast and furious."

He leaned out to the window sill.

"That's eight dollars, Mister."

"Eight dollars?? When'd this go up??"

"Just today. My beef supplier has doubled his prices."

Sarah looked at him from the sides of her eyes, but before she could speak Adam spoke.

"Ladle up Sarah, ladle up. Keep this stuff going if you want your rent money."

Outside the line now stretched back to the oaks with an intermix of truckers and movie fans, all hungry for the smell of Sarah's cooking, and not another hot grill within ten miles.

The confusion of noise outside grew from louder voices, challenges of cutting line, threats of serious punches, to car horns of those filling the parking lot to overfull, and then joined by exasperated long-distance truckers trying to get around a major heavy hauler blocking the highway. Finally Adam had to go outside for crowd control, turning over the food operations to Sarah, while Stumpy stepped in to flip French Fry baskets, and I fried burgers and heated buns.

Tater Millpond had shown up with a few friends after he heard about the movie and was doing a brisk business of selling parking places across the highway for $5 a-piece, even though the land was actually the Finton County Fair Grounds. His brother, Slick, helped for a little while until Slick's wife Vidalia showed up saying she wanted to try to get a job as an extra on the set. So Slick and Vidalia walked across the highway and down through the large crowd gathering around the Park'N'Pump. Tater watched them walk down, and punched his friends laughing and pointing at the couple, as the crowd melted back before them like Moses parting the red sea.

"Lotta' burned noses happening down there!"

Vidalia had splashed herself with her best perfume, but as it mixed with her own notorious natural aroma, the eyeballs of those folks too slow to make a path for her, teared up and their sinuses slammed shut.

A long-faithful trucker had arranged his load delivery so he could be at Tooey's Crossroads in time for lunch, but it was a poor decision since he was hauling a three-story historic brick house to another part of the state. His trailer had to straddle the center line to keep the house between the telephone poles and power poles on either side, but he had never planned on the traffic he was encountering. And the traffic never planned on having to deal with a full road wide load creeping along at four miles an hour. Cell phone calls to the sheriff resulted in a request for an overflight by a passing state police chopper, and the dispatch of two deputies to deal with the traffic snarl.

Officer Mike Daniels came south from Millersville in his squad car with the siren blaring, but since things had been slow so far that week, Clifford Tibideaux had been south of the Crossroads cutting grass along Route 535 when he got his call, so he came shooting north in his modified Kubota Tractor/Cruiser. Before he could even begin to turn in at the Park'N'Pump, Clifford saw Tater Millpond over on County Fairground property and headed straight for him, his upward pointing manifold exhausts shooting flames and the cutting deck sending rooster tails of grass clippings into the backdraft and making a swath of neatly trimmed grass behind him as he dashed across the field.

Daniels wound up having to run road interference and escort the house truck out of the county, after he finally found the driver who had just left the truck sitting in the middle of the road while he got in line at the Park'N'Pump. The driver had refused even on a threat of jail to step out of line and lose his place. Daniels finally gave in and handed the driver enough money to get him one too, which by then Adam had raised to $10.

Watching the action across the highway and realizing

what Tater had been doing , Adam grabbed a piece of cardboard from the store counter, wrote $10 on it and sent Thurmond Hooker out to the field next to his great grandfather's statue across the Swamp Road to start renting out parking places. Next he brought up two sticky signs, both saying High Test, and slapped them on the front of the gas pumps. Below those words he wrote in magic marker "$4/Gal." He spent the next few hours selling cokes for $3, packs of Nabs for $2, and individual cans of beer for $5 each, until his shelves were almost clean. And still the crowd grew. By 1:30 both gas pumps were empty, and still the crowd grew.

Adam had called Al to open the Tavern early, but to skip happy hour. We ran out of chili and Coleslaw by 2:00, even though Sarah made extra, and still sold plain hamburgers until they were gone by 2:30. We even cleaned and fried the man's trouts and served them with deep fried frozen French fry cutlets until they were gone. By 3:00 there was no food left in the refrigerator to cook. By 3:30 all the beer in the Tavern was gone and Al was selling drinks of half shots at full price. And still the crowd grew. Effrim stood on the porch to the Park'N'Pump dutifully reporting the scene to his cream tube.

It is an absolute sea of humanity, brought together by curiosity, by the lure of stardom, the glitz and romance of make-believe. Hungry for excitement and hungry for any food anyone will sell them at almost any price, it is almost a sea of locusts, but at least they appear to be happy locust. Some want to watch it, some want to be watched watching it, some want to be a part of it, and some want no part of it at all for any of us. Witness, Sister Doris Greenwood, of the Union Rest Baptismal Sisterhood.

At the highway edge of the undulating crowd stood a solitary figure in starched Lime Green Habit, holding a large sign on a pole above her, proclaiming to the crowd "Sinners!" and preaching fire and brimstone for them to be gone from this site of movie-going madness. "You will all regret this day!" she yelled. One elderly couple did actually turn around and head back to their car, but mostly the crowd just flowed around her.

Out at the highway an old Volvo parked on the shoulder of the road blocking Doris Greenwood's protest circuit, and from it emerged two teenagers making up the entire student body of the Finton County Community College Cinematography Technology Program. They withdrew hastily constructed protest signs of their own to counter the unwarranted censorship promoted by Doris's protest, and proceeded with an anti-anti-movie protest demanding creativity and free speech. Within moments, the blue-jeaned students and lime green wrapped pseudo-nun were flailing each other with their protest signs. The dueling protestors drew their own crowd, into which waded Tater Millpond's friend Beetle, who started taking bets on the nun, which was followed by Clifford Tibideaux to break it up after leaving Tater once again handcuffed to the front of the Kubota.

The car from the Millersville radio station finally arrived only seconds before the van from the television station and fell into a bidding war in front of Thurmond Hooker for the last parking space in Tooey's field. The television people finally acquired the spot for $110 in cash and a promise to Thurmond that he would be able to say "Hi" on camera and pull down on his ear for his wife the way Carol Burnett used to on her TV show. The radio station car had to slalom its way through jumbles of haphazardly parked cars and incoming ones along the highway. The driver finally pulled onto an unoccupied space of the shoulder three-quarters of a mile back toward Millersville. Eager groups of people were still arriving and quick-stepping down the middle of the road to the crossroads, trying to get there before it was all over.

As the communications technician extended the satellite dish on top of the television news van, he looked over the crowd and saw Effrim on the porch of the Park'N'Pump. He stared in amazement at the sight of Effrim's lemon yellow leisure suit and his bald-crown faded red afro, thinking at first it was a local clown, until he saw the body language of a reporter. He clapped his hands several times and yelled out the name of the lead reporter to get her attention.

"Katie! Katie! Get up here, quick! You've GOT to see this!"

With make-up towel still stuffed around her blouse collar, Katie climbed the ladder at the end of the van and mounted the transmitter base next to her technician. She looked at him in question, but he only gave her a wide-mouthed toothy grin and pointed at Effrim. Katie looked out and frowned under the afternoon sun to make out the details, and turned back to the technician. By then he was handing her an earpiece and pointing his directional sound microphone at the store. She closed her eyes as the reflector center found Effrim and fed her his voice as if he were standing next to her. Her eyes popped wide open.

"Wonderful voice. Who's he reporting for?"

In answer she was handed a sleek pair of binoculars.

"What th-?? What kind of microphone is tha-?? It's a tube of – I can't tell, but.!! He's broadcasting into a tube of – something??"

The technician frantically shook his head, wide-eyed and almost giggling.

"Look at him! Look AT him! He's not BROADCASTING to anyone. He's talking to himself and he sounds like –"

"Yeah, I know."

"Well, Katie. You wanted local color. There it is."

"Go get him, Ted! Now! Get over there and bring him back, right now!"

She almost pushed Ted off the van roof, and only barely retained her own control dismounting the ladder. Moments later Ted was threading back through the crowd, escorting Effrim with gentle pressure on his elbow, steering him toward the van. Katie offered her hand.

"Hello. Can you tell me your name?"

This reporter has seen it all today, ladies and gentlemen. Now even the news is reporting that news is being reported. Those here to tell the story are becoming the story.

Katie was surprised by the response and the method of the response and stood there in silence considering what to do next. Ted cleared his throat and leaned forward to make a comment, but Katie shot up her hand, fingers spread wide. She looked Effrim directly in his eyes, but they seemed focused just over her left shoulder. She moved into the center of his vision and he shifted his gaze back over her shoulder. Katie turned back toward Ted and spoke in a whisper.

"It's almost like Autism…"

Autism is statistically growing as a reported phenomena in this country and other modern industrial societies, but many researchers are now taking the position that while there is incident growth among the American population, there is also tremendous growth in diagnoses of the condition, as well as the willingness of families to publicly admit the condition exists among their children. It is also noteworthy that in the pursuit of accurate medical reporting through public media, there is also a growing tendency to misdiagnose the condition based on superficial comparisons with other conditions.

Katie stared at Effrim's face, looking for some

recognition in his expression of her nearness to him, but he kept his attention focused beyond her left shoulder.

"Get him a mike, Ted."

"Katie, are you sure."

"No. Get him a mike."

Ted brought out a short range transmitter microphone and tried to place it in Effrim's hand while pulling at the hemorrhoid tube, but was unsuccessful. Effrim clenched his fingers around the tube, but gently touched the microphone with the fingertips of his other hand. Ted stopped pulling on the tube.

"How 'bout if we tape them together?"

Effrim said nothing, but slightly loosened his grip on the tube. Ted retrieved a small roll of masking tape from the van and offered the microphone again. Effrim walked his fingers around both the tube and the microphone, and Ted carefully wrapped a band of tape twice around the tube and microphone. Effrim focused his eyes on the microphone. Katie put her arms around Effrim and turned him by his shoulders to face the crowd. She looked back at Ted.

"Activate the mike and tell the cameraman to aim the lens at anything this guy talks about."

Then she whispered into Effrim's ear.

"You're on."

And let go of him, stepping back. Effrim stood silent looking at the crowd and then looking at the microphone in his hand. Ted rolled his eyes at Katie and shrugged his shoulders. Katie just stared at the back of this strange little man they had found in southern Finton County.

Effrim took in a deep audible breath and exhaled it across the dimpled surface of the microphone head, making the needle of the recording monitor in the van jump off the baseline and then settle back down to zero. Ted looked questionably at Katie. Katie nodded at him, but slipped her hands into her pockets and crossed her fingers. Effrim looked out over the crowd in front of him and closed his eyes. Then he opened his eyes, looked around the field, and began to speak.

From the highway all around the Park'N'Pump, in the parking lot beyond, and all around Big Al's Tavern is a sea of people's heads and innumerable varieties of hats. The crowd has flooded out across the gravel road and seeped into the field across from the store, where knots of people gather around the old confederate statue and new arriving vendors selling trinkets under bright colored umbrella stands.

Every mobile vendor of any consumable has descended upon Tooey's Crossroads, and each new stand is immediately awash in people eager to expand the excitement and notarize their attendance with a memorial trinket, gaudy accessory, or balloon for their child.

Even Lively's Funeral Home has set up a display tent, showing off their latest design in bronze and stainless steel, filled with lollipops for the kids.

A single report of a small film company shooting a few scenes of a modest movie has generated an instant carnival attracting thousands to a rural intersection normally home to less than 10 people.

Katie leaned next to Ted.

"Are you getting this?"

"Yes. We are recording locally, but…"

"Send it. Send it all."

"What about your lead in."

"This little man is my lead-in. Transmit it now."

At a satellite receiving station on the top floor of a high rise building three hundred miles away a technician received an incoming signal and notified the newsroom three floors below. He was already listening in to the transmission when his intercom crackled and the news anchor for that station requested the feed. Within seconds, the telephone rang with a call from the anchor.

"Is this an old recording? Part of a lead in?"

"No sir. It's a live transmission from Katie's team on the road."

In the newsroom the old man smiled and shook his head, the body language of the man drew the attention of his staff. He pushed a button on top of the speaker sitting on his desk and turned to his staff.

"Listen."

... report of a small film company shooting a few scenes of a modest movie has generated an instant carnival attracting thousands to a rural intersection normally home to less than 10 people.

Why are they here? What is it that draws them? Thousands of dollars, weeks of planning and advertisement are poured into productions of carnivals, circuses, plays and concerts, but here a couple phone calls on a quiet Summer day in southern Finton County has brought people from all directions.

And the crowd is an entity of its own. No longer made up of individual people, but a mixture of them, and we apply terms normally used for oceans. There are seas of heads, waves of the crowd, tides of the crowd, ebbs and flows of the crowd. The crowd is only sporadically returned to groups of individuals when it parts wide for people like Vidalia Millpond, or shies from Doris Greenwood, or lines up for anything ladled out by the hands of Sarah Kozlowski.

The sound of a helicopter filled the background of the transmission.

It looks like maybe the state police will have to land here after all, they have been circling overhead much of this afternoon, and...no,...wait this is not the state police.

Back at Tooey's crossroads the private helicopter hovered overhead looking for a safe place to land, but finally raised back into the air and drifted across the highway to the county fairgrounds, where it slowly descends, landing not far from a strangely equipped black and white tractor, with a Sheriff's office emblem on its hood. As the helicopter settled onto the ground, the passenger side door opened and out stepped a state trooper followed by a trim little man in an expensive looking gray pinstripe suit. The state trooper eyed Tater Millpond for a moment, then began leading the man in the suit to the middle of the crowd, getting people to step aside as they made their way. The trooper made a beeline for the television van, and asked Katie if the man in the suit could make an announcement from the roof that the people needed to hear. Ted handed the man a bullhorn and a built-in microphone and assisted him climbing the ladder to the roof.

"People! People! I have an important announcement about the movie!"

Silence spread out from the van ending with a raucous laugh back at the front of the Tavern, which was cut short by an elbow to someone's side so they could hear the man on the television van.

"People! I am Lester Van Treno, Vice president of New Calabash Films!"

The crowd roared with welcoming yells, whistles and applause.

"NO! NO! You must listen! There has been a terrible mistake. Listen!"

It took several moments before the crowd settled down enough for the man to continue. As quiet settled in someone yelled out.

"When will the shooting start?!?"

And the crowd erupted again. Van Treno held up his hands for quiet and finally the crowd responded.

"There is no shooting here! Listen to me! There will be no movie here!"

Absolute silence swept among the crowd, and only the sound of gravel under the tires of the last arriving car drifted into the air. When Van Treno spoke, the bullhorn almost sounded too loud in the quiet air.

"This is all a rumor! We are not filming a sequel to *Swamp Detective*! Not here or anywhere! The movie was a bomb!! The only places it showed more than two nights was at the Millersville Roxy and a Drive-in over in the next county!"

A soft mummer drifted over the crowd.

"I don't know how all this got started, but no such release ever came from our company. This has all been a rumor!"

In near silence Van Treno dismounted the van and returned with the trooper to the waiting helicopter. The silence remained as the helicopter powered up into the air and then nosed down slapping the air, paddling its way out of sight. People stood where they were staring at each other in silence. Effrim's voice floated among the crowd.

A man once told me that there was no such thing as Santa Claus. I felt cheated when I heard that, and I begrudged the man greatly for trying to take that belief away from me. But he could not take away the experiences that my belief had brought me up until that moment. He did not rob me of all my Christmas's past. He did not take away the trembling excitement of a dozen Christmas eves trying to go to sleep, so Santa could come during the night, or the memories of a dozen happy Christmas mornings. I will always have those.

The excitement of today did not disappear just because they won't be shooting a few movie scenes in the nearby swamp. The hamburger or hotdog eaten at lunch is no worse – or better – because of what you hear now; the trinket no less gaudy; the crowd no smaller; the smile you shared with a nearby stranger earlier today no less genuine; no less freely given.

Maybe that's what really separates us from the animals. Maybe what really makes us a crowd of people instead of a herd, is our ability to celebrate as a group. Maybe, maybe, at the very bottom line of it all, we need to celebrate, and so we look for special reasons, and the most special reason of all is that we are people - and we NEED to celebrate together. We need to leave our rooms, our houses, our offices, and our cars and come rub elbows with each other.

Without the people, this is just a lonely intersection between an old asphalt highway and a dusty gravel road, bounded by the swamp on one side and Indian Rocks on the other. It's only worth remembering because of the people, in all their variations. Because of the people, it's Tooey's Crossroads. And we have spent a fine sunny day together.

Katie leaned close to Effrim and kissed him on the cheek.

He looked into her eyes and then down at himself.

"Reckon Ted has an old shirt I could borrow?"

He unwound the tape from the tube, handed the microphone back to Ted, and then gently dropped the tube into a nearby trash can.

It was after midnight before the crowd finally left. Adam and I stood out on the porch after he locked the door and turned out all the lights. Even Big Al had sold out of stock and closed early, leaving the tavern rarely dark on the other side of the gravel parking lot. The moon was full and laid tree shadows on the gravel and painted shadows of the porch columns on the planks where we stood. We were the only ones left anywhere near Tooey's Crossroads. He turned to me with a big grin.

"We did damned good today, Pug. More than I usually make in three months."

The parking lot and field across the gravel road were covered in trash.

"This'll take days to clean up, Adam."

Adam twisted his back trying to ease a knotted muscle in his back, and shook his head.

"Nah. Mike Daniels said he'd get up with the county roads people tomorrow and they'd take care of it."

Adam slowly descended the worn wooden steps down to the packed dirt and stood in the moonlight.

"Adam?"

He stopped, with his back toward me.

"Yeah?"

"Did you start that rumor?"

He slipped his hands into his pockets and jingled his car keys and sighed. He looked up at the moon for a moment, then gave a small chuckle.

"Pug, you remember that injured woodpecker you found when you first came here on work release? The one you kept in that little cage out back by the trash dumpster 'til it got strong?"

"Yeah."

"I even sold all those old maps I had printed up to find him down in the swamp. Got'em Xeroxed down at the county library that weekend for three-cents each. Sold'em all for five dollars apiece today."

"You started it, didn't you?"

He walked over to his old Chrysler and took the cardboard sign off the windshield that read, "Tooey's Rent-A-Car" and tossed the sign into the back seat, then stood by the open driver's side door while he fished his car keys out of his pocket. He looked out at the Millersville Highway then back at me, his eyes in moon shadows under his forehead and his scalp shiny through his thinning hair, his smiling lips and teeth silver in the moonlight.

"Yeah," he said.

PUG GREENWOOD

MOONRISE

During my Wednesday afternoon trash rounds in Millersville, I came across a battered cardboard box set out at the curb for Thursday morning collection. It looked like an old storage box, with a metal label holder half pulled out at one end and the card once there gone long ago. Inside was a CD of Ella Fitzgerald songs laid on top of a loose bundle of frayed white shirts, still heavy starched, but faded to yellow and scented with Old Spice. There were a few narrow ties under the shirts and a little stack of newspapers from 1976 at the bottom. I wondered what was in those old papers that was once important enough for someone to save, but not anymore. The CD looked to be in good condition, and I had always heard of Ella, but never knowingly ever actually listened to her sing before. When I got back to the cabin I left the other stuff collected that afternoon and tossed into the trailered boat still hooked to the Jeep, and went to the little junk shed out back to fish out the combination CD/Radio/Cassette player I had found the week before. The batteries in the player were still good, and although the cassette cover was pulled off and the cord gone, it still twirled the CD player when I turned it on. Now I had a CD to play in it, so I dropped in the CD, pushed the button with the little triangle on it, and set it on the porch to play while I fixed supper.

Next to Buford Ledbedder's, Ella's was the purest singing voice I had ever heard. Her voice drifted into and around the cabin and just seemed to fill the air, not pushing other sounds out like jukebox music, but going where it was welcome. Supper was over and the player was on its third time through Ella's songs when the sunset over the trees behind the cabin. The evening was still shirt-sleeve weather, so I set the camping chair off the porch so I could see the sky from it, and placed Ella on the ground next to the chair. I blew out the lamp in the cabin and returned with a glass of Tennessee Whiskey and lime juice, then settled into the chair in time to see the sky dim to dark blue and the first stars come out. Ella's voice stretched out to fill the rest of the field to the tree lines, and as the moon rose, the evening birds and crickets and cicadas all settled down to quiet, listening to Ella sing.

I was deep into the chair with my feet propped up on the little foot support that extended out from the chair frame, but hadn't taken my first sip when I heard a scratchy little voice close beside the chair.

"Ah hemm."

There beside me was that chubby raccoon holding a little clear plastic communion sip cup he had pulled out of some church trash pile, holding it up in both paws toward me, begging for some of my drink. I leaned over to pour a dribble into his cup and he tossed it back like a thirsty farm hand at quitting time, offering it back up for more before I could even roll back into my chair. So, I poured him some more.

"Donald, how come you only show up when I'm drinking?"

The raccoon shrugged his shoulders, keeping the cup held in both paws in front of him, and settled down further onto his haunches with a faint sigh. I rolled back into the fake canvas curve of the camping chair and leaned my head against the backrest, watching the moon rise clear of the trees, sipping my drink, and listening to Ella sing to us. The wind had stilled and it seemed that even the trees had stopped their evening swaying to listen to Ella sing 'Stardust', while the moon rose higher, drawing back the laced curtain of its tree shadows and painting us all in silver light. And I dozed off to sleep in the chair.

Just another quiet night in southern Finton County, with not much going on that anybody could see from a passing car along the Millersville Road. Just another rusting town limit sign along a road slipping fast under the car, holding nothing more than the narrow world of the high beams. The occasional flash of gray plank or crumbled red brick next to the road, joined by a lonely overgrown driveway, or a neat parallel line of peonies leading up to an empty spot among overgrown grass, points out a home place still existing only in the memories of people living over the hill, and waiting for someone to hear its story.

YOU ARE NOW LEAVING FINTON COUNTY

Y'all come back, ya hear?